LLOYD McNEIL'S LAST RIDE

ALSO BY WILL LEITCH

LLOYD McNEIL'S LAST RIDE

A NOVEL

WILL LEITCH

HARPER

An Imprint of HarperCollins*Publishers*

HarperCollins books may be purchased for educational, business, or sales promotional use. For information, please email the Special Markets Department at SPsales@harpercollins.com.

FIRST EDITION

Library of Congress Cataloging-in-Publication Data
Names: Leitch, Will, author.
Title: Lloyd McNeil's last ride: a novel / Will Leitch.
Description: First edition. | New York, NY: Harper, 2025.
Identifiers: LCCN 2024056829 | ISBN 9780063238565 (hardcover) |
ISBN 9780063238572 (trade paperback) | ISBN 9780063238596 (ebook)
Subjects: LCGFT: Humorous fiction. | Novels.
Classification: LCC PS3612.E35926 L56 2025 | DDC 813/.6-dc23/eng/20241209
LC record available at https://lccn.loc.gov/2024056829

25 26 27 28 29 LBC 5 4 3 2 1

To my family

*Parenthood offers many lessons in patience and sacrifice.
But ultimately, it is a lesson in humility. The very best thing
about your life is a short stage in someone else's story.
And it is enough.*

—Michael Gerson

*I never saw any of them again—except the cops.
No way has yet been invented to say goodbye to them.*

—Raymond Chandler, *The Long Goodbye*

ALIVE

1.

M y God. It really is so beautiful.

How have I never noticed how beautiful this is? How have I never even *looked*?

I had to stop. It bowled me over. I had pulled my cruiser over on the side of the freeway, right on I-85, one of the busiest interstates in the country, with pickup trucks and Teslas and big loud Harleys zipping by, all missing me by just a few feet. I didn't put my lights on. I didn't stop a motorist. I really hadn't planned on doing anything at all. I was just looking up, like it was a normal day, and then I saw it, right there in front of me, and it was so beautiful that I had no choice but to swerve to the side of the road and stop.

I mean, look at it.

Millions of years ago, there was a cell, and that cell turned into a bacteria, and that bacteria became a fish, or something like that, I think I remember it being a fish, and then the fish pulled itself out of the sea and started walking on two legs, and then after a while it became a monkey, and, well, fine, so maybe I don't have all the exact details of human evolution right, what do you want from me, I grew up in the American public school system in the 1980s, you're lucky I can put my finger on our country on a map. I'm doing my best.

The point is that billions and billions of things had to happen over the scope of space and time for human beings to even exist in the first place. And then human beings had to be different from animals, smarter, or at least more inventive, they needed to be able to reason and use logic and understand object permanence and learn that they will someday die and invent tools and make machines—machines like wheels. Then they had to turn those wheels into moving vehicles, and then they had to create engines, and then they had to harness energy to power those engines, and all that led to cars. Cars! When they had cars, they needed roads for those cars to drive on, because now people could go from their homes to their jobs from many miles away, but only if they could create a complex series of roads, and exits, and side streets, and ramps, and everything they might need to allow people to get from one place to another. They needed materials, they needed asphalt, and concrete, and metal, they needed all of that to make those roads, and then they needed scientists and geologists and architects to tell them where to build the roads and how to keep them from falling apart. And they needed to do this *in every single place on the planet*— everywhere, all of the time. They spent thousands upon thousands of work hours, millions upon millions of dollars, huge swaths of their entire lives, figuring out a way to help humans move themselves around. We have built roads that rise hundreds of feet into the air to carry dozens of machines that are heavier than any animal on earth.

We were once fish! And now we can make this!

It's incredible, right? Look at it. They call it Spaghetti Junction. Its official name is the Tom Moreland Exchange, where I-85 meets I-285 in Atlanta, a spiraling, labyrinthine octopus of highways and on-ramps and off-ramps and speed limit signs and EXIT ONLY THIS LANE that will take you anywhere you want to go. Want to go to downtown Atlanta, or through, all the way to Selma and Montgomery, Alabama? I-85 South will take you right there. I-285 will take you to Truist Park so you can go see a Braves game in the suburbs, or you can keep going to get on I-20, which goes as far west as Scroggins Draw, Texas, if you've got a hankering for Scroggins Draw. I-85 North gets you all the way to Virginia. From those places you can just keep driving, as long as you want, until you hit water. Or you can stop at an airport, oh yes,

4

that's another thing we humans have done, we've created *machines that soar through the sky*. You can go to Paris, or China, or Antarctica, or Timbuktu, shoot, someday we're all going to go to Mars. This road will take you anywhere.

And we made it. Some guy drew a picture of it, and a bunch of other guys found all the other parts to put it together, and a whole different group of guys got hammers and screwdrivers and cranes (cranes! Machines that lift the heaviest things miles into the sky that you can control with a joystick!) to build it, and they did, they built it, and anyone who has ever been in this city, this crazy gorgeous city, Atlanta, my Atlanta, anyone who has been here has used it, and they've never once stopped to think about it, how it's a miracle that it exists, how it's a miracle that any of this, that any of us, is here at all—you, me, the president, the guy on television dancing while trying to sell you all these sandwiches he made just for you, just for all of us.

It's a road in the sky that will take you anywhere. It's a miracle.

And we made it.

My God, look at it. How have I never looked at it before?

Why aren't you here with me looking? Why isn't everyone? Why don't we just *look*?

Dr. Lipsey was asking me about Georgia football. That's the last thing I remember from before. I'd known about Dr. Lipsey's personal, uh, issues for a while—the women, the drugs, the "investment opportunities"—but so much of it always came down to the gambling. Dr. Lipsey was, to put it mildly, a degenerate gambler.

"Big game for the Dawgs this weekend," he said from across the desk, sweating a little. He was always sweating a little. "That line hasn't budged a bit. I thought there'd be a little late money in on the Rebs, but it's holding steady. You heard anything? Isn't your ex from up there in Athens? She's heard anything?" He was always sweating a little and he was always looking for information that might make him whole again.

"I don't think Jessica is scouting any practices, sorry," I said. Jessica hated football, always had, which is why Bishop hated it too.

Dr. Lipsey had called me that afternoon, on my off day, on *his* off day, which he made a whole deal of telling me was something he never does, and he said he wanted me to come in immediately. I'd thought it was something bad—why would he call if it weren't something bad?—but starting our appointment with another gambling question had eased the weight on my chest a bit. Maybe he really did just want some info on the Georgia–Ole Miss game? He was forever in the hole.

"Just bet on Kirby, I guess," I said. "You know I don't watch much football."

"Right, you're more into that *Euro* football," he said, tapping his fingers on his ornate marble desk. I'd always thought his desk was too fancy for a doctor. That was much more of a hedge fund guy's desk. "Well, if you hear anything, lemme know. That line is super fishy."

I looked at him. The maw in my stomach growled and stretched. "So, uh, what's up?"

I hadn't told anyone I was here. I hadn't told anyone, about any of it.

The headaches. The headaches had been coming for a couple of months, but they'd gotten bad in the last few weeks. At first I thought they were just typical hangovers, maybe just a little bit worse because I'm old now and everything's a little bit worse. But then they were still there even when I didn't drink, and then these little spasms started happening, these sharp lightning bolts, first behind my right eye, then my left, and then they were just firing all over the place. I tried to ignore it.

But the bolts got stronger, and larger, and they were happening more often, so often that even my partner had noticed. We were making a coffee run when one of the bolts fired so hard that I nearly drove the car off the road—he'd had to grab the steering wheel so I didn't plow over a stroller on the sidewalk.

"You should, like, call a doctor or something," he'd said. We've only been partners for a few months—Officer Anderson is his name, nice kid, earnest, even knew some of Jessica's family up in Athens— but I did think it was a tad too early in our relationship for him to be giving me medical advice. But that night, I fell asleep on the couch watching an old soccer replay and woke up with the room vibrating blinding white light as someone tried to carve a hole in my eye socket with a coping saw.

So that was when I called my old friend Dr. Lipsey. And after a day in a long white tube, there I was, in his office, at his desk, with the marble top, and a real-time crypto stock ticker, and a signed photo of him and some tattooed UFC fighter.

Dr. Lipsey gave me a very serious look—a serious look I'd never seen from him before, a serious look I hadn't thought him capable of making. He licked his lips and took some papers out of his desk drawer. He clicked his tongue. He was sweating more now.

"Well, Lloyd, I gotta tell you . . . it ain't good," he said.

The maw twisted and snarled. I felt a hot sensation at the back of my throat.

"Well, that's straightforward," I said, and I was impressed I was able to sound out a word with so many letters in it.

Dr. Lipsey shuffled the papers around, collated them a bit in his hands, and then took out an X-ray. I thought he might have one of those light fixtures on his wall, the ones you can turn on so you can see the X-rays more clearly, but he didn't. It was just a printout of an X-ray. It looked like some kid photocopied his butt.

"Well, Lloyd, this," he said, pointing with his pen to a dark blob that looked like every other dark blob on the paper, "is exactly what we were hoping not to see. And the tests, well, they brought back exactly what we were hoping they wouldn't." He popped a Nicorette in his mouth. It's strange to be told you're dying by someone who's chewing gum.

But that's what he told me.

THE WORD WAS *GLIOBLASTOMA*. IT WAS AN ODDLY RHYTHMIC WORD WHEN I heard it aloud. It sounded like some '70s concept album from Pink Floyd or something, or the Who maybe—*Roger Daltrey presents "Glioblastoma!"*

Glioblastoma, Dr. Lipsey would explain, is a brain tumor. "But that doesn't quite do it justice," he said. Here I had been my whole life thinking that the worst thing that could happen to you would be that you'd get a brain tumor. Apparently there was a word that rendered the term *brain tumor* insufficient.

Dr. Lipsey explained that a brain tumor is scary, obviously, but that we know what to do with tumors. Tumors even have their own verb: *Excise.* You *excise* a tumor.

"Don't think of it like that," Dr. Lipsey said, chewing his gum like a cow, or more like Burt Reynolds, actually. You cannot excise glioblastoma. It is, as Dr. Lipsey said while clenching both his fists and pushing them into the air, *aggressive*. He said it with a little more relish than I would have liked. He put some real mustard on it.

"*Aggressive*," he said. "Think of it like a superaggressive weed. No, no, more like a tree . . . hey, did you ever see the movie *Evil Dead*?"

"I have not," I said, and still he chewed.

"Well, there's this tree in *Evil Dead*, and it's an evil tree, which makes sense, it's a tree in a movie called *Evil Dead*. It's not a nice tree. And it has these branches, you know, like trees do. Well, these branches expand, like they're fingers that just keep growing. That's what glioblastoma is. It's like the root of a tree, with branches that grow really fucking fast."

He extended his fingers when he said this and made this weird rictus grin, and for a moment I thought he was going to shake them and yell "Jazz hands!"

Dr. Lipsey picked up the photocopy that he called an X-ray and pointed to what was apparently the front of my skull.

"So right now, the glioblastoma is right here," he said, poking the spot with his pen again. "But because it doesn't grow like a normal tumor, we can't just cut it out and plop it in a pan."

"Do you really plop those in a pan?" I don't know why I asked that.

"Well, maybe *plop* isn't the right word, but point is, you can't just scoop it out," he said, putting his hand over my photocopied skull and spreading out his fingers. "It grows too fast, and it gets all over everywhere. By the time we'd get in there, it would already be over in this part of your brain, and then this one. And even if we could get in there in time, the thing about glioblastoma is that it has all different kinds of cells, which means whatever we'd zap it with would work on some kinds of cells but not other kinds."

He wiggled his fingers over the paper, and then put his other hand behind the paper and wiggled *those* fingers.

"So it just grows and grows and grows, Lloyd, really fast, stupid fast." He flattened his palms on each side of the paper and slammed it down violently on the marble table. "And then it's everywhere."

I stared at the paper. Dr. Lipsey had ink all over his fingers. Everything he was telling me made sense, and it certainly seemed very bad, but it still felt like he was talking about someone else—like the photocopied skull he was pointing to was a theoretical photocopied skull. It wasn't *my* photocopied skull.

"So, uh," I said, and I realized that though there were surely a million questions I should be asking, I couldn't think of one. I had this odd urge to just respond with nonsense words. *Banana. Aardvark. Nittany. Corset. Gerrymander.*

Dr. Lipsey took his hands off the paper, swiveled his chair back to face me, and leaned forward.

He was no longer chewing. He loved all his job gave him—the money, the huge condo in Buckhead, the Jag, the pretty young girlfriends, the membership at the River Club in Sewanee, the ability to fund what I was pretty sure was a rather serious cocaine problem. He was a doctor—a neurologist! Being a neurologist is a pretty goddamn good life. You get whatever you want in this world when you're a neurologist.

But this was the shitty part of the job. You could see it in the little fret line in the middle of his forehead. This is why his hair was already so gray.

"You . . ." He paused. "Well, Lloyd, you really should know that if this is a glioblastoma, and I believe that it is, you . . . you don't have much time."

Just over his left shoulder there was a picture of him on a golf course somewhere with the governor of Georgia, both wearing baggy golf shirts that were still too small for them. They looked like goobers. I stared right at it, as if, if I looked close enough, I would be somewhere else, someone else.

"How much time?" I heard myself say, still staring at Gov. Kemp's nipple protruding through his sheer lime-green shirt.

Dr. Lipsey coughed into his hand.

"How much *time*?" I repeated.

"Honestly . . . three months? Maybe four?" he said. "Four might be pushing it."

"Oh," I said. I decided I was glad we were talking about someone else.

He stood up.

"Listen, Lloyd, I know this is hard to hear, and we have counselors who can help you, and of course we'll run some more tests, but this is the situation we're facing here," he said. "And we need to be, er, a bit proactive about this. A glioblastoma as fast-moving as yours, well, we're going to run into some cognitive issues sooner than you might be expecting."

My eyes finally shifted from the picture to him. "Cognitive issues?"

"Uh, you know, we can talk about that later."

"But not too much later," I said. My legs were getting back under me again.

He put his hand out to shake mine. It was time for me to leave, for him to let me do the next part on my own. "No," he said. "Not too much later."

I stood up. My vision focused. My head cleared, or at least it felt like it did.

I looked down at the floor. My feet were still there. I was a little surprised.

"So basically what you're telling me," I said, "is that I'm fucked."

Dr. Lipsey chuckled. I didn't mind. I was not against a chuckle right there.

"Yeah," he said. "You're fucked."

I shook his hand again, and then I left. I didn't call anyone. I just drove to the precinct, sat at my desk for about twenty minutes, then got in my cruiser and decided to drive. I came to the intersection of I-85 and I-285. I looked up. And then I pulled over. And now here I am.

Are you looking? Do you really see?

3.

The hood of the cruiser is still warm. The fan's still running, trying to cool the engine down. It's hot out. I'd say it's unseasonably hot for September, but this is just how hot Georgia is in September now, and will surely remain for the rest of my life, and my son's life, and his son's life. Every year's just gonna get a little bit worse.

How many times have I looked at Spaghetti Junction? Thousands—has to be. I used to sit traffic duty out here when I first joined the force. It's always bumper-to-bumper here, especially if you're trying to get on I-285. The McNeil family house is in the Old Fourth Ward, so I'm not usually up this far north, but Jessica grew up in Athens, so every time we'd go see her family, we'd get stuck right here trying to get back to the city.

How many times did I sit in Bertha, my beloved Big Bertha, my light-blue 1992 Chevrolet Caprice, the indestructible monster I still drive today, right here at this interchange, with Jessica and Bishop sitting silently, waiting out the traffic while not really seeing a thing around me? How much did I miss? How much energy—how much time!—did I waste here? For *nothing*. I did not appreciate the family in my car, and I did not think about how someday we would be a family no more. I did not think about time on this earth and how fleeting it is. I did not think about how it looks up there, the stunning beauty of all that concrete and asphalt and human ingenuity, how truly beautiful it is, how truly beautiful it all is and, I realize now, always has been.

I just sat there, caught up in dumb bullshit, paying attention only to things that do not matter, as life and hope—and beauty!—glided right past me.

And now, idiot, it's too late.

"Hey, Lloyd, that you?"

A cop, one who apparently knows me by name, has pulled up behind me, which is probably what I would have done had I come across a man in khakis and a short-sleeved button-up sitting on top of a police car alongside the freeway in the middle of rush-hour traffic.

He peers at me behind his Oakley sunglasses and cocks his head slightly to the left.

"You all right, man? Uh, what you up to out here?"

I've met Morgan a couple of times, Chris is his name, I think, and he is a friendly enough fellow, but it's fair to say if you were to rank all the people in my life that I'd want to be the first person I saw after I found out I'm going to be dead in three months, he'd be unlikely to top the list.

I turn to him.

"I . . . I . . ." The words will not come. Have I even spoken before? Did I ever know how? I suddenly am not sure.

Morgan lowers his Oakleys. His eyes are kind.

"Ah, Lloyd," he says, and he extends his hand to me. I take it, and he eases me off the hood. "Let's get you out of this heat."

My feet hit the asphalt, which cracks a bit as two pebbles stick to the bottom of my shoe. I look at him.

"Look at it, Morgan," I say, pointing to that maze of roads in the sky. "Isn't it incredible? Isn't it just the most amazing thing you've ever seen?"

ALERT

THE TEN GENTLE EDICTS OF LLOYD MCNEIL

Edict No. 1: This is going to happen to everyone. It's OK.

Bishop. Bish. Hey. It's Dad.

Remember when you asked me to help you with that paper about World War II in the fifth grade? When we did such a bad job that your teacher called me to make sure you weren't a Nazi sympathizer? Yikes. That was my fault. You had a "not" in there, and I think I accidentally took it out, or maybe I put one in there that wasn't supposed to be there, I really don't remember, but whatever it was, we really messed it up. That's your dad for you. Definitely a guy you should listen to for life advice, a guy whose words should be left for you as the lasting testament for you to remember him.

So yeah: we're not working in your old man's comfort zone here. But, well, I got some pretty disturbing news yesterday, and I'm trying to work through it, and this might be the only way to do it. By the time you read this, whenever that is, you'll already know what happened, so there's no need to get into the details of it here. It doesn't really matter anyway. I'm gone. I suppose it's a good thing you won't see me at the very end. It can get bad. Your grandfather told me how his dad, a proud man who'd rather you see him naked than scared, was a shell of himself at the end, how, right before the lung cancer got him, when it was all pain and rattles, he would get so terrified that he'd start shaking and crying and couldn't even complete a sentence. Him and your grandpa didn't talk much about real-life stuff, weren't close like that, not the way you and I are. He figured it would be dignified at the end, that his dad would be on his deathbed, and he'd look at his son, your grandpa, and say, "Son, you've been a good son," and Grandpa would say "Dad, you've been a good dad," and they'd give each other a flinty nod and then he'd die and that would be that. But that's not how it was. There was the horror of staring into the void—and a guy Grandpa had never seen before, shitting himself, all alone.

I won't let you see me like that. You're gonna have to remember me from this.

I'm going to miss a lot. No prom. No graduation. No college—I wonder where you will go. Wherever you want, I bet. I won't get to give you job advice, help you negotiate with your boss, how to let them know what your value is, how to let YOURSELF know what your value is. I'll never see you bring home a girl, or a boy, I guess it could be a boy—my guess is it'd be a girl, but what do I know, it doesn't matter anyway. I won't see you get married. I won't meet your kids. I won't get to be a grandpa. It's all going to happen without me.

But that's not why I want to write to you. This isn't about me. This is about you. This is about you, losing a dad, losing someone who loves you more than he would have thought anyone could ever love anything. Your grandpa and I didn't always get along, and one of the main reasons I've tried so hard to be the best dad I could to you was because it was so hard for him to do the same for me. He couldn't get out of his own way—I know that now. But he was still there. He screwed up a lot. He wasn't the best dad. But he WAS there. I have to give him that. He didn't leave. He always showed up. He was always there.

But I can't even do that for you.

So I thought I might just sit down and write down what I can, while I can, the things that might help you, things you can turn to because you won't be able to turn to me. That's what this is. I don't know if it will help. I don't know if any of this will even be good advice. But I know I need to do it. I've got to be for you as long as I'm able—even after I'm gone.

Feel free to reject all of this. It might just be the rants and ramblings of a scared, sad middle-aged man. It probably is.

But I think I need to do it.

My first gentle edict is a simple one: This is going to happen to everyone. It's OK.

Do not let my death be bigger for you than it should be. I am going when you are still too young. Thirteen might be the worst possible age for a child to lose a parent. I am sorry about that.

But it shouldn't sink you. Everybody loses their parents eventually. That's a good thing. That's all any parent could hope for—to go before their kids. This is the natural order of things. Parents die. All your friends' parents are going to die, just like their parents are going to die, if they haven't already.

The timing stinks, I won't deny that. But what you're going through, it's not unique to you. It's just happening to you first. This can make you useful. You can help people, when they go through it, because you will already have. They'll turn to you, because you will understand.

You have so much life ahead of you, and that life won't stop because of this. It's gonna hurt. It's gonna hurt a lot. It makes me want to scream, it's going to hurt so much. But it's not the end. It's not even unusual.

You're going to be OK.

All right. That's the first one of these. I don't know if this helped you. But it did help me.

So thank you.

4.

"This shit is so good, Dad," Bishop says as he slurps down a piece of tuna sashimi, a piece of seaweed dangling off his left lip. I don't dare tell him to brush it off. He is so happy, here, perhaps never more purely a blissful kid than he is when he is eating sushi. I want him to savor every second without me hectoring him about something. "Can you imagine what this tastes like in *Japan*?"

I sit across from him at MF Sushi in Inman Park, pouring more sake into the little ceramic cup thing they give you. I never understand why they make those so small. Do they not have glasses in Japan? Are their hands unusually small or something?

Bishop, who always loves to make fun of me for not liking sushi, like I'm a '60s dad who thinks Paul McCartney's hair is too long, tells me that there's a certain kind of sushi that will kill you if it is prepared improperly. "They have it at this restaurant, I think," he says. "Want to order it, Dad? Let's roll the dice." Can you imagine dying in between an Orange Theory and a CVS? Because you ate the wrong piece of fish?

But I'm here, just like I'm here every Wednesday night, because this is the night every week I get with Bishop, and this is where he always wants to go. His stepdad Gary got him into sushi, always raved about how he fell in love with the great sushi restaurants of New York City back when he lived there in his twenties, when he was trying to make it as a writer before he moved back to Atlanta and took a job working for the parks department. Gary went on and on about this when I first met him a few years ago, that night at the Mexican restaurant around the corner from where Jessica was living back then, the night she told me that she'd met someone. She said we both knew this day was going to come, that I really should start dating, c'mon, Lloyd, it has been a few years, and then all of a sudden he was there, introducing himself, complaining about the Silicon Alley media economy of the early aughts and letting me know he still thinks he's got a book in him someday, telling me he had been intimidated to meet the cop ex-husband but this has all been great, hasn't it? I shook his hand and nodded along to his stories and said good night and told Jessica it was fine, nice guy, I'm happy for you, and then I walked them out to their car, waited until they drove away, and then went back inside and drank until the guy who runs the place asked me if it was OK if they closed up for the evening. Nobody ever tells a cop to leave.

At a certain point, Bishop knocks over the plastic container that says BISHOP on the side, holding the Invisalign he took out of his mouth to eat.

"Don't lose that thing," I say. "Your mom is still mad at me for last time."

"She wasn't mad at you, she was mad at me," he says, holding an industrial-size glass of Sprite with both hands. "You always think she's mad at you. You always think everyone's mad at you."

I stare at him. A thirteen-year-old boy is quite a creature, a lunatic mix of total lack of self-awareness and an extreme, almost crippling self-consciousness; it's an age where you react to everything you do about ten, fifteen seconds after you do it. He is growing fast, almost too fast for his body to catch up, with his legs and hands now far too big for his torso, like he's constantly bumping into himself.

Yesterday, it was *yesterday*, this was a scared boy in the crowd after a United game, grabbing and holding my left leg like the wind would lift him up and float him away if he were to let go.

He still knows nothing, but now at some level he knows he knows nothing, and thus he assumes the pose of knowing everything. But then there are moments when he is still a child, and he will see something that delights him, and his face will light up and he will bounce around the room like he is Daffy Duck. He is thirteen years old.

"I don't think your mom is always mad at me," I tell him. "I think your mom has enough on her plate without worrying about me."

"You're kinda weird tonight, Dad," he tells me, literally picking up the little bowl of soy sauce and drinking it straight, like a psychopath.

"How's that?" I say. I am trying really, really hard not to be weird.

"You keep looking at my shirt, or something a few inches below my face," he says. "I keep thinking I spilled something on myself."

"You did," I say, looking at the growing pile of stray fish corpses scattered around his side of the table. Teenagers are so disgusting. "I'm starting to think you're only so hungry because you keep missing your mouth."

"It's sushi, Dad, it's supposed to be messy," he says, waving me off, along with the burgeoning toxic event he keeps dipping his sleeves into. "I don't know, you're just . . . weird. It's like you're off in your own little world."

"Sorry about that," I say.

He pops an edamame in his mouth, doesn't even take it out of its pod, just tosses it in there and chews, then spits it into the wicker bowl. Also I think he's chewing gum while he's eating. So gross.

Then he burps. "Whoa, excuse me," he says, and then high-fives me.

"Nice one," I say.

"Thanks, Dad," he says, gives a little fist pump, and stands up. "I gotta pee!"

He sprints past the sushi bar toward the bathroom like he's the only person in the restaurant. Every time a kid pees, it's a sudden, out-of-nowhere emergency.

I watch him prance through and around the tables, his hair bouncing left and right. He hops down the hall, turns around a corner, and steps out of the way as a woman comes out of the bathroom. Bishop makes a big theatrical here-madam-let-me-lay-my-jacket-over-this-puddle-for-you gesture as he steps backward, and she laughs. He makes eye contact with me, shrugs like a silent movie actor, turns around the corner, and disappears as he closes the door behind him. I love him so goddamn much.

I sit and I stare, still seeing his outline, his eyes, his hair, his grin, still there. I sit and I stare. I know where he is. But it still feels like I cannot find him. It feels like he is gone.

5.

Jessica knew we weren't supposed to be married earlier than I did. She helped me deal with it.

We'd met on a dating app, a librarian from Athens and a cop from Atlanta, two normal lonely people with two normal lonely jobs. She was quieter when we first met, more recessive, more likely to keep dating a guy because he had a steady job and a full head of hair and was kind to her. I didn't really know much about who she really was back then, and she didn't either—neither one of us were thinking much about that. We were both in our late twenties. I loved her, and I think she loved me. I was nice to her, and she was nice to me, and it's hard to find people who are just nice to each other. We felt grateful we'd found each other, which at the time we thought was enough but was never going to be—at least not for her.

I just wasn't enough for her. I know that now. We've talked about it. It's fine.

Jessica had a steady family life and a happy childhood in Athens, and I, uh, didn't always, which made the two of us stick together almost for theoretical reasons: we wanted not to be the sort of people who split up more than we actually wanted to be together. We didn't have knock-down, drag-out fights, because knock-down, drag-out fights required more passion than either of us could muster. Every day we were together was a rational decision for her: *Will today be better if I just stay with him?* That question kept ending with a yes, but eventually, she realized that the problem was, she kept asking it. She wanted more out of the world—expected more out of the world—than I did.

It's all right. I'm really OK with it. I couldn't admit it to myself then, but I knew it, really, the whole time.

But we had him, Bishop, and that kept it going longer than it probably should have. Even as we grew further apart, as her world expanded and mine contracted, we always had Bishop. "You're such a good dad," she would always tell me, and she always said it in a way that sounded like she was saying it to herself more than she was saying it to me.

Even now, when we have nothing else in common, Jessica and I can talk for hours about Bishop.

I hadn't known if I'd be a good father or not. I had certainly vowed to be, like so many other sons like me, sons who had tough demanding fathers, sons who would sit in their room and hide, trying to be quiet, to disappear, promising themselves that when *they* have a son, when *they* are a dad, they'll treat them right—they'll be a *good* dad. I won't scream, I won't drink, I won't call my son a pussy all the time.

That was the word Major Lawrence McNeil would use: *pussy.* He didn't use *pussy* as a term of direct address; it wasn't, like, on our Christmas card. It's just what he was forever imploring me not to be.

Oh, don't be a pussy, it's just a spider.

Christ, kids crash their bikes all the time, why are you being such a pussy about this?

Those kids are always going to be targeting you because you're the son of the chief of police. You have to show them you're not a pussy! They'll never respect you until you do.

But I dunno. I guess I was a pussy? I might have just been a pussy.

Bish never knew his grandfather. I suppose I am grateful? But I am not sure.

6.

stare at the television. There is an ad for another pharmaceutical product. I take another sip of bourbon, Buffalo Trace. I drink my bourbon on the rocks, sometimes even with some Diet Coke, I don't need to impress anybody.

The actors in these pharmaceutical commercials all look happy. They make *you* want to be happy. To be healthy. To be well.

I see all these people, and all these commercials, and all these drugs. All this effort! All this money! Scientists working in big labs, wearing the goggles and lab coats, pouring things into beakers, lighting Bunsen burners, wearing big green plastic gloves, working jobs they spent years in college studying for, amassing unfathomable student debt, building their whole lives, a family, a new car, a big house, finally getting those loans paid off, around the construction of these little pills. Then they spend years testing these little pills, trying to see if they work, making sure there's nothing in them that will kill you, and then when they're satisfied that they'll work and that they won't kill you, they give them a name and they go out to sell them, and then they hire actors, some of those actors are British, and they make commercials, and they tell the actors to smile, above all smile, let everybody know that someday, if you take this pill, you will not suffer, you will not hurt so much, that maybe, just maybe, you will not die. All this brainpower, all this time, all this money, all these drugs, all this *effort*, all done in the name of making you believe that you will be better, that everything you feel, the weariness in your bones, the pull of gravity on your skin, the erosion of your body, the decline of your spirit, it can be reversed, or at least stalled. You can look like these people! They look so beautiful! They look so happy! That could be you!

All this effort. *All this effort.* And it all ends the same.

We are all going to die, no matter how much Rinvoq we take. It's happening. Maybe you go peacefully in your bed at the age of ninety-eight. Maybe you get cancer. Maybe you fall down the stairs and break your neck. Maybe the UFOs come and wipe us all out. Maybe it's an *Evil Dead* tree in your brain. It's happening. I've always known this. We all have.

The lightning bolts have been bad tonight.

7.

So lemme get this straight, Lloyd . . ."

Officer Perkins is a thick-necked squat who's been down south for about a year now after being run out of his Jersey precinct for what he ominously described as "an unfortunate rest stop incident." Perkins is one of those mouthy young cops who hasn't gotten his nose broken by somebody here yet but is gonna. He, and the rest of us, and really the city of Atlanta, will all be a lot better off when he does.

"Lloyd here, after working here for, shit, fifty years now, however old he is, how the fuck old *are* you by the way, just decides yesterday that he's gonna go just sit on his squad car and stare at 285," Perkins says. He is standing in the middle of our office, raising his voice and gesturing like he has everybody's full attention, though none of the guys are looking at him, which is only making him raise his voice more. "Motherfucker just gets out of his squad car and squats down on the hood! To look at the freeway! You go blank on us? We need to get you into a home?" He has a wide, meaty nose. It would crack and flatten in a most satisfying manner.

I wondered if anyone would even know, or care, what happened with Morgan yesterday. I should have known: police precincts are like high school locker rooms, we're all catty little bitches, nothing stays quiet around here. I don't look up from the reports I've been mindlessly filling out. I stopped a guy for speeding a few days back, before I saw Dr. Lipsey, a million years ago.

"He's not the one beating it to Grindr all day like you." The room erupts. Perkins smirks, but he also shrinks and walks away. From behind me, my partner, emerges Senior Officer Wynn Anderson. He's a young guy, transferred here a couple of years ago from Athens, a real up-and-comer in the force who's nevertheless currently stuck with a middle-aged legacy cop who hasn't sought a promotion in fifteen years as a partner. Anderson sits at his desk, across from mine. He's a massive kid, with a big thick beard and a broad chest, and the hours he has been putting in at the gym since moving to Atlanta are paying off: there's no baby fat on him anymore. He is, as Bishop said when Anderson came with us to sushi one time, "swole." He looks like an upside-down Trivial Pursuit wedge. But there is a kindness to him that everyone picks up on immediately. I've always found that the biggest, burliest, most intimidating cops are the nicest, calmest ones, like they've learned how to control their anger their whole life because if they hadn't, they'd have snapped some guy's neck years ago. It's the little ones you gotta worry about.

Anderson's big break came a couple of years back, when he was the responding officer to a scary hostage event in Athens. Anderson got in there, subdued the crazy woman who had pulled a gun in a pharmacy, and got everybody out of there in one piece. Made him a bit of a celebrity cop for a while, which got our people up to Athens trying to recruit him and bring him down here—lot of good press to be had for hiring a high-profile white cop everybody likes, here in the big city. Joke was on him, though. Atlanta's a lot less exciting than he imagined, particularly in one of the city's safest neighborhoods. He thought he'd be out keeping the streets clean. Instead he's busting speeders, responding to noise complaints, writing tickets for underage drinking, and listening to me talk about my kid.

Anderson opens up a Tupperware container and takes out two sad, wet pieces of what might have once been grilled chicken. He sees my revulsion. "Gotta keep it lean today," he says. "It's leg day."

"You know me, I consider every day leg day," I say.

He takes his chicken-type substance over to the microwave, starts it up, and walks back over.

"So," he says, "you all right? What *was* yesterday about? Morgan said you were pretty out of it out there."

I like my partner, I admire my partner, he may well be running this place someday, but I am not ready to talk about this with him.

"Yeah, uh, the AC in the cruiser conked out on me, and I got a little sweaty in there," I say. "Just pulled over to get a little bit of air. Morgan just happened to pass by when I was outside the car. I had been just about to leave."

Anderson looks at me skeptically. I'm a shitty liar, always have been. The hard part of lying is *remembering* all the lies you told to get you to the current one. It's more work to keep all the lies straight than it is just to tell the truth in the first place. I'm honestly surprised people do it so often. It's exhausting.

"Uh-huh," he says. "I hadn't noticed any issues with the AC."

"Yeah . . ." I say. "Must have been a battery thing or something. I'll take it into the shop this week to make sure. Gonna be hot out there next week."

The microwave beeps, and Anderson gives me a you're-full-of-shit-but-whatever head shake as he gets up and walks into the kitchen. "To be continued, Lloyd," he says.

I'm sure that chicken is going to smell like boiled piss when he gets back, so I finish up my paper on the speeder and walk it over to put it in the plastic folder outside my CO's office.

She's in there, watching Braves highlights on her phone. She does love her Braves. She sees me through the window, nods, and waves me over. She doesn't look up as I walk in and sit down at her desk.

"Did you see that game last night?" Ellis says, still staring at her phone. "Them boys are rolling right now."

Sergeant Desiree Ellis, or "Ellis," as she has always demanded we all call her, is the only person in this precinct who has been here as long as I have. She's also the only one, other than me of course, who was here when my dad was still in charge. We were briefly partners back then, back before she zoomed past me and everybody else up the ranks, and she had a way of doing everything in a way that made her look great and made me look bad, at least in Dad's eyes. She wasn't doing it on purpose, or at least I don't think so. The job just meant more to her, more than it ever could to someone like me, who was born into it, who never had a choice. She told me once, back when we talked about things like this, that she was watching the news as a teenager and saw that the chief of police was a Black woman. Her name was Beverly Harvard, she was the first Black woman to ever be the chief of police of a major American city, she was in charge when the bomb went off during the Olympics. "I saw her and thought, 'I want to be her, I want to be the boss,'" Ellis told me. Dad, shortly after taking over for Beverly Harvard himself, saw that ambition instantly. He recognized it as yet another thing his son lacked.

Which is one of the many reasons she's sitting at that desk right now, and I'm sitting across from her.

"I didn't, no," I say. "I guess they won?"

"Right," she says, putting the phone down, glancing at me, then looking at her computer screen. "I forgot, soccer guy. How's the boy?"

"Huge," I say. "Gonna eat me out of house and home. I think he literally grew out of his shoes while we were having dinner last night."

"That happens," she says. She just sent her second son off to college. Her kids are too smart to become cops.

"Don't sweat that report, it's some speeder off McClendon I tagged a few days ago, I just forgot to log it," I say.

"You know I'm just gonna have the GSU intern plug it into the computer anyway," she says, sipping coffee from a mug that says "Stupid People Keep Me Employed," with a picture of handcuffs on it. "Though the little shit's so lazy I'm going to have to remind him twenty times. None of these kids want to work."

"We didn't either," I say.

"Well, you didn't." She briefly peers down her glasses at me before

31

going back to her screen. "But you still went out and did your job." She takes another sip of her coffee. "They just don't do anything they don't want to do. Imagine how that would have gone over in our day."

I think of the picture outside her office that I passed by when I walked in, the picture I and the rest of the officers look at every day, almost as much as it looks at us—looks at me, really. The man is sitting ramrod straight, his hat rigid and low over his eyes, his uniform crisp and pressed, not a wrinkle or crease in sight. He has a slight grin, maybe not a grin, more like a subtle smirk, as if he knows he has power over you and is a little amused by your inability to do anything about it.

But it's the eyes that get you. He had the most piercing blue eyes, cold, iced eyes, eyes that you could feel staring at you even in the dark. Those eyes saw everything, and they judged—me, Sergeant Ellis, everybody in the precinct, everybody in the department, criminals, judges, reporters, mayors, you, your dog, your great uncle who never even met him, presidents, kings, God himself. Major McNeil saw all, and all that he saw displeased him.

"Can you imagine what Major McNeil would do if we tried to pull that?" she says, looking back to me, her voice lowering, as if simply saying his name would conjure him and his judgment somehow.

"I can," I say. "I very much can."

She chuckles darkly. "Oh, I'm sure you can."

I see him every day. Everybody docs.

8.

Did Dad just think I was a pussy?

I certainly wasn't him, anything like him, a fact that once brought me considerable shame—and not just from him. Major McNeil commanded respect, demanded it, grabbed you by your shirt until he got it. Major Lawrence McNeil was commander of Zone 6, the area of Atlanta we lived in—Old Fourth Ward, Little Five Points, Cabbagetown, Inman Park, all of it—and he ran Zone 6 like it had been siphoned off from the rest of Atlanta specifically so he could be in charge of it. He was tall—so much taller than me, forever—and lurked over everyone, barking out orders and indulging no disorder, discord, or disruption. He actually had a sign on his desk that said this: NO DISORDER, DISCORD, OR DISRUPTION WILL BE INDULGED. Weird sign, right? There was no picture of my mom and me in his office, but there was that.

He was respected by the men and women who worked under him, or at least feared, and so resolutely focused on his corner of the world that he was able to run Zone 6 as his little fiefdom even as more reform-minded police chiefs and mayors, with little success, occasionally tried to rein him in. Until he just got the big job himself.

Zone 6 was a primarily Black neighborhood back then, before all the white tech hipsters showed up and made everything expensive (and more than tripled the taxes on our house), but Major McNeil was able to overcome the even-then-still-problematic optics of a white zone commander in charge of a Black neighborhood by keeping the crime numbers lower than nearly every other part of the city while relentlessly consolidating his own power. Dad's office was also covered with newspaper articles about himself, all orchestrated through his press agent—himself. He was seen—in a city that often seemed, from the outside anyway, to be careening out of control—as the steady, firm, unyielding hand of the law. "The Man Keeping Atlanta Atlanta," the *Atlanta Journal-Constitution* once called him—he loved that one. On the cover of *Atlanta* magazine—the issue that came out when he got the chief job, which adorned the walls of his office both at work and at home—he looked like a statue that had been standing over the city for decades.

I was a cop's son—I was *the* cop's son—which meant I was a cop before I'd ever even thought of being a cop. Shoot, I was a cop for Halloween, every Halloween. It was all mapped out for me. I never questioned it; I wouldn't dare. *Little Major*, that's what all the guys at the precinct called me, and I hated it, hated it, hated it. Little Major sounds like the name of a little dog riding in a motorcycle sidecar, maybe wearing goggles; Little Major is definitely something you are constantly patting on the head. I learned to smile and pretend like I was OK with it.

My classes were never that important. It was all just pointing to being a cop and working for Dad. I ended up going down the road to Georgia State for college, got my criminal justice degree in four years, and was working in the precinct two weeks after graduation. The plan was for me to be Dad, sooner rather than later. That was Dad's plan, anyway. If I'd just stop being such a pussy.

And I was a pussy. I can admit it now. At least by Dad's definition, and maybe by a lot of people's, I dunno. Maybe tougher kids would have rebelled against all this, would have at least done some light vandalism to piss off their father. Maybe he would have respected me more if I had done that. The thing is, though: I *did* kind of want to be a cop. I didn't want to be the type of cop Dad was, taciturn and unrelenting.

But I did see how cops could help people, how people needed cops, how a cop had a higher mission than one of those schmucks just sitting in a bank collecting a paycheck all day before heading home to mow the lawn in silence. At GSU, I discovered that I liked poring through all the books, absorbing all the theories, analyzing all the debates on the different styles of policing. I also liked that the job was, at its core, designed to help people, to solve the problems of people who cannot solve their problems themselves. I liked that I could help.

I know how a lot of people feel about cops. People like my dad are very much responsible for people feeling that way. If you ran into my dad on the street, or any of the number of men who loyally served under him, you would be more likely to see him as the cause of your problems rather than the solution to them.

I remember when I was a kid, we were walking home from the precinct—it's perhaps not a coincidence that all my childhood memories of my dad involve either going to his office or leaving it, rather than, like, watching a ball game or something—when we came across a drunk old man on the street near our house. I don't really know if he was old; when you're a kid, everybody who isn't a kid is ninety. But even at the age of nine, I knew he was probably homeless, and definitely sauced to the gills. He swayed side to side as he walked, like he kept trying to lean on imaginary stepladders. He saw me and my dad, in uniform, walking toward him, stopped, did a little mock salute, and said, in diction that was exquisitely, expertly slurred, in a singsong voice, "Mr. Officer, please don't let your boy put me in the hoosegow. Don't put me in that hooooooosegooowwwww." He then tapped my head and let out a little spit.

I thought we were going to walk right past him, pretend like we didn't see him at all, but when we had just gone by him, Dad turned on his heels so quickly I felt a gust of wind. In one motion, he grabbed the man by the back of his neck, lifted him up like a kitten, smashed his face against the hood of a parked car, whipped out his baton, and smashed the man's left knee with it. The man howled in pain, but Dad had him turned back around and sprawled back-down on the top of the car before anyone could react. As I stood there and stared, Dad picked the man up with both hands and pulled his face to his own so that their noses were touching.

"You touch my son again, I'll take this gun here and I'll cave in your skull with it," he said, evenly, almost calm, a thick blue vein coursing out of the center of his forehead the only evidence that anything was happening at all. "Do you understand that?"

"Yes sir," the man said, and I think he was already crying.

"If I see you on this street again, this will be worse," Dad said. "How about that? You understand that?"

"I do," the man said.

This all happened in about ten seconds. Dad was too efficient to make any sort of extended scene. He got his point across. He gave the man a light shove into a park bench, and the man sat there, his head in his hands, as we continued our walk home. Dad didn't say another word about it. Mom had a pot roast on the stove, and it was not mentioned again.

This is what it was like to grow up with Major McNeil. This is what it was like to be Little Major.

Yet, still: I became a cop. Being a cop could be a way to make a difference—to help people feel not just safe, but *comforted*. There is something about the job, when it is done well, and I do think I do it well, that can be inherently calming. There is a chaotic situation, one in which people with extremely different views of a conflict find themselves unable to resolve it and therefore in need of a third party, an impartial observer with no connection to either one of them. A cop should soothe, should listen, should empathize, and should thus then be able to restore order. When people are heated, a good cop can use academic, intellectual, even dispassionate, strategies to cool them down. I realized that I could be this kind of cop.

I had learned, after all, to be that kind of son.

I liked all that stuff. That's to say, I liked all the stuff that Dad had told me would be useless once I was actually in the job. That was all "hall monitor geek shit" to Dad. Dad was about force. But I hated— still hate—that whole notion. Dad knew I hated it. He knew I hated a lot. I hated all the tough guy bullshit. I hated my gun. (I still hate my gun.) I hated having to puff my chest out to assert my authority. I hated the "shit themselves" look that Dad tried to teach me, the look he said "makes them want to shit themselves the minute they see you walk up." I hated all of it. At the core of it, though, I have to be honest: I hated *conflict*. And that's all being a cop was in my dad's world. Just one conflict after another, all day, every day, confronting people on one of the worst days of their lives and muscling them into submission. Everything was a battle, all the time, and you better win, or else there is no order in the world, only chaos. It was nothing but conflict. And if you hate conflict, there isn't a worse job in the world for you than being a cop. Yet here I was. A cop. A pussy cop.

He was wrong, though. I'm a good cop. I'm just not his kind of cop. He had vowed to make me one, from the day I was born, and I have to admit, if he had stayed on me as long as he planned to, he might have gotten there.

But it all fell apart on him in a way he never could have seen coming.

9

The first woman's body, well, parts of it, was found after the other three, even though she'd been killed two years before any of them, in the same place they'd been found: in a dumpster. Her name was Karen Middleton, a thirty-five-year-old single mom of two who disappeared shortly after leaving an exercise class in Kirkwood, one of the last places in Atlanta you'd ever expect to disappear from. Her twelve-year-old daughter had called 911 when her mom never arrived home. Her ex-husband had been at work all day, and we cleared him pretty quickly. No one even thought it was a murder. Dad had put Homicide on it, but there was no physical evidence, no video, and it never even made the news. Dad kept after them about it, but what could you do? Karen Middleton was just gone.

But nine months later, there was another one. Veronica Winters, a forty-one-year-old softball coach at Maynard Holbrook Jackson High School. She had stopped by a Walgreens after practice and somehow hadn't made it back to her car. It was still sitting there when her body was found, still warm, outside an alley behind Dr. Grierson's OB-GYN practice in a strip mall next to an ACE Hardware store. Security camera footage caught Ms. Winters leaving through the automatic doors and turning toward her car, but nothing else, not where she went, not who might have stopped her. Her legs were still dangling over the side of the dumpster when an employee at the ice cream place around the corner found her, as if she'd been hoisted up there by someone in a hurry. She still had her car keys in her pocket. Her plastic Walgreens bag, containing a refill on her Xanax prescription, some face cream, and an opened value-size box of Junior Mints, was lying in front of the dumpster, with three Junior Mints on the ground beside it.

Veronica Winters instantly became the biggest story in Atlanta, and it happened right here in Zone 6, the old precinct of the current chief. Dad went on television and said, in his clipped, pursed way, that the department was not yet considering the death a "certain homicide." He took a lot of heat for that phrase, "certain homicide," even though I remember at the time him privately not only thinking it was a murder but pushing the homicide guys to connect it to the disappearance of Karen Middleton. The *Atlanta Journal-Constitution* columnist, who didn't know that, wrote, "Major McNeil has a much higher threshold for certainty than most of us do—definitely more than that woman does, who, despite what he tried to tell Atlantans at his press conference, is certainly dead." Dad was being cautious, but people didn't want caution. They were scared. And they wanted Major McNeil to be a lot more certain than he looked to be. He took some hits on that one.

But then everybody moved on, like they always do, to the new tragedy, the new thing to scare you. Homicide was still digging up dead ends two years later when everybody got the opportunity to remember. Forty-four-year-old Helen Watsma, a real estate broker, was found lying at the bottom of a dumpster outside Dr. Singh's office in Little Five Points. The killer, perhaps irritated by the quiet, decided he no longer wished to go unrecognized. He had taken his time with Helen Watsma. She lay at the bottom of the dumpster, neatly posed, arms folded, wearing a light-blue dress that was barely rumpled. There was a note in steno paper on her chest, with the words CERTAIN HOMICIDE written on it. They called him the Dumpster Diver.

The chief was more prepared for the press this time. Major McNeil was on television for three consecutive evenings after Helen Watsma was found, confident, poised, and dead-solid sure that the killer would not get far. "We're going to get him, and we're going to get him soon," my dad said, and he looked directly into the camera when he did so. There wasn't a person watching, including me, who didn't believe him. After all, Dad had been on this since Karen Middleton. It was widely assumed that it would not take long to find the perpetrator. The crimes had taken place in the middle of the day, in an affluent up-and-coming neighborhood, and they did not seem to have been planned out in a particularly meticulous manner. We had a pool in the office about when we'd get the asshole. The longest anybody had was a month.

But that month passed. There were no killings, but there was no arrest, or even many leads. The precinct started to get letters from a guy calling himself DD, claiming he was responsible for the murders and trying to taunt my father, the guy from the TV, into some sort of "cat-and-spider game" (the exact, and weird, term the letters used), but none of these missives had any specific details, and we all assumed it was just some crank. But they got leaked to the press anyway, and they ran with the story of a killer specifically taunting Major McNeil. At one point, during an interview with 11Alive News, the reporter asked my father if he thought the killer was targeting these women as part of a personal vendetta against him. "Do you *think* I have any serial killers in my life?" Dad growled. "Jesus, I have no idea." This became a headline too. McNEIL: I HAVE NO IDEA.

Dad aged twenty years overnight. The television networks and newspapers turned on him, something they'd been waiting to do for years—you don't get built up as much as Major McNeil built himself up without being primed for a fall. Here was the man who promised to keep Atlanta, like Zone 6, not only safe but *unchanged*, a man who now couldn't stop what seemed to be a madman who was snatching women—white women, *educated* white women, the very people who had moved to this neighborhood and turned it into a place that Major McNeil could claim he had personally been protecting—right there in the middle of the day.

Dad closed ranks. He stopped calling press conferences, but that just made the reporters gather outside the building and, eventually, his home. I even got dragged into it. The *Atlanta Journal-Constitution* ran a sidebar on "Major McNeil's Nepotism Hire" that seemed to imply that Dad would have had time to find the serial killer if he hadn't been spending so much time giving his unexceptional son a desk job. I was twenty-four years old and didn't know what more to do but watch. I had no idea what was happening either.

Two weeks later, thirty-six-year-old Meghan Hampton, a fitness instructor, was lying on *top* of a dumpster outside Dr. Landing's office in Little Five Points. She also had her arms folded over her, and a little manila envelope was tucked under one. When they opened it at the lab, they found a jawbone, three severed toe bones, and a femur. They turned out to be Karen Middleton's. There was a note in the envelope: MORE. I remember this one most vividly because Ellis was the one who discovered the body. I'd been out late the night before, and she was covering for me. Dad put her on the task force. That was her last day as my partner.

But they got nowhere. And it wore him down. Dad would just come home, long after my and everybody else's shift was over, head straight for our den, shut the door behind him, turn on a baseball game, and drink. I still lived in the house, a cop sleeping in his old bedroom. Mom told me to leave him be. We were good at leaving him be.

The final victim came one week later—Wendy Johnstone, a thirty-eight-year-old waitress at the Outback Steakhouse on Peachtree Road. She showed up in yet another dumpster with a knife in her chest, a new wrinkle. There was no note.

Dad had his heart attack two weeks later. Mom had been out at the grocery store—we were going to have some of the guys from the precinct over to watch the Dawgs game. She found him cold dead in the kitchen. He was in his uniform, even though he hadn't gone to work that day. It was crisp and pressed. We had a huge funeral, with all the firing of the rifles. I didn't cry. It was the least I could do for him.

DD sent a note to the station the day after the paper put his funeral on the front page. BYE, it read.

10.

"You look like shit," Sergeant Ellis says.

"I always look like shit," I say.

"True," she says, placing the speeder report in a filing cabinet that I have a sneaking suspicion she only keeps around for my benefit.

Ellis graduated from the academy alongside me. She'd grown up in Mechanicsville, one of the higher-crime areas in the city back then, nothing at all like the safe and gentrified Little Five Points. She was a natural from the beginning. When we were both assigned to my dad's precinct, she stood out immediately as the one who had her shit together. We were all young idiots back then, and we had this sort of hazing ritual where we'd have a target shooting contest when our shift wrapped, and whoever won got free beers at Pal's on Auburn Avenue. She won, every time, and ended up outdrinking all of us too—she was always the only one still on her feet at the end of the night to make sure everybody got home. By the end of our first month, she'd color-coded everybody's food in the fridge, organized the fantasy football league, and led us all in arrests. She was also, we discovered, a history buff; she actually minored in it in college.

My dad took to her instantly. They used to talk about World War II battles together. He loved all that; I think he couldn't help but be envious of a time when there was order and everybody had to pull together to beat the bad guys. Dad had a way of dressing me down by talking directly to Ellis, like I wasn't in the room. I remember one time, he came by the desk we shared back then. He stood behind me, facing her, and said, "Ellis, I saw you nailed the target test last week, nice work. Make sure you tell your partner that he needs to work on his sight alignment. As you know, you want equal light on either side of the front sight post. Equal height: equal light." He put his right hand on my shoulder, sighed, and walked away. Ellis had the courtesy not to say anything.

Ellis benefited from being the partner of Major McNeil's son; for an ambitious cop like her, it provided real proximity to the boss. We didn't talk much, and we sure didn't socialize. But she wasn't a bad partner. She could have made it a lot worse for me, that's for sure.

I remember one of our last shifts together. There'd been a B&E at a Home Depot, some junkie who didn't know chain stores had alarms and cameras, I guess, and I responded near the end of my shift. The place was closed, and the night manager let me in. "He's up there by the lumber section," he told me. "I think he's asleep." I walked over to that part of the store, a little too casually, and as I was approaching the indeed-sleeping junkie, he suddenly leaped up, had to have been five feet in the air, and began screaming, "They got me in the gonads! *They got me in the gonads!*" That's a word you don't hear much anymore.

It startled me, and I went to my gun. I unholstered it, but I was falling backward a bit and slipped on a wet spot on the floor. To catch myself as I fell, I instinctively put my right hand behind me, which made me drop my gun, sending it flying. It landed on the floor, skittered past the power tools, and, as I watched in slow motion, slid down a grate left open by the janitorial staff. Down it went. I heard it fall, then, after about five seconds, clang off a pipe and clatter down the sewer, gone forever. As far as I know, it's still in the Chattahoochee River somewhere.

I sat there, flat-assed on the floor of a Home Depot, a wet cop without his gun. There is nothing more humiliating, emasculating, for a cop to lose his gun, particularly a cop responding to a sleeping junkie in a hardware store. I panicked. How would I explain this? What would the guys at the precinct say? Worst of all: What would Major McNeil say?

My radio buzzed. "McNeil, Ellis here, you wrapping up?"

I pulled out my cell phone and called her.

"Uh, it's Lloyd," I said, feeling like a pussy. "I lost my gun, Ellis. I lost my gun."

"Oh for fuck's sake," she said. "Where are you?"

"The Home Depot on Ponce de Leon," I said.

"Stay right there," she said and hung up. I sat back down in the water and stared at the sandpaper aisle. She was in the store ten minutes later. By the time she got to me, she had already talked the night manager into not pressing charges, she had gotten the junkie cleaned up and a ride to the shelter, and she had concocted my cover story.

"You and I were shooting at the range, and your gun malfunctioned," she said, picking me up gruffly and putting a towel on the back of my neck. "We reported it damaged—I've already done that—and we placed it in the wrong box for repairs, and now it has been misplaced. It happens all the time. No one will ever care."

"Wha?" I said.

"Just shut the fuck up, Lloyd," she said, pushing me out the door and out to my squad car. "This never happened. But hang onto your damn gun next time, would you?"

We never discussed it after that, and you can be damned sure I never lost my gun again. She got promoted to the task force a few weeks later and rose through the ranks. After the guy who took over for Dad got transferred up, she became the youngest Black female zone commander in the history of the Atlanta Police. She has now run this precinct for ten years. She hasn't relented one bit: she's going to become chief. I don't know how, Lord knows they throw every obstacle in front of her they can. But she's indestructible. She's the cop Dad wanted. And she knows it.

"When's the last time you slept, Lloyd?" she asks me. She stands up from behind her desk and walks over to me, pulling up a chair just to my left. "No pissing around here, you look awful."

I do not know the answer to Ellis's question.

"What day is it?" I say.

"That's the wrong answer, Lloyd," she says. "And now you're pulling your cruiser to the side of I-85 in the middle of the day? And spacing out? What's that about?"

"The car was—"

"Bullshit," she says. "That car is fine, and everybody knows it."

I say nothing.

"Anyway, you look like shit," she says. "Go home. Don't come back to work again until you're better."

"Yes, ma'am," I say, following orders as ever, and head to her office door.

"Also," she says from behind me, and I turn around. She whips a handkerchief at my chest. "Your nose is bleeding."

I put the white napkin to my face and then look at it. She does appear to be right.

THE TEN GENTLE EDICTS OF LLOYD MCNEIL

Edict No. 2: Learn to drive a stick.

Your grandfather taught me how to drive on Bertha, which was a four-speed on the column back then, before we put the stick shift on the floor because, well, because it looks cooler to shift your car on the floor than it does to shift it on the column. You probably don't even know what a stick shift is. They don't make cars that aren't automatic anymore. But if someone only knows how to drive an automatic, they don't really know how to drive a car. You're just pushing a button in an automatic. You might as well be starting a blender.

You have to *feel* a car, to understand when you are giving it power, what it is doing with that power, what it needs from you, what you want to give it. It's a dance, shifting a car, revving it up, hitting the peak, shifting, revving back up again. You increase the tension, you push it to its limit, and then you release that tension. A car is not a device, or a gadget. It's a living, breathing thing. It's something you must feed. You do not simply own a car. You *provide* for a car.

We've lost this. They've put distance between us and our cars. They've put computers in charge of them. You can't even change the oil in these new cars without some sort of code. But the right car is an extension of you: everything it does is a direct result of your physical movement. When you get in a car, you have a responsibility, to yourself, to the car, to the people on the road, to understand what the car needs from you. What you are making the car do—what *you* are doing. To truly understand that, you need to learn to drive a stick shift. That's how you find the rhythm of a car. It's how you find your own.

I don't know if you want Bertha or not. I hope so. But even if you don't, you have to care for her. You have to respect her. You gotta learn to drive a stick. It will be hard at first. But everything worth doing is hard at first.

Plus: someday, you watch, you'll find yourself in a situation where no one else knows how to drive stick, and you do. Shifting a car, man, it looks cool. You look like a movie star when you shift a car. You look like a guy who knows what he's doing. You look like a guy in charge. Be a guy in charge. Be one with your car. Shift the goddamn thing. And then get out there on the open road, Bish, and just floor it.

11.

Here's what the pamphlet they gave me said I'm in for:

Some brain tumors present themselves through neurobehavioral or psychiatric symptoms only. Hallucinations and even psychosis have been reported in brain tumor patients. These symptoms can be very unsettling to patients and their informal caregivers. This combination of temporal displacement, hallucinogenic visions, anxiety about expiration, cranial pressure leading to psychic outburst and emotional confusion and, of course, the immense physical trauma caused by the tumors can lead to harrowing scenes for caregivers and professional staff, as well as obviously the patient themselves. Ask your doctor about techniques for dealing with the psychological stress and mental toll on you, and your loved ones.

And here's what I found on the glioblastoma Reddit group, because it's not like I was going to sleep or anything.

u_screamingmeemie: No memory. Can barely walk on his own. Has Tantrums like a 5 year old. Repeats the same meaningless questions over, and over, and over, and over again. And again. Doesn't make sense any more. Picture an

advanced stage of Alzheimer's, that's what he is.
Oh and he's mean too. I am beyond tired. Why
are we keeping him home ? Why keep him like
this ? He drives us absolutely crazy, and we are
constantly angry at him. Judge me for my lack of
patience, I'm sorry but I don't care. I do not want
this. I do not want to hate my dad. This is not
how we pictured the last days should be.

u_Betty248: my dad just punched his
granddaughter in the face. i hit him back without
thinking. it felt good i am so so sorry

I was eight, too young to quite grasp what was happening to my
aunt Marlese. But I knew she wasn't Aunt Marlese anymore. That part
was clear.

Mom told me in the car on the way to see Marlese that I should appreciate this particular visit, that this was family, that *you never know
with family.* Aunt Marlese was staring blankly forward, wrapped up
in one of the quilts my grandmother had knitted for her while she
was sitting across the room from her for the last month, gaping at the
turned-off television. The left side of Aunt Marlese's head had been
shaved, and she had a new cherry-red scar that ran just above her ear.
There was some drool on the left side of her lip. She wasn't moving,
but she wasn't sitting still either. She just sort of sagged.

Aunt Marlese's head lolled to the left, a cue ball coming to a stop
at the end of a felt table. She lifted her head slowly. Then she saw me.

"Lloyd! Lloyd! Mama, it's Lloyd! Mama, do you see, it's Lloyd!
Come here, Lloyd!" Aunt Marlese said. I didn't even think she would
know my name. "Come sit next to me! Oh you beautiful boy!" Her
voice slurred, but it was suddenly strong and loud. My grandmother
scampered over to her to keep her from falling on the floor. Aunt

Marlese turned her head back to her mother. "Mama! Mama! It's Lloyd! Come closer, Lloyd!"

She tried to put her left arm around me, but she couldn't quite lift it. It was more like a twitch. "What a good boy you are! Tell me about your school! Are you in school?"

"Uh, OK," I said, looking at my mom, and then back to her. "Um, well, I'm in the third grade, and I—"

Then she started screaming. Full-on wailing, like someone had just stabbed her with something, and twisted it. *"Aaaaaaaieeeeeeeee!"* she howled, and began spasming, knocking over Grandma's water bottle and sending the remote control spinning across the floor. "It *hurrrrrrrrrrrrts!!!!"*

She turned to my grandmother. "Mama, help me! HELP ME!!!!"

Mom gasped, took me out to the car with her, and drove home. We didn't go see Aunt Marlese after that.

I am not sure I want to make it to Christmas.

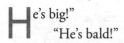e's big!"

"He's bald!"

Bishop gives me a quick look and cocks his head slightly to the left.

Can I say it?

Yes. Go ahead.

"He's a motherfucking wall!"

Then Bishop continues to join up with 42,500 other screaming Atlanta United fans, all standing, jumping, and clapping their hands over their head.

Brad Guzaaaaaan!

Brad Guzaaaaaan!

He's big!

He's bald!

He's a motherfucking wall!

Brad guzaaaaaaan!

Brad guzaaaaaaan!

This chant originates from the Gulch, the supporters' section of Mercedes-Benz Stadium, where several thousand Atlantans bang drums and wave flags and sing songs for two hours during every Atlanta United home game. We've had these season tickets right next to the supporters' section since Atlanta United, our Major League Soccer team, came into being in 2017. We never miss an Atlanta United home game. Bishop knows all the chants, has known them since we first started coming here when he was six years old.

Vamos, vamos, vamos ATL!

Vamos . . . A . . . T . . . LLLLLLLLL!

This is our place. This has always been our place. The plan has been for it forever to be our place.

The occasion of my allowing my thirteen-year-old to scream "Motherfucking wall!" in my face arose because of a fantastic save by Atlanta United keeper Brad Guzan, who is indeed big and indeed bald and indeed a motherfucking wall. Guzan is a former World Cup goalkeeper for the US national team who is now nearing forty, which is slowing him down but not making him any less impenetrable. He is the only keeper Atlanta United has ever had, the team's captain, and Bishop's favorite player since he was in the first grade.

"Guuuuuuuuuuuuuzzzzzz," Bishop yells, his mouth half full of M&Ms.

I took him to his first game when he was six, so small that he had to fold the seat down and stand on it just to be able to see. It wasn't the game that entranced him anyway, at least not at first. It was obvious to Bishop, and to me, that by coming to an Atlanta United game, he was instantly part of something different. It was his first real collective.

To most of the country—and really to most of the area surrounding the city who never actually come here—Atlanta is less a city than it is an avatar of southern culture. You could see why people not really paying attention might think that. It's the biggest city down here, the place that hosted the Olympics, the home of Jimmy Carter and Ted Turner, the epicenter of SEC football, the airport where you can get a connection on the way to Denver or Florida or Mexico. It's the home of Waffle House, and Jeff Foxworthy, and country music stars—the place where white people in Mississippi and South Carolina go when they're going to "the City." In the popular imagination, Atlanta is The South, and most sports teams down here, they market themselves accordingly. When you go to a Braves game, you hear country music and "God Bless the USA," and you do the Tomahawk Chop, and you celebrate Christian Heritage Night, stuff like that. It's the sort of stadium where it can feel like you're standing up for the veterans every half inning.

What's immediately striking—and what makes you feel, every game, like your feet are floating above the ground for the entire two hours—about Atlanta United games is that they are about *Atlanta*. Because the team is so new, it was able to invent itself in its own image. And that image is of the new Atlanta, the current Atlanta, the Atlanta that is diverse and young and progressive and inclusive, a 48 percent Black city, Black owned, Black led, Black run, an Atlanta that has rebuilt itself, an Atlanta that is surrounded by the sins of the past and is determined to be a rebuke to all of it.

The opening hype video features shots of people marching through the streets of Atlanta, chanting, drumming, young, *ready*. (You can *almost* see my house in one shot.) They're young and Black and Latino and Asian and white, all together, a conscious mission statement from the very beginning: *This is what Atlanta is. This is who we are.* There's a flag in the corner of the stadium with a Five Stripes Atlanta United logo in rainbow colors emblazed with "Y'All Means **All.**" There's an LGBTQ+ fangroup, All Stripes, that's right in the middle of the Gulch. To look into the stands is to see a cross-section of races and genders and nationalities and everything that makes this city a place that so many young people want to be.

This is not my father's Atlanta, the place he insisted on it being long after the city itself, and even its police force, had begun to move on—to try to recover from the decades of pain and ruin. This is today's Atlanta: different people, with different backgrounds, cramming together and intermingling in new and thrilling ways to produce a unique community all their own. This is what I want my Atlanta to be. It is a place I am proud to protect.

Not for me. For my son. For him.

Bishop took to this instantly. He's a city kid at his core, always was, and this is what a great city does: it makes you feel like a part of something, in tune with a larger hum, connected to a world that's bigger than just yourself. I do not know where he will go in his life. But I know that he will always come back here.

"Dad, that's a *terrible* call! There's no way he was offsides!" Bishop turns to me and points at the opposite end of the field. If I'm being honest, even after seven years of being a season ticket holder, I don't always understand the intricacies of soccer, and no matter how hard I try, I can never tell when someone is offsides or not.

"Yeah, crap call," I say, trying to be as vague as possible. Suddenly the entire stadium erupts. A horn blares, and two eruptions of fire blast from in front of the Gulch.

"Gooooooooooalllllllllllllll!"

Our whole section leaps in the air, and water bottles go flying in the air above us. Bishop is screaming and dancing.

"Almada! Did you see that? That was incredible!" He reaches out his hand to high-five me.

When we first started going to games, when Atlanta would score a goal, I would put my hands under each of Bish's armpits and lift him. I'd then drop him down to where his feet hit the ground and yank him back up, and each time he touched the ground he would do a little hop, like he was flying, like he could soar into the sky. He would look at me the whole time with such joy, his mouth round and wide and his eyes sparkling, *Higher, Daddy, higher*, and we would celebrate each goal this way, his hands in the air, his arms spread out, the two of us surrounded by forty-five thousand of our best friends but also just the two of us, alone, smiling and yelping in each other's faces. *Up* he would go, *down* he would go, *higher, Daddy, higher*.

He is too big for me to do that anymore, and he wouldn't let me anyway if I tried. But every time Atlanta United scores, I think of how I used to lift him. And I know that he thinks of it too.

Now, though, now we just high-five. It is enough.

"Goalllllllllllll!" I scream, louder than I usually do, maybe louder than I ever have.

13.

I told myself I was going to tell him tonight. I spent all day working myself up to it, writing it down, practicing it in the mirror. I couldn't get it right.

Bish, listen . . . we need to talk.

That was a good start. But it was hard to figure out where to go from there.

Hey, so you know how you always say that you like Gary but you'll never think of him as your real dad? Well . . .

Yeeeesh.

I found myself trying everything.

OK, so you know how normal brains don't explode? Well, mine's not like that.

Hey, good news! You don't have to sweat which house you're going to spend Thanksgiving at this year!

So it looks I'm gonna have to put these season tickets in your Apple Wallet, uh, forever.

In the end, I was just going to do the whole "There's no good way to say this, so I'll just say it: I'm dying. I'm sorry" thing. Straightforward.

But I just couldn't do it. I picked him up at his mom's, and I thought I'd tell him before the game, but Gary wanted me to hear this song he wrote, so we barely got out of there in time, and I couldn't exactly tell him at the game, in public, and then the game went into extra time, and before you knew it it was ten thirty and he has school tomorrow and I just kept finding excuses not to do it and then I hugged him good night and he yelled "BRAD GUZAAAAAAN!" as he got out of the car and then I was home.

I don't know if I would be helping him by telling him. I worry that the only reason I'd be telling him is that, well, there really isn't anyone else I would tell. I'm not telling Jessica, or Sergeant Ellis, or my partner . . . and honestly those are the only other three people who would care, something I hadn't realized until I thought about it just now. Would I be telling Bishop for my benefit, or his?

As I sit here, watching political news on cable like any of it is going to matter to me anymore, I'm glad I didn't say anything.

Does a son want to spend the last three months with his father crying and scared?

Or does he want to do soccer chants and eat sushi and make armpit noises?

I think the answer is obvious.

He doesn't know these memories he's making with me will be his last. That will make them more vivid as the years come, not less. He doesn't need to know. It will be one of the last gifts I can give him.

Which means it's just me here. I'm gonna have to do this alone.

14.

I've never liked thinking about money. Jessica and I never really fought, even when it wasn't going well, and I honestly think part of that is that we didn't really worry about money that much. It's not like we were rich or anything. She was a schoolteacher, I was a cop, you don't usually see either one of those on the *Forbes* list. But one of the nice things about being a cop or a teacher is that the pay scale is laid out for you. Sure, you can work your way up the ladder and become a staff sergeant or a commander or even a chief, and you'll get plenty of raises along the way, but if you're ambitious enough to push yourself hard enough to do all that, you're not doing it for the money anyway. (The only way any cop ever gets rich is stealing.) There's no confusion about money. If you can just hold onto your job for thirty years or so, you know exactly what you're going to make, pretty much year by year until you're done.

I made about forty-five grand a year when I started, went up to about sixty-five grand a decade later and am taking home about ninety-five grand now. Not bad, sure beats McDonald's, but again, no one's ever going to get rich doing it, no matter how good a cop you are.

Because of this, I have never worried too much about money. I just live within my means and make sure not to get fired. Sometimes I splurge on a nice bourbon. This plan works. It could work for you too. I should have my own call-in radio advice show.

However. This plan only works if the set income is consistent—if it is never, say, cut off unexpectedly.

I HAVE A LITTLE DESK JUST OFF THE KITCHEN TABLE WITH A COMPUTER ON IT, though I always forget it's there. Another nice thing about being a cop is that you don't have to sit and stare at a computer all day, so my desk ends up just being a place where I dump all my bank statements and all those official document things that come in the mail and I sometimes forget to open. Everything just stacks up there. It exists in a strange purgatory of being too important to just throw away but not urgent enough to open.

But today I dug into the statements. Because for the first time since I became a cop, it is suddenly very important that I know how much money I have.

I would have thought that if I learned I only had a few months to live, money would be the last thing on my mind. Death is supposed to focus the brain on what matters most in the world, and money is, theoretically at least, not supposed to be at the top of that list. You can't take it with you, after all.

But Bishop can. He's going to need every penny I can leave to him. He is five years away from college, and he is smart, stupid smart, absurdly smart, *thrillingly* smart. He's going to go to a great college, which is wonderful except for the inconvenient fact that great colleges are considerably more expensive than shitty colleges. The kid has a future that makes my heart leap just thinking about it. He's going to be able to do anything he wants. But he's going to need some help from me. And I'm not going to be here to give it to him.

We thus need to do some accounting.

My ex-wife has a public service job that pays even less than mine. Gary, God bless him, works at the board of elections, a job that is just unchallenging enough to allow him to go play '70s rock covers with his fellow middle-aged Rock Dads three nights a week without it affecting his job any—I shit you not, the name of his band is the Grateful Dads—but also a job that pays him less than if he just put on a blouse and waited tables at the Texas Roadhouse. The primary provider for Bishop is me, and we've all assumed that would be the case moving forward. I never planned on retiring early, if just because, well, what else would I do with myself? I'm comfortable here, we know exactly how much I'll be making every year, I could do this for twenty more years, no problem.

But I'm not going to be doing this for twenty more years. I might not be doing this for twenty more weeks.

Currently in my checking account I have $12,432.55, right on the button, though I don't know if my Spectrum internet autopay has gone through yet, so give or take eighty bucks there. I know that's too much money to have in your checking account, but I just like knowing that it's there—that if for some reason I needed an immediate suitcase of cash, I could get it. That situation has never come up, but you never know.

I do have a pension plan, but it's been slashed in recent years. The state of Georgia has been running out of money, like every state, I guess. The way it's supposed to work is that I can retire at the age of fifty-five, twelve years from now, and get thirty bucks a month for each year of "creditable service," which, in my case, would be thirty-three years. But they max out at thirty years, so that would have been nine hundred bucks a month pension after I retired. And while you can transfer it to a spouse (which I don't have), you can't transfer it to your kid (which I do). Never mind that, uh, I'm going to be dead anyway. So that doesn't do us any good.

I also have a savings account. There's $11,122.18 in there, money I got when Mom died. There used to be twice that, but I've been using it to pay the mortgage on the house. It's our family house, and it's now in my name. According to Zillow, it's worth $258,800, though I bet we could get a little bit more. But I still owe about $110,000 on it, and besides, I'm dead in three months. Who exactly would sell it? Is that even the right play? I can't give it to Bishop yet; he's only thirteen. I could transfer it to Jessica, or make her a trustee—I trust she'd do right by it and eventually give it to Bishop, but who knows what her and Gary's situation is going to be like in five years? Gary has two kids from a previous marriage, and an ex-wife who is always referred to in vague, menacing terms. He'd want to be a part of it, and that's fair, but he's even more feckless about this stuff than I am. Would they just sell it? Then what would Bishop do? Would he even want it? I don't want him hanging around this place, with all the ghosts that are already here, with the ghost that'll be added when I'm gone. He should go see the world in a way I never did. He should get the hell out of here.

But that's a whole different question. Right now, we're just talking about assets. And there ain't many.

After looking for it for about an hour, because I knew it had to be in there *somewhere*, there's a life insurance policy. It is worth less than I thought. If a piano fell on my head tomorrow, my direct beneficiary—Bishop—would receive . . . $50,000, held in an account until he turned eighteen. That's not much of a life insurance policy.

So that's what I've got to show for my time spinning around this earth. Twelve thousand or so in a checking account. Eleven thousand in savings. A house that I can't do anything with that isn't even close to being paid off. And a life insurance policy worth fifty grand. I should have done better. But I thought I had more time.

I spread all the papers out in front of me on that kitchen table.

There is not enough. There is not even close to enough.

15.

My father was always unhappy. You don't realize that when you're a kid. You think the yelling is your fault, or the drinking is just something everyone does, or that all people are just like that, that the weight he carried with him to every room, the sense of unease that hung in the air right before he entered and right after he left, was something that was a part of all adult men. And I knew he had a hard job. Of course it wore on him. But he made it harder on himself. He refused to allow himself—and thus anyone who worked for him, who looked up to him, or was his son—to be human. He thought being a cop, a great cop, the *best* cop, meant setting clear, specific, unbendable rules and regulations for himself and everyone in his life, really everyone in his city, and never yielding one inch. But that's not how the world works. Pretending that it does helps no one. And it makes everyone despise you—the people you're policing, the actual human beings in your life, the world at large. They stop listening to you and start waiting for you to fall. I think deep down he understood this. But all he knew was to double down.

We had our moments. Most of them involved Bertha.

Dad brought home Bertha when I was fourteen years old. It was an old cop car—most of the fleet was Chevy Caprices back then—and it had just been through a pursuit that ended with it ramming into a medium on I-20, over by the Carter Library. They were gonna junk it, but Dad put in a claim: he had a kid who would have his license in a couple of years, and he thought we could work on it together, maybe get it drivable by the time I turned sixteen. That's what he told me: Fix this with me, and you can have it. So for the next two years I'd come by the cop impound garage after school, and we'd work on bringing that car back to life. We replaced the front frame entirely, banged out all the dents elsewhere, and completely rebuilt the engine. Dad loved cars, loved how they worked, how every part of the engine connected to every other part, how everything had to work in tandem or the whole thing would break down. And I loved it too. Working on the car was like figuring out a puzzle—like solving a mystery. Dad and I rarely talked when we were under the hood, but as a tandem of amateur mechanics, we worked together well, a series of grunts and nods and *hand me that would ya?*s, night after night in that garage. It was a big job, but it was one we knew how to do. And we did it. I had it done and painted—I never knew why he chose that shade of blue—in time for my sophomore prom. He flipped me the keys. "Be careful with this Big Bertha, she's got some kick," he said, and that's how she would be forever known from then: Big Bertha. Every time I look at her, I know that I've held every piece of that car in my hand. Dad did too. It outlived him. It will outlive us both.

I am thinking a lot about this sort of stuff lately.

Dad has been gone twelve years now. I do miss him. He was not a monster. But I think I miss the person I didn't know, or only rarely got to see—the guy in that garage. I do not miss the man he showed to people, to his family, to his son. That man, I understand now, was in many ways a creation, an attempt by him to harness the world into some sort of order. I do not think that man was really my father. I miss the man that I never got to see, the one who so rarely poked his head out from underneath, the one afraid we'd all see him as flawed, as fallible, maybe even as broken, as he surely was—as we all are. I miss having the chance to have known that guy. That's what I miss. That's what I dream about, when he shows up in my dreams. He will be around the corner, I can't see him, but he's whistling, something I never remember him doing, but it's definitely his voice, what his whistle would sound like. He is just whistling down the street. That guy had to be there somewhere. I just never got to know him.

So I vowed to try to be that imaginary version of him. Like sons since the beginning of time I, in ways I only now understand, have constructed my life in direct contrast to my father's. The only two things I really knew about him was what he was like as a father and what he was like as a cop. So I just did the opposite of what he did.

My father believed that sons were not supposed to be friends with their parents; they were supposed to learn from them, fear them, and obey them. So from the beginning, Bishop was my best friend. That's a lot to put on a kid, particularly when his parents are divorced, but Bishop took to it immediately—as any kid whose dad doesn't foist a lot of rules or punishments on him probably would. We have always been goofballs together—there isn't a fart joke that we haven't mastered—and we have always been equals. He does not fear me, and I do not want him to. We are affectionate with each other in a way I never was with my father, can't even *imagine* being with my father. And it feels good.

But the difference between my father and me has always been far more profound at work. Being Major McNeil's son came with so many burdens and expectations that I decided quickly after he died to release myself from all of them. I thought about quitting but I had a new son and family to support; I couldn't start over. So I decided to stay a cop but be . . . different. I would not be a hardass. I would not be ambitious. I would not dedicate my career to finding the killer who might have destroyed Dad. I would not give in to his demons. I would not treat my city as a place of constant threats—that was not the Atlanta I wanted to live in, and certainly not the one I wanted to police. I became . . . meek? A pussy? Is that right? I don't think it is. That's probably too harsh. I just—I just went with the flow. I became the cop I think people wanted to see rather than the one Dad thought I was supposed to be. I think that's it. I did my job. I wrote my tickets.

I responded to all my calls. I did everything I was supposed to do. But I did it as a part of the community, not as someone above it. I rejected the way Dad saw his job, saw his city, saw his place in it. I made the job something I could work with. I made it something I could do.

It was strange for people at first. Major McNeil's son wasn't a ballbreaker—he *was* kind of a pussy, actually. Guys at the precinct used to give me hell about it, guys like that Perkins kid, too young to know better. But once they realized I *wasn't* Major McNeil, that I was just a regular guy who wore a uniform and tried to stay out of everybody's way, they accepted it. I even like to think they absorbed a little bit of it themselves. I wasn't Sergeant Ellis. I didn't want to run the place. But I did the job.

I even have a whole gimmick I do when people start filming me. Oh, this is a thing for cops now. People will just walk up to you and stick their phone in your face, like they think they're about to catch us beating on somebody. I can appreciate the dedication to police accountability—Lord knows we haven't earned a lot of trust in that regard—but in practice it ends up feeling a lot less about these folks being intrepid citizen journalists and more about people looking for Instagram clout. Pro tip, kids: you're a lot less likely to stealthily film somebody in the middle of an illegal activity when your phone is in selfie mode and your face is taking up half the frame. (Also: our body cams get better resolution anyway.) But I also don't understand cops who get grouchy about this either, who stick their hand up, yell at the person filming, and sometimes even try to take the phone away entirely. That only makes you look like you have something to hide.

So I've got a shtick. I do my best Ned Flanders. It's a whole script.

"Good to see you, fellow citizen!" I say, looking into the phone's camera, smiling as widely as I can, using what Bishop calls my game-show-announcer voice, *Tell 'em what they've won!* "Just your friendly neighborhood public servant, here to keep the peace!" I then wave like an old-timey guy from the 1920s saying goodbye to an ocean liner. They never quite know what to do. They usually smile—they'll even laugh, wave back, maybe even remember that cops can be dorks too. There are surely dozens of videos of me doing this, sitting on dozens of phones, unwatched, forgotten. But I keep doing it. It certainly cannot hurt.

I'm a good cop. I take a lot of pride in being a good cop. And I should be upfront about this: I'm a good cop, in many ways, because my dad died when he did. It's true. It didn't have to be like that. But that's why I had to be different—for Bishop, for this job, for myself. I had to make sure everybody heard me whistle.

THE TEN GENTLE EDICTS OF LLOYD MCNEIL

Edict No. 3: Don't shave against the grain.

The McNeils are not a hairy people. Honestly, we're barely mammals.

It has always been a disappointment that I can't grow a good thick cop mustache. That should be the divine right of every police officer. But it was just never happening for me. I tried once early on in my career, but nothing would fill in. I ended up with some wispy little brown thing on my lip, like I'd left some chocolate milk there. It was pathetic. I lasted a week.

We're just hairless, we McNeils—we're like dolphins. No chest hair, no back hair, no ear hair, smooth as a mole rat everywhere. Your mom always said she liked that when we were dating, said she hated beards brushing up against her cheek, but I think she was just saying that to make me feel better. Gary's got a thick full beard. You can always see his sweaty chest hair busting out whenever he's onstage with his band, I don't know how he doesn't get some of it caught in his teeth. I bet he has to shave twice a day.

Not us. You don't know this yet, you're only thirteen, I'm not even sure you've got hair on your pickle yet. Ha, sorry, that's a weird phrase. Your great-grandfather used to say that: "I've been a Dawgs fan since before I had hair on my pickle." It's probably a good thing they don't use that phrase anymore. I'm a little worried just typing it is going to get me put on a watch list.

I suppose it's possible that the Hairless McNeil Curse will pass you by, that you're looking like Bigfoot by the time you're sixteen. But I doubt it. I like to think our hairlessness means we're more evolved than other men. We're further away from the Neanderthals—we're further along the evolutionary chain. Let's go with that.

Still, though: every man's got to learn how to shave. And it's the job of a father to teach him.

I'm not going to make it to your first shave. This is my only chance.

So:

1. Rinse your face with warm water. It can be hot if you can handle it, but warm is fine. Only sociopaths shave with cold water.

2. Fill the sink half up with water once rather than leaving the faucet running throughout your entire shave. Water is expensive, and besides, you gotta save the earth.

3. Splurge on the sensitive skin shave lotion. Being a Hairless McNeil means you won't shave as often as everybody else, which means you're going to have soft skin. Take care of it. Girls hate cuts and bumps, it'll make you look like you have acne even if you don't.

4. Same thing with the razors. Don't get those disposable ones, you'll slash the shit out of yourself. Get the triple blades, you'll need all of them.

5. Shave with the grain. *This is very important.* You want to shave in the direction your hairs are growing, not against it. Otherwise: bumps.

6. Go slow. There aren't many moments in your life that you get entirely to yourself. Shaving is one of them. Take your time. The outside world can wait.

7. Remember to get right under your nostrils and on the sides of your mouth. Those are the places that are most annoying to have hairs you missed. You'll end up having to pluck them.

8. Use aftershave lotion, not cologne. It's lighter, and it smells better anyway.

9. Hairless McNeils probably only need to shave twice a week. Try to plan out your shaves for big occasions, like a date or an important meeting. Most people won't overtly notice if you go through four or

five days without shaving, but you'll give off a subtle vibe of being unkempt, like you don't have enough respect for yourself. Think of shaving like putting on a crisply ironed shirt.

10. Clean up after yourself. Wipe down the sink. Live like you care about where you live. We're not savages.

Print these out and tape them next to the mirror. And hey: maybe you'll have better luck with the mustache than I did. Good luck.

16.

"Sir, do you remember why you took all your clothes off?"

This is one of those questions that, if you have it to ask it, the answer doesn't matter all that much.

The naked man looked up at my partner, who was shining a flashlight in his eyes even though we left lunch early to respond to this call. Senior Officer Anderson likes his flashlight, likes pointing it directly in the face of anyone we're talking to. Says it's important "to see if their pupils are dilated." I don't think this is a real thing, and I'm not sure what difference it would make even if it were, but it makes him feel in control, and that's what a cop needs more than anything else.

"Eggs?" the man says. "Eggs, I think." He is no longer lying on his back, as he was when we got here, before we woke him up from what appeared to be a rather deep sleep—a deeper sleep than I personally can remember having in a while. He has pulled himself up and is now facing us, sitting, legs spread, giving us a pristine view of his testicles resting lazily on the freshly lacquered porch. This is a nice house, one that I suspect usually has fewer balls lying on it than it currently does.

"Eggs," I say, and I take out a fake notebook and pretend to write in it. "Got it."

Anderson smirks. He bends down to try to make eye contact with the man, but he's way too big to get that low. He looks at the homeowner, the woman who called the police and informed us that there was a stray naked man on her porch that she'd appreciate us dispatching for her. Through the window, she watches us while half hiding behind some drapes. Making sure she sees him, Anderson subtly nods his head to a wicker chair and turns back to her. I see her nod from the window, then sneak back behind the drapes. I'm pleased to see him do this; I taught him to. It's not your chair. You are a guest in their home. You work for them. Make sure they know that—and feel it.

Anderson pulls the chair across from the naked man and sits down in it. Well, he tries to. This is a chair meant for a child, or perhaps a tiny woman, not a six-foot-six, 250-pound mammoth, a fact Anderson realizes too late, when his ass is already lodged in it and can't get out. He stands up for a moment, and the chair goes up with him. He shimmies for a second, can't dislodge it, then does a little hop, which only gets him in there tighter. With my eyes on the naked man—I hope he can't see me try not to grin—I walk behind Anderson and bop the top of the chair with my fist, finally wrenching it loose. It clangs down to the floor, and the naked man looks up. He definitely saw me grin.

Anderson ends up just sitting on top of the arms of the chair. Close enough.

"Let's try this again," Anderson says, clearing his throat and stretching his back a little. That looks uncomfortable. "Why are you not wearing any clothes?"

The man is slightly more alert than before we arrived. Seeing cops does that to people.

"Um . . . hot," he says. His face is freshly scratched up, and he has a short string of drool hanging off the right side of his mouth. "It was hot. I got hot." I hear footsteps from inside the house and inch my way toward the door, just in case.

"Uh-huh," Anderson says, and looks toward me. Whatever this guy's high on—opiates are generally a safe bet, probably heroin, he's pretty sedate, no one does PCP anymore, in the old days I'd be worrying about this guy jumping through a window—a paramedic's going to be more helpful to him than anything we can do. The procedure here is to make sure he remains calm, get him stood up, cuff him—for his protection as much as ours—put a blanket over him so the hiding lady in the house no longer has to look at his bony ass, call the EMTs, let them get some fluids in him, and take him to the ER. There probably won't even be any charges filed, unless the homeowner insists, and likely not even then. This is not an arrest situation. This is a keep-the-peace situation. This is a get-this-man's-balls-off-this-woman's-floor situation.

"Can you tell me your name?" Anderson asks the man.

"Frank," the man says.

"You got a last name, Frank?"

The man's eyes are coming more into focus. All told, he looks . . . rested. Good for him.

"Jefferson," he says. It's dawning on him that he might be in a little bit of trouble. "Frank Jefferson."

"Well, Frank Jefferson," Anderson says, "I'm Senior Officer Anderson. It's good to meet you. We need to get you off this nice woman's porch, OK?"

Frank Jefferson the Naked Man lowers his head and picks it back up. "Yes," he says. "I understand. We should do that." He pauses, turns slightly toward the front door, and sees me standing there. "I'm sorry," he says to me, and the door, and maybe the nice woman with the porch. "I'm really sorry." He then begins to softly cry.

Anderson stands up, and the chair skitters across the floor behind him. I hope he didn't scratch it—this is a great porch.

"So my partner over there," Anderson says, "his name is Lloyd . . . Say hi, Lloyd." This is another thing we try to work on: referring to other cops during arrests by their first name rather than their rank and surname. It personalizes the experience, reminds everyone involved that we're all human beings here. Some of the older guys on the force hate it, but I find it works. I've got a friendly name. Who doesn't like a Lloyd?

"Hi, Frank Jefferson," I say. "I'm Lloyd."

"Hi, Lloyd," Frank Jefferson says. He has a Georgia football tattoo on his left forearm. Go Dawgs.

"So Lloyd here, he's gonna cuff you," Anderson says. "He'll be gentle. We just need to get you off the porch. We're going to put a blanket over you. You've got to be cold."

Frank Jefferson nods. "I'm not hot anymore," he says. He's no longer crying, but he doesn't look any less sad.

I walk behind him, my hands open out in front of me, trying to make the least threatening face I can. This isn't hard: I have a very unthreatening face. One of the reasons Anderson and I work together so well is that we can play off this contrast. Our version of good cop, bad cop is intimidating-mountain-of-a-man cop, small-mild-guy-named-Lloyd cop. It's a combination that defuses most situations: perps are simultaneously terrified and reassured to see us.

I put my left hand on Frank Jefferson's shoulder. His skin is freezing to the touch.

I tap him slightly. "I'm going to take your arm now," I say. "Let me know if it hurts."

"Thank you," he says with a grateful sigh. "It's fine."

I cuff his arms behind him without incident—I'm an excellent cuffer, I can do it without twisting anything, five stars on Yelp, you're welcome. I then escort him to the front steps of the porch, where he sits, and Anderson puts a police blanket around him.

"Some guys are coming to take you to the hospital and get you cleaned up, OK?" he says. It consistently astounds me how such gentle sounds can sometimes come out of the mouth of such a large man. "We're gonna wait here until they get here, all right?"

"Yes," Frank Jefferson says. He looks at his feet. He's more sober now, which has to make all of this worse. "Thank you."

A door opens behind me. A young woman in workout clothes comes out. She is rattled, but sure in her movements. She walks around me and Anderson, down the steps of her front porch, and turns around. Her eyes are red, and I can see she's still a little scared, but also that it meant a lot for her to come out here.

She is holding a plastic cup with a straw coming out of it. She puts it in front of the man's face.

"Here," she says. "Drink."

He looks at her, but only for a second. He then puts his lips on the straw.

"Thank you," he says, and then he drinks.

17.

One of the funniest things about being a cop is that our presence always seems to make rich people more nervous than poor people. You'd think it'd be the other way around, right? Poor people sure as hell go to jail more than rich people do. That's not how it works out, though. When a rich person sees a cop in uniform, you can almost hear their sphincters tighten and pucker. They talk to us like they're trying to disarm a bomb, like even the slightest misstep in syllable will cause their whole life to explode.

There are many of them here. We're at the Ritz-Carlton in downtown Atlanta, which is the home of the only Jittery Joe's location in the entire city of Atlanta. Jittery Joe's is the coffee shop of Anderson's hometown of Athens, and he complains about missing it constantly. It makes him feel like he's home.

"Is that what you imagined you'd do?" he says, sipping his matcha. "Peeling high and naked people off the floor? Is that why you became a cop?"

I stare at him.

"Yes, exactly that," I say. "You should see the paper I wrote about it when I was five."

"I'm just saying that there has to be more action than this," he says. "I knew we wouldn't, like, be taking out gangbangers every night, but seriously, all we do is write tickets, deal with noise complaints, and sit around the office. Can't we at least get a cat out of a tree once in a while? It's just a little depressing that today is the most exciting thing that's happened in weeks."

We've had this conversation so many times that I can tell even *he's* bored by it at this point.

"I'll say it again: I don't know why you think you'd somehow be happy with someone shooting at you," I say. "The quiet part is the good part. When it's calm, that means everything's fine. If you wanted action, you should have joined the army."

"Harrumph," he says, and he actually enunciates it like that, *harrumph*, like he's a cartoon character. Anderson's pretty clever for a child giant.

"Look, maybe you'll—"

A voice comes up from behind me.

"Lloyd? Lloyd, is that you?"

When I turn around, I see a face that's vaguely familiar, but only vaguely.

"Uh, hey, uh . . ." I extend my hand, trying to bail myself out. "Great to see you!"

He's a younger man, maybe early thirties, definitely white, wearing a custom suit that fits him perfectly—snug, but loose and comfortable. I have never had a suit like that.

"Lloyd, man, I thought that was you!" He clasps my right shoulder, and I think he's about to go in for a bro hug, but he stops himself, perhaps realizing it'd be weird to hug a cop in the lobby of the Ritz-Carlton. "Holy shit. It has been forever." The more he talks, the closer I feel like I am to recognizing him.

Anderson knows me well enough at this point to understand that I'll sit there for days trying to figure out how I know this guy before I'll actually ask him, so he steps in.

"Hey, Senior Officer Wynn Anderson," he says, extending his hand. "Good to meet you."

"Oh, sorry, Senior Officer Anderson. I'm Michael," he says. "Michael Cetera. Good to meet you too."

Of course. Michael Cetera, Michael Cetera *Jr.*, actually, is the son of Sergeant Mike Cetera, one of my father's old friends from back in their academy days. He was more of a ham-and-egger than my dad, and a devout Catholic, so devout that apparently the pope never let him use birth control, seeing as he had seven kids. I used to run around with Michael's older brother Thomas, I think he was No. 5, back in high school; it always struck me as kind of lovely that Mike Sr. waited until his seventh and final kid to finally name one after himself. He was a MARTA cop, one of the guys who patrolled Atlanta's sad excuse for a mass transit system, mostly writing tickets for people who tried to jump the fare and running off panhandlers. It was basically the safest job on the force, which is why what happened to Mike Sr. was so uniquely awful.

It was rush hour on a Thursday, sometime in the mid-1990s; I was still in high school, I remember that. Some teenagers were running through the Arts Center stop on the Red Line, causing chaos and thinking they were indestructible, like teenagers are put here to do, and Sergeant Cetera motioned for them to slow down, finally stopping one right as he was about to pass him. According to my dad, just as Sergeant Cetera was about to say something to the kid, another teenager—it would later be a point of considerable debate at the trial just how well these two teenagers knew each other before they found themselves chasing each other through the MARTA station—came zooming through behind both of them. He saw Sergeant Cetera, tried to stop himself and turn around, slipped, and went barreling into the other teenager. That teenager then smashed into Sergeant Cetera, who fell backward onto the tracks. Video footage of the incident shows him starting to get up as the second teenager extends his hand to try to pull him up. Sergeant Cetera grabbed it, but the kid wasn't strong enough to pull him up, and by the time two bystanders realized what was going on and went over to help the kid, a train arrived. The video cut out after that. From what I understand, Sergeant Cetera was not killed instantly. But he never made it off those tracks.

I never knew Mike Jr. well. But he looks just like his dad.

"Michael!" I say, too loud, almost like I've just remembered it or something. "Wow, it's terrific to see you. You look sharp!" His suit does in fact look like it cost more than my house.

"Ha, naw, I got this off the back of a truck," he says, then looks at Anderson quickly and lowers his voice. "I'm just kidding. I didn't steal it."

Anderson waves his hand in front of his face.

"So, Lloyd, how are you?" Cetera says.

There's an Evil Dead *tree inside my brain that's going to make me insane and then kill me. And how are you?*

"Oh, same old, same old," I say. "Just trying to show the new guy here the ropes. How are you? You do look like a million bucks."

Michael tugs the sides of his lapels and then smooths them out, like a dapper gangster in a '50s film. "I'm a lawyer over at King & Spaulding, just up Peachtree a few miles. You know King & Spaulding?"

"Yes, I know King & Spaulding," I say. King & Spaulding is one of the biggest corporate law firms in the world. That suit *did* cost more than my house.

Look at Mikey Jr., the seventh of the Cetera Cop Kids, taking over the world. "Congratulations, Michael," I say. "I'm sure your mom is very proud of you. How is she?"

"She's great," he says. "She got remarried a couple of years ago. Twenty-five years later, she at last gets hitched again. Nice guy. Partner at another firm. I think they're in the Bahamas right now. Shoot, they're always in the Bahamas."

The first time I met Barb Cetera, she was picking up shifts at a Waffle House for a little extra cash. Now she's in the Bahamas. And her son looks like DiCaprio in *The Wolf of Wall Street.*

"Well, Lloyd, I have to say, it's quite something to run into you here," Michael says, putting his hand to the side of his mouth conspiratorially. "Truth be told, I hate this place, but I gotta meet my client, he's an old Duke buddy of mine, he practically lives here. It has been too long. I'm glad to see you still out here keeping the streets safe." He turns to Anderson. "And nice to meet you, buddy! Keep this guy out of trouble, would ya?"

"Great to see you, Michael," I say. "Say hi to your mom for me."

"If I can find her!" he says, already down the hallway, hands waving behind him.

"You run in some high-dollar circles," Anderson says as we head out the revolving doors onto Andrew Young.

"He's the son of a cop, actually," I say. "A friend of my dad's."

"Man, he must be smart as shit," he says. "How smart you gotta be to get the scholarships you need to afford to go to Duke law school as the son of a cop?"

"Yeah," I say, and something stirs in my brain. I suppose you could say this is how it all got started.

18.

So: I have an idea.

19.

How many cops do you think died in the line of duty last year? There's a website, the Officer Down Memorial Page, that compiles the numbers nationwide. I played around on that site for several hours last night. I learned a lot.

Being a cop is a dangerous job, no question, and it sure isn't paid like one. Though I guess they don't decide a profession's pay structure by how dangerous it is. What a world it would be if they did, right? You'd be a lot less irritated by how much bank CEOs make if they were dropping like flies on the job. Think they'd take that deal? Sure, you can make fifty mil a year, but you also run the risk of being taken out by a perp at any random moment. I'd take that deal.

In 2021, nationwide, 722 officers died in the line of duty. That's a lot. That's actually three times as many as five years before. But you've got to put that in context. Of those deaths, 503, two-thirds, died of getting COVID-19—not a problem a decade ago. As with all professions—other than, say, college professor, I'd guess—there was a dramatic increase in on-the-job deaths among police officers because of illnesses from the pandemic. But if you take those out there were 148 on-duty deaths in 2023, about one every two days, nationwide. Eight died of a heart attack. One drowned.

The two most common non-COVID-related ways that officers die on the job are:

- Gunfire (48 deaths)
- Automobile crash/vehicular assault (45 deaths)

When we think of a cop dying on the job, we probably focus on these two. A bad guy shoots a good guy. A good guy crashes his car chasing a bad guy. If you were to write a story about a cop dying, you'd likely come up with one of those. The website doesn't break down the car crashes, which ones resulted from a high-speed chase and which were just the sort that happen to everybody every day, but nevertheless: those cops were on duty. They were in their patrol vehicles. They count.

So: these are the deaths that make the front page of the paper, the ones we have the big services for, the ones that stop time. There are 93 of those.

At the last census, there were 708,001 full-time police officers in this country. That's more cops than I bet you thought—basically one out of every 468 people. It's still five times fewer cops than there are nurses: Did you know one out of every 65 jobs is a nursing job? Also, you should see how many baristas there are.

Sometimes lately I get to looking stuff up on the internet and I completely lose track of how long I've been doing it. I woke up in my chair in the middle of this last night.

Anyway! The point is that out of 708,001 cops, only 93 of them died in some sort of violent interaction with someone committing a crime. That's one out of every 7,612 cops. Again: that's more dangerous than being a CEO. But being a police officer is officially the *twenty-second* most dangerous job in America, behind, among others, crane operators, crossing guards, cement masons, delivery drivers, power linemen, iron workers, garbage collectors, and, at No. 1—the most dangerous job in America, drumroll please—loggers. Maybe they should arm loggers.

I went through all this googling partly because I couldn't sleep and partly because the lightning bolts were attacking last night and partly because what I am thinking about is starting to make more and more sense, and thus I am trying to make it more and more real in my mind. The fact remains: it's a lot harder to get yourself killed as a cop than you'd think.

Which might be why it pays so much when you do.

———

20.

After I ran into Michael Cetera Jr., a little seed popped into my brain. Well, a figurative one—I'm not sure there's enough space left up there for anything else but the *Evil Dead* tree to grow. Michael Cetera Jr. went from a cop's kid who would be lucky to get a partial scholarship to Kennesaw State to a kid who went to Duke Law School and now hangs out at the Ritz-Carlton all day for reasons *other* than the finest matcha in all of Atlanta.

And this happened because his dad died.

Not just because he died: because he died in the line of duty.

Do you know how much money the Cetera family got when Mikey Sr. died? I do. I looked it up.

When Mikey Sr. died, his family received a lump sum of two years' salary, which, as far as I can tell (and this figure is from ten years ago), was roughly $150,000. But that's not all. The police union has a formula that's meant to take care of the families of officers killed on the job for years to come. It's a bit complicated, and it changes a little depending on how an officer dies—you end up getting more if you're killed by a gun than by a car—but it's roughly two-thirds of your monthly salary . . . *forever*. Here's the exact wording from the International Brotherhood of Police, Atlanta chapter:

> If the member is killed in the line of duty and the surviving spouse
> or designated family member elects the optional family benefit, and

if the member's monthly salary at the time of death is $5,000, the spouse is entitled to:

66⅔% x $5,000 = $3,333.50

In this case, the member's spouse or designated family member would receive $3,333.50 a month until his or her death.

After twenty-three years of doing this, my salary is $95,000, or $7,916.67 a month. Seventy-five percent of that is $5,937.50. A month. That would go directly to Bish, every month, *for the rest of his life*. That's in addition to the two years' lump salary, $190,000, he would get upon my death. Well, he wouldn't get any of the money until he turned eighteen—from what I understand, it sits in some sort of escrow account until he's an adult. But that's even better. Then he can use it for college, and besides, I don't trust that kid not to lose his phone every three months, I sure don't trust him with a hundred and ninety grand.

But seriously, *do that math*. By the time Bish goes to college, if his dad were to go the way of Michael Cetera Jr., he would have $190,000 from my initial two-year salary plus, at $5,937.50 every month for five years, another $356,250, for (Bob Barker voice) a grand total of . . . $546,250. And that's not even accounting for the $5,937.50 he'll get every month after that.

I'm sure I'm getting some math wrong here, and when you account for taxes and all the lawyers that will dip their beaks in, it'll end up being less than that.

But it'll goddamn sure be more than $50,000. That much I know.

So, you tell me: $50,000 for my kid (minus house payments) if I die of the brain tumor that's destroying me by the second. Or $546,000 for my kid, plus a steady income for the rest of his life, if I die from being a cop.

What would you do?

I think I know.

AWAKE

THE TEN GENTLE EDICTS OF LLOYD MCNEIL

Edict No. 4: Don't worry about what anyone who
doesn't know you might think about you.

Here's something that I realized more recently than I should have: *Nobody cares about you.*

Hey, nice thing to hear from your dad, right? Well, I mean, *I* care. Your mom cares. Gary cares. Your stepsister, she cares, I'm sure, though I don't really know her very well. Everything I know about her came from you, and you seem to like her, so she surely cares about you too. Your friends care about you, the real ones, the ones that'll last, they absolutely do. You'll find a mate someday. That person will care about you. Maybe there will be kids. They'll care about you. There are a lot of people who care about you! There isn't a person out there who truly knows you that wouldn't care about you. You're pretty great.

But people who *don't* know you, those are the people who can really mess with you. It blows my mind—OK, so maybe that's not a phrase I should be using so loosely, haha—how much of my life I've spent worrying about what people think about me. When I was a kid, I worried that they only saw my dad when they looked at me. When I got older, I worried that they thought I was too much of a nerd, too passive, too quiet. When I became a cop, I worried that they would think I wasn't a very good cop. When your mom and I got divorced, I worried that they'd think I was a failure, or a bad husband. When your friends came over, I worried that they'd think your dad was a loser. All the time with the worry. All the time walking around, convinced the world was looking at me, judging me, mocking me. All the time feeling like I was coming up short.

All the time living for an imaginary audience of people I couldn't see.

That's the thing, you see. Who were these people? Who were these people who, in my mind, were staring at me all the time, evaluating my decisions, leaping to conclusions? Who was I trying to please?

No one. There was NO ONE. A writer your mom used to love and quote to me all the time once said something like "You won't care what other people think about you when you realize they don't." (I don't know if I have this quote right. You can look it up if you want. She's probably quoted him to you too.) When I got older, and particularly when I began getting a little bit more comfortable with what I was and stopped fretting about what I wasn't, I started thinking about this quote all the time. Because it's totally true. *Nobody cares.*

That kid in class who gets on your nerves but is also kind of cool, and you want to think YOU are kind of cool? He's not thinking about you at all. He's not! He has his own problems. He has his own life, and his own worries, and his own insecurities, and all the issues that everybody has. Even if he had a strong opinion about you—and, again, he won't—he doesn't have time to dwell on it. He's got enough on his plate! He is surely walking around the world scared of what people are thinking about him too. He's not thinking about you. None of them are. These people that we tell ourselves are out there passing judgment on us, documenting all our mistakes, deciding what kind of person they believe us to be . . . they're not doing any of that. They are NOT REAL. They exist only in our own heads.

Because you know what he's really doing? He's thinking about himself. Just like you are. No one notices what you're doing, just like you don't notice what they're doing. Pick a random person from your life that you don't know that well. Maybe a teacher. Maybe a kid at school. Maybe one of the people who sits near us at the Atlanta United games. How much do you think about that person? Do you have a list of specific beliefs about them? Do you think they are nice? Do you think they are mean? Do you think they are successful in their life? Do you think they are respected by their co-workers? Loved by their family? Respected in the community?

You don't have any thoughts about any of that stuff, do you? Why would you? That's THEIR life. You have YOUR life. And yet that person, like so many other people, has a little running voice in their head. *What do they think about what I'm doing right now? What does **he** think about what I'm doing right now?* And you don't give a damn! Which is good! You have your own problems.

And that's what I'm saying, Bish. Keep that in your mind at all times. They're thinking as much about you as you are about them: barely, or not at all. You don't answer to them. You answer to YOU.

That's the secret, I think. All those fears, all those worries about other people, they're really about you. The theoretical person out there that you obsess over trying to impress is actually just you. The questions are coming from you. The call is coming from inside the house.

So: Can you answer them?

Because if you can answer them truthfully, if you can live your life in a way that makes sense to you, that is true to the people who know you and thus love you, if you can realize that those questions are just little pinpricks in the brain and don't really exist outside it . . . well, then, you win. You made it.

I don't know if I got there in time. I was always so concerned about whether the guys on the force thought I was a good cop, whether I was worthy of being your grandpa's son. But those people didn't really know Major McNeil, and they don't really know me. So any thoughts they might have—and, again, they're not having many, they're all lost inside their own heads just like I was—don't matter. Am I the cop I want to be? Am I the father I want to be? Am I the good citizen that I want to be? Can I look myself in the mirror and say, "I am a good person. I am doing my best," and not be lying? That's all that matters. Because no one else was ever asking those questions. Just me.

I understand that now. Probably too late. But also maybe just in time. Because now you know it. You can know it a lot earlier than I did. Don't forget it. Make yourself happy. Be true to yourself and the people who love you. Nobody else is real. Nobody else makes a damn difference at all.

21.

"So let me get this straight," Dr. Lipsey says, taking his feet down from his desk, leaning forward and giving me a suspicious look, "you *don't* want me to file this to insurance?"

It was past midnight last night when I left a message with Dr. Lipsey's answering service. I had to see him—immediately. It must have sounded frantic to him, but, well, it was pretty frantic. I'd been lying in bed, staring at the ceiling, trying to figure out the answer to a fundamental question, *the* fundamental question: *Can I pull this off? Is this even possible?* I had not gotten yet to whether or not it was something I should do, would do, was even capable of doing. I just was trying to determine, were I to try something so insane, whether it was even theoretically feasible. I had also just thrown up for the third time. I wasn't nauseous, and I hadn't eaten anything rotten. The lightning bolts are sharper now, particularly at night, and they're definitely no longer little. The pain can be so immense that the only response my body has at its disposal is the vomit reflex, as if the bolts are something it can maybe expunge through the stomach. If only.

When it cleared, I put a cold rag on my head, followed the rhythmic *thrum* of the ceiling fan blades, and tried to figure out how it could work. How could I do this right? No one could find out what I was up to, obviously. They'd ruin the whole thing, stop the money going to Bishop, render all of this pointless. I had to be careful and do something most cops are terrific at doing and I am lousy at: think like a criminal. This, after all, is insurance fraud. As far as capital crimes go, it's hardly the most venal; I find it difficult to imagine I couldn't make a good case to St. Peter about the whole thing, if I had to. But I still could not get caught—before it all went down, but also after. That would be the worst: to get myself killed and have the whole thing unravel anyway. In death, I'd be known not just as a hapless failure but as a hapless crook. And Bishop not only wouldn't get the money, he'd be forever known as the son of the cop who couldn't even die right.

That's not what we want.

So, the first question I had to answer: *Who else knows I'm dying?* Before I could come up with any sort of tangible plan, I had to make sure it didn't explode on the launching pad. I still hadn't told anyone—not Bishop, not Jessica, not Anderson, not Sergeant Ellis.

But one person did know—had known before even I did. And that guy didn't know yet, not at midnight, that I would need him to keep a secret.

Fortunately for me, I had a sense he was good at keeping secrets.

Before I can respond to Dr. Lipsey's rather reasonable question as to why I would call him in the middle of the night begging him *not* to submit a claim to my insurance company that would theoretically save me out-of-pocket costs of nearly $150,000, Dr. Lipsey, briefly, remembers that he is a doctor and I am his patient.

"Oh, yes, uh . . . how *are* you doing, by the way?" he says, still chomping on his Nicorette.

Since I last saw Dr. Lipsey, I have lost ten pounds off a frame that wasn't particularly stocky in the first place, I've unclogged clumps of my hair out of my shower drain three times, and I've lost one of my back teeth. I thought I'd been hiding all of this well, but Dr. Lipsey noticed it immediately, and I can't tell if it's because he's a doctor and it's his job to notice when his patients start wasting away or if everybody has been noticing it and has just been too polite to say anything. I suppose it doesn't really matter.

"I've felt better," I say. "But I'm holding up. Lightning bolts coming more often. Particularly at night."

"Yeah. That's going to keep getting worse. The only thing that's going to help that is a fuckload of morphine. But we're not there yet." He looks down his glasses at me. "At least, I don't think so?"

"It's fine," I say. We have more pressing issues than the pending explosion of my brain. "That's not why I'm here."

He sits up straight in his chair and begins to rub his hands together in a way I first thought was out of nervousness but am starting to think is actually out of anticipation. He's excited. There's no question about it. Some people just love when crazy things happen out of nowhere.

"Yeah, so, I didn't really understand your message," he says. "What's going on? I have to file everything to your insurance, unless you brought a couple of suitcases full of unmarked bills with you. It's kind of an absurd thing to ask. Maybe you're farther along in this thing than I thought."

I learn forward. As I begin to speak, I realize, to my surprise, that I'm pretty excited myself.

"Well," I say. "How'd you like to make a little money?"

I'VE KNOWN DR. LIPSEY FOR ABOUT TEN YEARS. I MET HIM WHEN RESPONDING to an alert at his place in Buckhead, a fancy new condominium in a ritzy building that was shiny and clean and expensive and had huge tall ceilings but mostly seemed empty and lonely. Me and my partner back then, Officer Walt, had responded to a security alarm going off, which was the only thing that ever really happened in Buckhead.

When we knocked on Dr. Lipsey's door, he opened it only slightly. He seemed nervous and antsy, and that was *before* he realized he had two uniformed officers on his front stoop. As he peered past the chain on the door, I noticed that his eyes were shifty and his pupils dilated—he was extremely high on drugs.

"Officers!" he said. "How funny to see you here!" He was wiping his cheek with his shirtsleeve for some reason.

Walt, also bigger than me, was always eager to do the pretend tough-guy cop thing. He lowered his voice the appropriate number of octaves and informed the good doctor that we were responding to an alarm in the building, and if he'd let us in, we'd do a routine check and then go on about our day.

"Yes!" he said. "I should warn you, I have some guests!" He was now scratching his left elbow. He coughed and seemed to realize he was yelling. "Ah, yes, so, we have a weekly card game, very low stakes, I assure you, just friendly friends, being friendly to each other, yes." He unlatched the door, opened it wide with flair, like it was the 1940s and he was courting a dandy lady, and showed us in.

"Holy shit," Walt said before I'd even gotten through the doorway. "That's Ellex Albert."

It was. The Atlanta Hawks legend sat at a round table covered in ash-trays, barely smoked cigars, and half-full bourbon glasses, surrounded by, from what I could tell, two members of the Atlanta City Council, a local TV weatherman, a lawyer who had billboards of his face all across the I-285 perimeter, and two young women wearing black dresses so tight that I was pretty sure I could see their lungs working.

"The Human Highlight Film!" Walt said, already next to Albert, shaking his hand and clapping him on the back. "Wow, it sure is an honor to meet you. My brother and I grew up *worshipping* you, man!" Lex, silky smooth as ever, invited Walt to sit down, and Walt, a six-foot-three, 275-pound man now hopping up and down on his front feet like his daughter at a Taylor Swift concert, gave me a pleading side glance. "Well, I'm sure Detective McNeil can, uh, check out the alarm without me, can't you, Officer McNeil?" he said, and I knew I'd be getting a few free beers at Rusty's from him for this one.

As I heard Walt disparaging Isiah Thomas behind me, I turned to Dr. Lipsey. He looked a little calmer. It paid to have Hall of Famers in your den.

"Do you have a security unit in the condo?" I said. "Can you show it to me? I just need to check it out, turn it off, and call it in. This happens all the time."

"Yes, yes," he said, and took me through a room with dim blue lighting that seemed to have several aquariums in it, including one built into the floor. "Just in here, Detective . . . McDonald, is that what he said?"

"McNeil," I said, opening the closet door and shining my flashlight inside. "Detective McNeil."

Then I saw a plate with a pile of cocaine about a foot tall.

I pointed my flashlight back to him, then to the cocaine, then back to him. "You're having quite the party tonight, I see."

I saw his Adam's apple lurch up, then down. But then he gave a lopsided grin, and I realized this wasn't the first time he'd had a cop in his condo. He extended his hand to me. "Dr. Frank Lipsey," he said. "Nice to meet you. I suspect we have a lot of friends in common."

In a cop movie I would have booked him right then and there, with a steely-eyed glare and probably a quippy one-liner, then called for backup, cleared the party out, got a statement from the Human Highlight Film, and made sure Dr. Lipsey either did ten years for possession or flipped on the guy who gave him all that coke. But you and I know that's not how it works. He walked me out to the poker table, introduced me to the two city council members, both of whom had known my dad, of course, and we all posed for pictures with Albert. (Walt even stayed behind after I left and played a few hands.) Would it have been different if it were a young Black kid rather than a rich neurologist with a Mount Rushmore of the city's elite in his condo? Sure, especially ten years ago, though today, who knows, nobody cares about possession anymore. But it wasn't some young Black kid; it was a wealthy neurologist who hosted high-stakes poker games and played golf with the governor and writes huge checks every year to the Police Benevolent Association. He wasn't going anywhere, and he and I both knew it. These sort of interactions happen all the time, in every city in the country, every city in the world, and you should know that I do not believe you are really all that shocked about it—or even as angry as you might pretend to be. I don't think you really care that Dr. Lipsey had connections to get himself out of trouble. It is how the planet works and always has.

After we talked to the poker-table crew, we walked over to Lipsey's kitchenette.

"So are we OK?"

"You need to get that shit put away," I said. I had some self-respect, anyway. "And please figure out how to turn your alarm off so this doesn't happen again, all right?"

Dr. Lipsey laughed. "You got it, Officer McDonald."

"McNeil," I said.

"Right," he said. "Sorry. Well, thank you for all your, um, consideration tonight. I hope you won't hesitate to call me if you ever need anything. After all, we're friends now. That's what friends do. Friends help each other out."

"Yeah," I said, trying to figure out even then what in the world I would ever need this guy for.

The point of this story is that after this incident, Dr. Lipsey and I were *connected*. That's how the world works too. In the years afterward, we saw each other occasionally. He showed up at a couple Police Benevolent Association functions, Bishop and I ran into him at a few United games, he always sends a Christmas card with a couple of cigars. But there aren't a lot of opportunities for a neurologist to hang out with a police officer, or vice versa.

And now here I sit, in his office, ready to make him some money.

I CLASP MY HANDS TOGETHER, READY TO MAKE THE SALE, LIKE I'M ON *SHARK Tank* or something. "As you know, I'm dying. Fast."

"Probably really fast," he says, looking me over.

It is remarkable how a person absorbs the information that they're dying. The last time I was in here, my entire world collapsed. Now it's just in the air, part of the decor, the doctor's tie, that paperweight over there. His saying it no longer means anything. It is just what the world is now.

Dr. Lipsey snaps his fingers in my face. I must have been sitting there thinking about that longer than I realized.

"You were saying something about money?"

"Yes, I was," I say, and I take out the steno pad I'd been scribbling in all night since I called his answering service. It starts with a header at the top: SHIT LIPSEY NEEDS TO DO. Beneath that, there are four boxes waiting to be checked, with questions next to them. If he can answer all four of these questions correctly, we can check all the boxes. And then we can do this.

I show him the steno pad.

"This is what we need to talk about," I say.

He takes it from my hand, squints, takes a pair of glasses out of his desk, puts them on, and squints again.

"Did you always have handwriting like this, or is this the tumor?"

I frown at him. "Fine, I'll read it to you."

"Thank you," he says, looking at the steno pad again.

I lay the steno pad out in front of me.

"OK," I say. "Just to be one hundred percent clear, you *haven't* filed anything with my insurance yet?"

He squirms in his chair slightly. "No, I haven't," he says. "I'm always a little behind on that. I'm not even sure I've logged your scans yet."

I take a pen out of my pocket and mark the first box, next to the word INSURANCE? with a checkmark.

"That's what I thought," I say. "Second question: Did we use your in-house MRI guy for the scans?" I'm pretty sure I know this answer to this question already. Dr. Lipsey told me the last time I was in here that because he does his scans in the office, he can sometimes double-dip, claiming there were faulty scans that didn't register and then charging insurance time and a half for them. It's amazing what people will tell a cop that they know won't arrest them.

"Yep, you saw Gus there," he says, and I notice he's starting to slowly bob up and down in his chair. He knows I'm up to something, and he likes it.

"And Gus didn't see the final scans?" I ask.

"He knows not to look," he says, smiling.

I check the next box: GUS? This is going great.

"So this leads me to my next question: The only people that know I'm dying, then, are you and me?"

Dr. Lipsey's face falls. "Wait, you haven't told anyone? You've got to be shitting me. You didn't tell your kid? Your wife?"

"Ex-wife," I remind him. I'm honestly sort of impressed he remembered I had a kid. "And nope. I'm keeping this close to the vest."

"No one at work?" I shake my head. He looks legitimately sad for me. "That's the most depressing fucking thing I've ever heard."

"I'll take that as a no," I say.

"I don't make a habit of posting on Facebook updates on which patients of mine are dying," he says. "Bad for the brand."

I check the third box: SECRET?

"So to be clear as possible, the only two people on this earth who know that I'm going to die by New Year's are sitting in this room?"

"Yep," he says, and I'm pretty sure he just licked his lips.

I start to feel a pain creeping in behind my left ear. I'm getting to where I can tell when the lightning bolts are coming. In about twenty minutes I'll see spots at the periphery of my vision. About a half hour after that I'll be on the floor. I better hustle.

I flip the page of the steno pad, where I have written a very simple equation in thick black magic marker so he can see it:

$536,000 ++++ SIX GRAND A MONTH. FOR LIFE.
>>>>>>>>>>
$50,000.

And then I explain the math. Dr. Lipsey learns about police

insurance, and the International Brotherhood of Police, Atlanta chapter, and Michael Cetera Jr., and "designated family member." He learns about how brilliant Bishop is, how much my house might sell for, how Gary's a nice guy but also a shitty guitar player with a loser job who won't be able to send my kid to college, how if nobody knows yet that I'm dying from a brain tumor, maybe nobody *has* to know.

I finish my pitch. It was a good pitch. But I still haven't said it out loud. Not to him, not even to myself. So I take a deep breath. He stares at me. He knows what I'm about to say. He can't wait.

"I am going to get myself killed. On the job. I am going to do this so that my son can have a shit-ton of money. I don't know how I'm going to do it. But that's what I'm going to do."

God. It feels fantastic to say it. It really does.

He grins. This is the most fun he's had at work in weeks. "It's like you're taking out a hit on yourself but hiring, like, humanity to do it," he says. "Fascinating."

I hadn't thought of it that way. He's right.

"Of course, the only way this works is if no one, not the insurance people, not my family, not any of my fellow officers, finds out about the glioblastoma," I say. "Which is where you come in."

I turn my steno pad to the final page. It is just one number. It is a big number. I point to the number, and then point at him.

He peers at it through his glasses. He inhales.

"That could go up a tick or two, you know," he says.

"These things are always negotiable," I say, and I scribble out that number and write another one. You can't take it with you.

He nods. "You've got a little color back in your face," he says. "Insurance fraud looks good on you."

I've probably told him more than he wanted to hear. I wonder if I could have just stopped at "money."

I turn back to the front page of the notebook and check one final box: **$$$$$$$?** That was the one I was worried about the least.

We talk for a few more minutes after that, but we've said all we needed to say. I promise I'll keep him updated, he writes me a prescription for *some* morphine that I have to take to a *very specific* pharmacy, and we argue for a while about whether I can pay him in cryptocurrency.

Then I shake his hand and say goodbye.

"I guess this is it," I say. "I don't imagine I'll be back here again. So thank you."

"Thank you," he says. His face says *What a story this will make someday.* "And hey, Lloyd: Good luck with your dying."

22.

am going to get myself killed."

That was the first time I said it out loud, there in Dr. Lipsey's office. I'd thought about it. I'd obviously considered it. That's all I'd done the night before, staring at the ceiling fan, letting the thought float around my brain, take whatever form it needed to, free to roam, no judgments here.

But I hadn't said it. Now I have. It exists in the world. Someone else has heard it. It's dialogue! Sure, the person I told is a shady drug addict, and I could probably convince him that the whole thing was a hallucination if I absolutely had to. But he's got skin in the game too. I promised him money. I made him a part of this thing. Which means it is now, officially, a thing.

Which means I need to formulate a plan. I have some ideas.

23.

Atlanta is not a dangerous city. This always comes as a surprise to people who don't live in Atlanta, specifically those who live in the suburbs, or other Georgia cities outside Atlanta. I don't watch cable news or local news, so I don't know *exactly* what they're telling people, but it kinda feels like they're scaring the shit out of everybody. Whenever I used to tell Jessica's family and friends in Athens that I was a cop in Atlanta, they'd look at me like I was on patrol in Afghanistan. One year at Thanksgiving, shortly after Bishop was born, her sister Sam, right there at the dinner table, told me that she was worried about her nephew growing up in a house where the father was engaged in "constant fighting with gangbangers."

"Don't you worry about retribution?" she said, pointing at Bishop asleep in the pack-and-play in the hall just outside her mother's dining room. "They take out hits on people, you know." I told her the most dangerous thing happening in our household was Bishop falling asleep on my chest while I was watching *Jeopardy!* She didn't believe me.

Sure, there is crime in Atlanta, because there is crime in every city. There is more crime in Atlanta than there is in Athens, or Columbus, or whatever boring-ass small town you may be from, simply because there are more people in Atlanta. More people, more crimes. But statistically speaking, you're much safer in Atlanta than you are in other parts in Georgia. According to the most recent crime data—and believe you me, they shove this stuff down our throats at the end of every year, I can recite this stuff from memory—you have a 1-in-137 chance of being the victim of a violent crime in Atlanta. That's higher than you'd like: obviously, what we all want to hear is that we have a zero percent chance of being a victim of violent crime. But 1 in 137? That's comparatively safe. There's a song a lot of the young guys on the force all like, those who have transferred in from other parts of Georgia because we pay better, called "Try That in a Small Town" by some big-hat, no-cattle dope—sorry, I don't know his name, I don't listen to country music. All those dudes look the same, some chubby chump in tight jeans, wearing a cowboy hat he got from Dick's Sporting Goods, driving a $90,000 truck with a bed they've never used.

Some kid was playing that song in the office one time. I asked Anderson, who also hates the song, what small town that guy was from.

"Macon," he said.

"You're shitting me," I said.

"Yeah, that small town's got a hundred fifty thousand people, a country club, eight private schools, and an independent film festival," he said. "There actually *is* a lot of stuff I'd love to try in that small town."

Anyway, Macon? A 1-in-109 chance of being the victim of a violent crime. That small town's a lot more dangerous than Atlanta. How about Brunswick, the island tourist city with the gorgeous views of the Atlantic Ocean? That's 1 in 84. You can name city after city in this state, and in this country, that's a far more dangerous place to live than Atlanta. But because we're the biggest city in the state, and because we have local news that has everybody convinced they're gonna get gunned down the minute they cross the city line, and because they get freaked out when they see large groups of people because they live in places where they have lots of space because *no one wants to live there*, they think this city is some sort of hellhole. Jessica's mom once told me she was too afraid to go to the Phipps Plaza mall in Buckhead, the richest area of Atlanta. There is a Gucci store in there. There is a Bottega store in there. You can buy a goddamn Tesla in that mall. You ain't getting shot in no

Phipps Plaza, please. People are so desperate to be afraid of something that they just decide that whatever place they're currently not in is a place that's trying to kill them. And because their towns are boring and sad, the only town they ever see on the news is Atlanta. So they decide Atlanta is dangerous. They decide Atlanta is gonna kill them. Also: *There are Black people there. They're actually in charge!* Christ. You know what? They can just stay home. Stay the hell out. I hear there's a special at Applebee's tonight. You won't want to miss it.

Sorry. I get a little fired up defending my town.

Anyway. Anyway! The point is that Atlanta is safer than everyone thinks it is. I'd like to think I've done my small part in helping to make that happen. I don't think my decades in this department have been a waste in that regard. I help people. I keep the streets a little safer. I add more than I subtract. That's all any of us can ask, whether we're a cop or a nurse or a teacher or just the guy whose job it is to scrape gum off the bottom of the tables at Starbucks. Just make the world a little bit better.

But—and it must be said—there is still crime in Atlanta. It is a big city, after all. While statistically speaking, *per capita* speaking, you're more likely to get killed in Brunswick or Jesup or Cordele than you are in Atlanta, there are more crimes, *in total*, in Atlanta than in any other city in Georgia. This will be the case forever, no matter how good a cop I am, or Anderson, or anybody else. You can't change human nature. Some people are gonna commit crimes, maybe because they have to, maybe because they feel like they have no other choice, maybe because they have a mental health issue, maybe they like watching people hurt, maybe they just don't give a shit about anything other than what they can get away with. It's going to happen. It's why I have a job, after all.

So I can defend my city all I want, I can put it up next to yours— safer than Indianapolis!—I can take pride in the good and noble people of Atlanta. But there are crimes here. There are violent crimes here. There is danger here.

All you have to do is look for it.

24.

If I'm going to get killed on the job, I'm going to have to work at it.

Don't get me wrong: There have been a couple close, or close-*ish*, calls. Walt and I turned on our lights one time to pull a guy with a taillight over, and the dude took off on us. Walt floored it through a red light to pursue him, and some kid in a truck, holding his phone in front of his face, never saw us and clipped the back of the cruiser. If he'd have been there a split second earlier, he'd have T-boned us and turned my bones into mulch. A few years back, a guy was holed up inside a gas station after a failed robbery, and when I showed up for backup, he started firing random bullets out the front window. One of them hit a tree about ten feet from where I was standing, which will only seem far away if this has never happened to you. Did my life flash before my eyes? No. But it'll get your pulse going, that's for sure.

On the whole, though: my regular rounds are unlikely to find me much peril. My neighborhood is too nice, my beat too friendly, the whole area too gentrified to stumble myself into a firefight on demand. I suppose I could cross my fingers that someone will bust into the Jittery Joe's at the Ritz-Carlton while Anderson and I happen to be there, guns blazing, or that a crew tries a violent heist of the yoga studios just up the road from the hibachi place, but I can't say that I like my odds.

If I'm going to find my death, I'm going to have to look for it.

The way I figure it, I've got a few options here:

DOMESTIC DISTURBANCE. By far the most common potentially violent situation I ever come across. It is thoroughly depressing what percentage of the "risk" of my job comes from dealing with drunk asshole men pounding on their women. People are generally not violent in public. There is a certain, almost subconscious understanding that there are expectations on us when we are in public, that we have to, in the purest sense, *behave.* Even if we are not violent or angry people, though, that implicit understanding goes away when you are in your home. Think about the worst fight you ever had with your significant other, or a family member. Did you yell? Did you scream? Did you punch the wall? Did you do or say something you regret? Now, imagine doing any of those things in a public place. You can't, right? No matter how upset you were, you'd dial it back, you'd save it for later, you'd try to find a private place to hash it all out. You would be calmer, by definition. But we are comfortable when we are home, and when we are comfortable, in familiar surroundings, without the prying eyes of the outside world, it is then we are at our truest, and often worst, selves. We unleash the inner asshole at home. It's where our emotions run hottest. It's where things can get most out of control.

I don't see people brandishing weapons on the street. I don't see people screaming in my face out in the world. I only see this in people's homes. I only see this when people feel the most safe being their worst.

Ideally, this is not where I want this to go down. There are too many innocent people there, a spouse, children, neighbors. The first thing you have to do when responding to a disturbance at a home is cool it down. You have to remind someone that they are not alone— that the world exists outside what they're currently going through. You turn down the temperature best you can. If someone is shooting at me here, they're not just putting me in danger: they're putting the lives of everyone else in the house at risk. This has to be the absolute first rule: *This can only happen to me.* I can put my life on the line. But not anyone else's.

But in the moment, if some asshole is putting his wife and his family in danger . . . well, I'll do what I have to do.

HIGH-SPEED CHASE. This is the simplest, I'd think. Someone tries to get away from the cops, the cops chase them, the pursuit gets out of hand, my car goes careening off a ravine or something . . . whammo, a cop fatality. It doesn't have to be a gunshot, or hand-to-hand combat, or anything like that. It can just be a fatal car accident. Those happen all the time. It doesn't even have to be a wild chase through the streets of Atlanta, really. If I die in a car crash, and I'm on the job and in uniform, it's an on-duty death. Clean. Easy.

A couple of obvious problems here:

1. I generally have my partner in the car with me. I can't guarantee I'm going to kill myself and not kill him.
2. I also can't guarantee that I'm going to die. Want to know the worst-case scenario here? I get myself critically injured but don't die, and I end up draining the bank accounts of everyone close to me, for the rest of my life, as they try to keep me alive as the medical bills mount up.

FIRE! You want a heroic way to die? Run into a burning building!

The downside here is, well, being burned alive. That strikes me as a particularly unpleasant way to die. Also worth pointing out: I am not in fact a firefighter. Getting shocked to death while working on a power line would also be a quick way to die, but that is something a lineman does, not a cop.

JUST WAIT. You know what an advantage of my job is? When something bad is happening in the world, when someone is scared, or in trouble, or trying to get themselves or someone else out of a dangerous situation, *I work at the place they call for help.*

Sure, my beat itself doesn't lend itself to all that many life-threatening situations. I had difficulty figuring out any way I could have ended up biting it when I came across naked Frank Jefferson on that nice lady's porch. The best I could come up with was "Trip on the stairs and drown in a mud puddle off the sidewalk." Hey, that would be fun. Fair to say, the level of difficulty on that one would have been high, and that was the most fraught interaction I had all week. Maybe I'll catch a break and come across a bank robbery while grabbing a bagel, but I'm not counting on it.

But still: there's plenty of crime. Not a disproportionate amount of crime, but still plenty. And I work in the exact right place to hear about it. Getting this done, done right, doesn't have to involve me seeking out situations of danger. I can just keep my eyes and ears open.

This is the right way to do this—the only way to do this. I will lie in wait. I will be ready. I will do what I have to do. The moment will present itself. The universe will provide.

The universe does need to hurry, though.

25.

woke up last night in the kitchen. I have no idea how I got there. I remember going to bed, like normal, even falling asleep a little quicker than I usually do: talking to Dr. Lipsey must have worn me out. And then, next thing I knew, I was standing in the middle of the kitchen, in my underwear.

There was a humming sound, and then, from behind me, a *ding!* I turned around, slowly, still confused, and was face-to-face with my microwave.

I opened it. There, steaming, with a button on the top starting to melt, was an old St. Louis Cardinals baseball cap. I'd won it at some Benevolent Association raffle a few years back. Some guy who used to play for them, Westhead, or something like that, had signed its bill in Sharpie. I couldn't make out his last name. Baseball players have terrible handwriting.

I have no idea where that hat was. I hadn't thought about it in years. And I certainly had no idea why, in the middle of the night, apparently while asleep, I took it out of where it had been stored for the last several years, carried it into the kitchen, put it in the microwave, and hit start.

But that is what I did. You definitely can't tell what the guy's name is now.

I burned my hand taking the hat out of the microwave, tossed it in the sink, and poured some water on it. It gave a short, sad hiss.

26.

See, that's the thing, man, it's just like Jerry said, ya know? It's magic, that's what music is. Wait, honey, was that what it was? Maybe it was that magic's in the air, and music is how we see it? Something like that? What did he say?"

Jessica pats Gary on the arm and then makes a subtle motion with her napkin across the bottom of her face. Gary has some pesto on the side of his mouth. He notices neither the motion nor the pesto.

"Point is, Lloyd, that's what it's all about, that magic, that feeling when you're onstage that you're elevating, like, you can really feel your feet lift off the ground." He points at me, then waves his hands in the air like he's conducting an orchestra of unusually intoxicated birds.

Bishop catches my eye and rolls his own. He gives a stealth grin. *What a maroon.*

"Cool," I say. All I asked was if Gary's band had played any shows lately. Just trying to make conversation here.

"Gary and the Grateful Dads are playing the Hyatt in College Park tomorrow night too, Lloyd, if you want to go see him float in the air in person," Jessica says, smiling. "Show starts at five, goes until Happy Hour Monday ends at seven. They make a mean Manhattan at the hotel bar too."

"Yeah, he'll be right there, Mom," Bishop says. "He'll bring all the guys from the station, won't ya, Dad? Anderson will love that, he can bench-press the bassist."

I catch myself looking at him a beat too long. Is this the last time I'm ever going to see him? This was one of my weekends with him—my last weekend?—and when he came over after school on Friday, he found me asleep on the couch with *Jeopardy!* turned on at full blast. I have no idea how that happened. I'd grabbed some sandwiches from Humble Mumble, I'd bought tickets for a movie that night, I'd made up his bed, cleaned up his bathroom, even checked the Roku in his room to make sure that he hadn't got logged out of Netflix, since that TV only gets used when he stays with me. It was just after lunch. I put the sandwiches in the fridge, sat down for a second, and next thing I knew Bishop was standing over me, backpack over his shoulder, confused. He was worried—he always jokes that I open the door to him like a butler—but I told him I'd been a little under the weather and, hey, maybe we just stay in tonight? "Cool," he'd said, shrugging, like it was weird that people ever made plans anyway.

So we stayed in. We watched some old movies and ate food that was bad for us and stayed up later than either of us usually do. On Saturday he came shuffling out of his room around noon, asked if it was OK with me if we just ahead and did that again today, I said yes, and then we ordered a pizza and watched *The Limey*. "You tell him I'm coming, you tell him I'm effing coming!" He must have screamed that line twenty times. That movie rules. That's all we did. We scarfed down pizza and lounged on the couch and watched movies and quoted our favorite lines and moved a cumulative total of about forty-five feet between us. I dozed off a couple of times—the exhaustion comes out of nowhere lately—and the lightning struck a few times, but nothing too bad, not really. We were just *there*. There were no deep conversations. There were no hints at what might be to come. There weren't many words at all. It was just the two of us, barely budging for thirty-six straight hours, occasionally fighting over the down blanket when it got cold at night, just quietly together, enjoying each other's presence, not making any sort of thing about it. It was the two of us, and only the two of us, relaxed with each other in the way you only can be with someone who loves you as deeply and easily as you love them. You almost don't even notice it.

After we finished *Haywire*, a very good movie that kicks ass, Bishop pulled himself up from the couch, put his plate in the sink, walked back to the couch, passed gas in my face, and said, "That was fun. That was a really good movie."

"Oh my God there's a deer in the car," I said, quoting our favorite line.

He laughed. "I'm going to bed," he said. "Good night, Dad." He gave me a little fist pound.

"Good night, Bish," I said. I heard him playing his favorite band, Hotel Arizona, from right here in Georgia, through the door. We had planned to see them headline the Shaky Knees festival next summer. I am sure Gary can take him.

And that was it. I could have said I loved him. I could have said something that he'd make sure to remember from what may well have been our last night together. I could have said something that he'd always be able to hold on to. But it wasn't that sort of night. It was better than that. "Get a good night's sleep."

"YOU LOOK TIRED, LLOYD," JESSICA SAYS.

"That's what I said, Mom!" Bishop says. "You know he was asleep when I showed up Friday. Dad! Asleep! At four in the afternoon!"

Jessica eyes me up and down. "Everything all right with you?" she asks.

"I'm fine," I say, trying not to cough. "It was, uh, a busy week."

Jessica does not believe me, but she is gentle about it. She has always been, at her very core, so kind. I see it in Bishop every day.

"They must be working you too hard over there, Lloyd," Gary says, and I've just remembered he is still here. "That's no way to live, working so much all the time. I know you're keeping the streets safe, but they'll work you to the bone. That's what I learned, that's why I got out of the rat race, these big corporations, all they care about is their bottom line, their profit mar—" Jessica pats his hand, and lightly shakes her head at him. *Not right now, Gary.*

He gets it. "Anyway, yeah, uh, sorry, Lloyd," he says. "You do look like you could use some rest, though."

When Gary told me that he was going to marry Jessica, those years ago, he did it in the strangest way: he promised to me that he wasn't an asshole, and he wouldn't become one. "I know you two have been divorced a while, and I know it's all right," he said, in between sets at a coffee shop I was supposed to pick up Bishop at. I didn't know Gary would be there then, either. He just sort of pops up. "This isn't about that. It's just that I know how much you care about her and especially Bishop, and, more important, to me anyway, how much they care about you. So I just wanted you to know that I'm a nice person." I started to say something, but he stopped me. "No, no, let me do this, man," he said. "I'm a good person. I'll be a good person to them. I don't know if that's enough. But you should know it anyway. So I felt like you had a right to know that." Gary was still a huge dork. But he was right. He is a good person. And that's enough. "It's fine," I said, and shook his hand. "Congratulations." I thought he was going to cry. I watched him play two Phish songs on acoustic guitar that made me want to stab myself in the ear with a knitting needle, and then I got me and Bishop the hell out of there.

"Thanks, Gary," I say, and he gives me an awkward shrug and a lumpy, antsy grin. I've always been able to make Gary a little nervous. I don't mind it.

They were all going to be all right here. It was going to be fine.

I stand up.

"On that note," I say, bumping up against my chair and scraping it against the floor, "I do think my expiration date for the evening has arrived."

Bishop stands up too—more quickly than I was expecting.

"Are you sure, Dad?" he says, with an oddly urgent surprise, like it hasn't occurred to him that I am going to leave, like he has forgotten I live somewhere else. "Gary was going to make milkshakes for dessert. He always makes milkshakes on Sunday."

Gary shrugs, but in a welcoming way. "I do make a mean milkshake, Lloyd," he says. "We've got plenty."

I look at Bishop, who is silent but suddenly desperate, even pleading me not to leave. "Yeah, Dad, we got Blue Bunny, it's super soft," he says. He is looking at me like he doesn't know when he's going to see me again. Which is how I'm supposed to be looking at *him*.

But I have to go. It is time. It has been a wonderful weekend. You gotta get out while you're ahead. You gotta know when it's time to walk off the stage.

"Thanks, but I'm supposed to pick up Anderson before work tomorrow," I lie. "His car's in the shop."

Bishop frowns, an expression right on the edge of devolving into something sadder.

"Well, I'll see you Saturday, right? United plays at St. Louis SC—I'm still coming by to watch, right?" he asks. We didn't have plans to watch the match. Bishop is coming up with this on the fly. "Right?"

I nod, so tired. "Yeah, Bish, that'd be great."

Jessica stands up, takes my left arm, and gently guides me to their front door. It reminds me of how she escorted her feeble grandfather down the aisle at our wedding—a weak man, at the end, getting the help he needs.

"You take care of yourself, OK, Lloyd?" she says, looking up at me, straightening the collar of my polo shirt. "Sheesh, look, your clothes are hanging off you. Get some rest, all right?"

"Thanks, Jess," I say. She is, and will always be, kind.

Bishop comes behind her and gives me a hug.

"Bye, Dad," he says.

I stare at him, and exhale.

"Bye, Bish," and then I turn around and walk out the front door.

THE TEN GENTLE EDICTS OF LLOYD MCNEIL

Edict No. 5: Write it all down.

When you were a little kid, when you were seven or eight or so, which, now that I'm thinking about it, was only five years ago, God, it feels like decades, anyway, back when you were eight years old, your mother and I had a shared Google document between us called "Bishopisms." It hasn't been updated in a few years, probably just because we've now both gotten used to all the smart things you say, but, man, the things that came out of your mouth back then just blew our minds so much that we had to document them. It took your mom forever to teach me how to use Google Docs, but in the end we both had to admit it was worth it.

I've been going through a lot of old files and papers and stuff lately, and I was downright tickled to stumble across the old Bishopisms.

Check some of these out:

What if life is someone else's fifteen-minute game, and we only think of it as a long span of years. But when they're done with the game, you're done.

Do you think if someone just kept eating and eating and eating, they would just explode? I've seen some people who look like they are close.

What if God is just a little boy playing with his sister's dollhouse? That would explain why people are so stupid.

Bish, you have always been such a talker. So confident, so certain that the world absolutely had to hear every word you had to say. At first I thought it was your generation, kids who have never been told to be quiet the way we're all told to, not willing to wait in line and wait our turn like our parents always drilled into our brains that we were supposed to do. But it's not your generation. It's just who you are. Your mom said you came out of the womb hungry, and while that probably seems really gross for you to think about at the age you're at now, it's true, and always has been. There is nothing passive about you. You don't tiptoe around, you don't ask permission, you don't recede at all. You are just you, gobbling everything up, eager to see it all, to find new things to do and new worlds to explore, forever. You just connect to the world in a different way than anyone else. You're special. I know every parent thinks that about their kid, but man, all due respect to other parents, but those other parents are wrong. Because their kids aren't you.

We knew this. So we wrote it all down. I'm so glad we did. I can still see your face when you said those things, it was more round back then, fuller—you've angled out, gotten sharper features already, since you started hitting the P-word. You had these little dimples, spots of freckles too, back then, and you still had a couple teeth coming in; you were missing one of your bottom front teeth when you said that thing about life being someone else's fifteen-minute game, and I remember how you lisped it a little as your top lip scraped the new tooth coming down there, *someone elsthe's fithteenth-minute game.* Would I remember that missing tooth now, if we hadn't written down what you said? Would that memory already be gone? Would what you said have vanished? Would it have mattered that that moment happened at all?

I write it down. Just in case.

I have not always been great about this, particularly in the last few years. Those moments go by faster than they used to, and I find the need to stay present for them more than when you were younger, to just try to catch up with you the best I can. It's harder to get your attention than it was when you were eight. It's not your fault. I'm happy about it. It's a good thing. The world out there is more interesting than your dad is; you've got more to learn from it than you do from me, that's for sure. Your brain is occupied by your friends, by your school, by all the things you're taking in constantly—all there is to learn and see and *be*. I can't compete with that, and I shouldn't. Any time I have your attention now, when we're connecting in a way little kids connect with their parents because they're the only people they *can* connect with, feels like something I have to hold as tightly as I can. I'm certainly not going to stop and write something down in the middle of it. I can't lose those moments while I have them. After all, I won't need to remember them years from now. Now is all I've got.

But you've got to write it all down. Because someday it'll be behind you, and you'll miss it. I hope you haven't noticed this, but I'm already starting to forget things. The doctor said my brain would start playing tricks on me, that I'll out of nowhere stop knowing things I've always known, and he wasn't wrong. It has. A big one happened at the soccer game. Did you notice? You asked me who we were playing next week, and I looked at the schedule and saw the New England Revolution. And Bish, swear to God, I could not for the life of me remember where New England was. Was it a city? A state? Was this another name for New York? Does the MLS have a team from London? That doesn't make any sense. I knew it was east somewhere, because of the conference, but I just could not get come up with what "New England" was. Did you see this? I just spaced out. I said, "Uh, New England," and thank you for saying, "Ah, man, I hate Boston sports fans," or I might have sat there trying to figure it out the rest of the game.

That is going to keep happening. Quickly. Next time you may notice.

God forbid you ever have to go through something like this, but even if you don't, you'll still want to remember, and to remember, you're going to need to write it all down. Because otherwise it's gone. And if it's gone—if memories of what we did on this earth just go away—then what the hell are we even doing here? I'm gonna be dead in the ground, pretty soon really, and if people don't remember what I did here, and once my bones are dust, then what was the point of any of this? What was this for? Just you. It'll just be you.

I don't know how much of me you will remember. Maybe it will only be this. But there will be other people to remember, other experiences you'll want to hold on to, other memories you'll want to return to years later, memories you worried would be gone forever, memories you didn't even know you had lost.

Look, another Bishopism:

Do you think birds look down on us and think we are ants but then are surprised how big we are when they land?

I was driving you to your first sleepaway camp at Lake Burton when you uncorked that one. I pulled the car over to write it down. I'm so glad I did. You'll be glad you did too.

27.

Anderson and I are just cruising down Peachtree back to the pre-cinct. Our shift started with Jittery Joe's, as it always does, just like it will end.

Well, maybe today won't end that way. I do know the score.

There is a crackle on the radio, and my ears prick up. But it's nothing. Just a dispatcher looking for somebody to pick up a hitchhiker who fell asleep in the road off 85.

SERGEANT ELLIS IS LOOKING AT ME STRANGELY. SHE HAS A THIN, ANGLED EYE-brow that rises nearly halfway up her forehead when she smells bull-shit. And she smells bullshit.

"You look worse than you did last week," she says. "You look like garbage, Lloyd."

We were on our way out the door to go make our rounds when Sergeant Ellis, whom I'd been studiously trying to avoid for this very reason, stopped us. She's very good at smelling bullshit. Which is why I've been trying to avoid her.

"You're late on your reports, by the way," she says. "That's the third week in a row. I'd expect that from most of the other idiots in this office, but it's very unlike you."

"That's my fault," Anderson says, lying. "Lloyd was with his kid this weekend. I told him I'd take care of it, and it just slipped my mind, Chief. I'm sorry."

Sergeant Ellis turns her head to Anderson, sharply, and her body pivots behind her, locking into place and directing all her energy toward him. She straightens her back and fixes him with a dead stare. I see his eyes widen, his lips twitch. She is a good foot shorter than he is, but still towering over him. I instinctively take a step backward. The room is suddenly fifteen degrees colder.

"Senior Officer Anderson, if you believe that standing up for your partner is some sort of excuse for you to perjure yourself to your commanding officer, to lie right in that commanding officer's face, you are very much mistaken," she says without her head moving so much as a centimeter. "I am going to assume that is not what is happening right now."

Anderson's face goes pale, and he begins to sputter something before Sergeant Ellis stops him.

"I highly recommend you choose your next words extremely carefully," she says.

He looks down at his feet, and then back up at her.

"I'm sorry, ma'am."

"What's that?" she says.

"I'm sorry, Sergeant Ellis, that's not what's happening right now," he says, ten years old, in big, big trouble. "I was mistaken. I'm . . . I'm sorry."

"That's what I thought," she said. "You can go out to your car now. Detective McNeil will be out with you in a moment." Anderson looks at me like a child relieved he didn't die but pretty sure his big brother's about to get murdered. *Sorry*, he mouths. I nod, and he slinks away, almost ducking, like there might be a sniper on the roof.

I turn back to Sergeant Ellis.

"Christ, you scared the piss out of him," I say.

"You gotta do that with the new guys," she says, smiling. "Always good to remind them I could cut their balls off at any second if I wanted to."

I laugh. "He's a good kid," I say. "He'll be one of the good ones."

"I know he is, and I know he will be," she says. "And I'm glad he has your back."

I grimace. "I am sorry about those reports," I say. "Just had a lot going on these last couple of weeks."

Sergeant Ellis has been standing in between me and the door out to the parking lot, but now she circles around me, to my right, and gives me a frown. I'm a lot shorter than my partner, so she doesn't have to rise nearly as high to be eye to eye with me.

"I don't know what's going on with you, and I figure if you wanted me to know what's going on, you'd tell me. But don't take me for a fool either. There is obviously something going on."

"Look, I—"

"Let me finish," she says, and her nostrils flare a little. "*Detective McNeil.*"

"OK," I say. "Sorry."

"Look, I've known you a long time, longer than anybody here," she says. "You always stay level, Lloyd. You always keep it straight. And you're not straight right now. Something's up."

I look away for a second and then turn back to her, but my eyes land somewhere around her left cheek. What must she be like to suspects?

"You don't have to tell me," she says. "I ain't gonna ask again. But if you're not going to tell me, then you need to take care of your own shit. Don't let it affect your job. It's tough out there."

She waves her hand at the photo of my father mounted on the wall outside her office. "Lord knows I don't need to tell *you* that," she says, and she clicks her tongue. "But I need you to be straight."

She lightly grabs my chin with her forefinger and her thumb.

"You going to be straight?" she says, starting to sneak in a slight grin. "I need you to be straight. You never know, Lloyd: I might actually need you to do some real-life police stuff at some point."

I look at her. She is also of course the last person on earth I can say shit about any of this to.

"Thank you," I say. "But I'm fine."

"You're not," she says, patting my arm, taking a gentle step backward, flashing a lopsided grin again. "But that's your problem, not mine. Not yet, anyway."

She opens the exit door for me. "Now please go make sure your partner has stopped crying."

28

Anderson is quiet for most of the next hour in the car. It always takes the male officers a little while to work their machismo back up after Sergeant Ellis rips them a new one; it messes with their self-image in a way that requires some time to heal. That's why I told him to scoot over so I could drive. He just needed to stare out the window and stew for a while. He wasn't really himself again until we pulled a guy over for running a stop sign outside a Jamba Juice and he got to puff his chest out a bit and be intimidating. Sometimes a big guy, even one as fundamentally decent as Anderson, just needs to feel like a big guy.

We drive around for another hour, and I listen to Anderson talk about his big incident at the pharmacy in Athens, how it was one of only three times he's ever even pulled his gun, how he feels like a phony sometimes when his old high school buddies think he's some sort of hero, how he thought maybe coming to Atlanta would have a little more action—be a chance to prove himself. He thinks this is unique to him, but of course it isn't. Every young cop goes through it.

"Jesus, Sergeant Ellis really did scare the piss out of you," I say. "You'll get over all this." I feel a dull ache over my left eye.

"Yeah," he says. "Probably."

There is a crackle on the radio. It's the voice of Lorene, a new dispatcher who hasn't really gotten the hang of everything. A few weeks ago she accidentally gave out Sergeant Ellis's cell phone number over the public ham radio system. Ellis got enough phone calls from creeps and reporters that she had to change her number—she really read Lorene the riot act over that one.

"Hey, y'all," she says through the static. That she starts her dispatches with "Hey y'all" is another sign that she's got some growing to do in this job. "We've got reports of gunshots fired in the four hundred block of Angier Avenue Northeast. Woman says it's the next-door neighbor in the—" She pauses and goes off air for a moment before crackling back on. "In the Bedford Pine Apartments, off Boulevard in the Fourth Ward. Cruisers in the area, please respond."

Anderson barely lifts his head. That's near our precinct, but not necessarily near us, not as long as we've been driving. That's a good fifteen-minute drive.

But: gunshots.

It's probably nothing—some kid setting off firecrackers, or, much worse, being an idiot with his dad's gun or something.

But I pick up the CB.

"Copy, Unit 217 responding, this is Detective McNeil," I say, and I'm surprised by how much authority it sounds like I have. My voice is deeper than usual. Anderson looks at me, widens his eyes, and mouths a *whoa*. "We're in the area, we're headed straight there, what's the apartment number?"

A pause, another crackle. "Copy, Unit 217, that's 461 Boulevard, Apartment . . . Apartment 4B. That's on the second floor."

"Any word on security at the front? We gonna need someone to buzz us in?" My voice is still deep—yeah, I sound like Batman.

"Hold, I'll check with the emergency operator for y'all, she's still got the caller on the line."

We wait as I put on the lights and siren and pull a quick U-turn, quick enough that a kid on a bike plows into a fire hydrant in front of us. Anderson looks at him, puts his hands in the air, and yells, "Sorry!"

Lorene comes back on. "No buzzer on the door, head on up."

"Copy," I say. "We're on our way."

I speed up, and I feel Anderson's eyes on me.

"What was in your coffee this morning?" he says.

"You said you wanted some more action," I say, staring straight ahead, head still throbbing, the lightning just a few beats away now.

29.

Nine and a half minutes later, we pull up to 461 Boulevard, the Bedford Pine Apartments in the Old Fourth Ward. I have a vague memory of picking up a girl for a date near here in high school.

It appears somebody beat us here: there's a cruiser already in front of the house. There is also a gaggle of people, people who apparently don't have jobs to go to in the middle of the weekday, milling around, occasionally looking up from their phones to notice us. Also, my head hurts.

"Harrison," Anderson says, clicking his tongue. Officer Harrison's a grinder like me, a few years younger, counting the days down until early retirement already. You can always count on Harrison to know what's going on and to wait for somebody else to do something about it.

We get out of the car and walk toward him. He looks nervous.

"What's happenin', Cap'n?" I say.

"Lorene said shots were fired fifteen minutes ago, but that's before I got here. I was just around the corner, so I pulled up. She told me you guys were on your way, so I figured I'd wait until you got here before investigating."

"That's the unit right there?" I ask, pointing to 4B on the second floor. A kid's bicycle with training wheels is parked in front of the apartment.

"Yep," Harrison says. "I heard some yelling up there, but no gunshots. I thought I might, uh, help establish the perimeter."

"A one-man perimeter, great work, they'll never escape that cage," Anderson says. I shoot him a look.

"Any sense of how many people are inside the unit?" I ask.

"Just heard the one voice, a man's voice, loud—yelling," he says.

"OK, let's—hey, whoa there, wait up," Anderson says from behind me, but I'm already up the stairs. The pain on the left side of my skull is escalating, and there's something running out of my nose, maybe snot, maybe blood—either way, no time like the present.

"I'll hold down the fort here," I hear Harrison say below me as Anderson runs to catch up.

I make it up the stairs, turn the corner, and bump into a teenager filming me with his phone. As I said, I always try to be aware of this; someone's always got a camera on you somewhere, particularly when you're a cop. Again: constant public relations. They want you to be an asshole, so they can catch you, and make all cops look bad. If they're really lucky, you'll do something shitty and they'll upload it and they'll get a ton of likes and you'll get your ass fired. So, you know, I just like to surprise them.

I stop in front of the kid and give him a thumbs-up and a huge smile. And I say my line.

"Good to see you, fellow citizen!" I put some real spin on it this time, like I'm in a '50s film strip. "Just your friendly neighborhood public servant, here to keep the peace." I put my hand out to him. "Happy to do my part for you, sir," I say. I see him grin behind the camera. I give him a little theatrical bow and then turn to the door.

Anderson has caught up to me.

"Boy, we're shot out of a cannon today, aren't we?" he says, following me to the front door.

I survey the foyer in front of the apartment. It's a mess. Amazon boxes and empty Gatorade bottles are strewn everywhere. The bike has two flat tires and is mostly rust and broken spokes. There's a plush giraffe lying wanly in a mud puddle; its ear is sludgy, wet and gross, and the poor thing only has one eye. There are two planter boxes with some old sad brown dirt in them. One of them is flipped over; neither of them has any plants. I see a Transformers lunch box, sitting open with a ziplock bag holding a half-eaten sandwich in it. Optimus Prime is pointing from the front of the lunch box, telling me that FREEDOM IS THE RIGHT OF ALL SENTIENT BEINGS.

Anderson steps in front of me. This is our standard procedure. He's the one who knocks and enters first. When a cop the size of a mountain shows up at the door, people tend to straighten up and pay attention.

But I stop him this time.

"I got it," I say, wincing as another lightning bolt stabs my left eyebrow. I put my left hand on his massive chest and gently push him back.

"Oh?" he says, smiling. "All right, all right, let's go, we got Dirty Harry here, let's do this."

I put my ear to the door and hear nothing. I take out my nightstick and rap hard.

"Hey," I shout. It's a thick door, and the nightstick makes a thick, deep thump. "This is Lloyd McNeil of the Atlanta Police Department. We received a call about a disturbance at this residence."

I'm greeted with silence. Anderson starts to take out his flashlight and shine it in the window when I rap the door again with my stick. I'm beginning to see little fireflies in the corner of my vision, another lightning precursor, and soon there will be dark clouds floating in from around the edges, little storms that will block everything out. The bolts are firing again, and I'm relieved that they're a little fainter than usual. That's a good sign. These are just going to be painful, but I like my odds of not blacking out and ending up on the floor of this apartment. But I'm still impatient. Clock's ticking. I look over at Anderson, who looks back from the window, shakes his head, and shrugs. *Nothin'.*

"Hey!" I yell as I knock a third time, even winding up with the nightstick so I thwack it as hard as I can, leaving a little dent in the door. This third knock does the trick.

Suddenly the madness within this apartment is revealed.

A child—a baby, maybe a toddler—begins screaming and wailing, a sound similar to the sound an ambulance makes in another, unfamiliar country. This causes a woman to cry out. I can't hear her over the child's wails at first, but then she repeats it, louder: "Help! We're in here! He has a gun!"

A man's voice. "Ah ah ah, shut up!" he yells, wildly, like the words are out of his mouth before he even knows what he is saying. There is a loud bang on the southside wall, catty-corner to the front door, and then I hear a stomping of feet toward the front door. I turn to my right and see Anderson already in position, on the edge of the stairway, his right hand on his gun, ready to pull if necessary. I'm in front of him, standing at the door.

There is a pause. I can hear the man breathing.

"Are you still out there?" he says, oddly hopeful, like he thought maybe we'd gotten bored in the last fifteen seconds.

"Yes," I say. "You need to drop your firearm and open the door."

The voice mutters, "Shit." I hear him take a deep breath. He then speaks again.

"Yo, officer, sorry, everything's fine here," he says, slowly enunciating every syllable in an obvious, elongated fashion, as if he is trying to order a dish in English to a server who does not speak it. "My girl and I just had an argument. But it's OK now. Everybody is all right. You can leave now. It's all fine."

Anderson is a couple of feet closer to me now, and he still has his hand on his gun. He lightly taps me on the shoulder, as if to ask me if I want to move out of the way. I ignore him. I notice the teenager has returned and is filming us both. I bet there's even more cameras aimed at us down on the street.

Heat rises in my throat. I feel a little woozy. I guess I'm going to give those cameras a show.

"Sir, I need you to open the door," I say, completely calm. I am surprised by my sudden comfort. "This is your last warning."

I hear a sigh, and then the child begins to cry. Another pause. The woman shrieks. "Put that thing down! Jesus Christ, what are you doing?"

A surge of pain attacks my left eye, one so intense that I take a step backward and bump into Anderson. I turn to him and put my hand on his chest to regain my balance. He looks at me with fear, and I can't tell if it's because of me or because of what's happening on the other side of the door. He now has his gun out.

There is another yell from the woman. I've heard enough.

As another bolt comes from above, like a helicopter dropped a spike from the sky and it landed in the middle of my skull, I put the nightstick back in its pocket. I lower my left shoulder, and I scream.

And I knock that motherfucking door down.

30.

A bird flies right into my face. That's the first thing that happens after I kick open the door, which smashes the man's head into the wall, which knocks over a coatrack and sends a Braves baseball cap skittering across the floor. At first I thought it was another of my bolts, one of my blind spots, another hole in my vision, but it wasn't. It was a bird.

I look to my left and see a birdcage leaning against where the coatrack presumably used to be. I guess I knocked that over too. The bird flaps madly around the room in the opposite direction, toward the kitchen, where I see a woman holding what looks to be a two-year-old girl in her arms. The woman only has on sweatpants and a sports bra; the child is wearing only training diapers; they are both soaking wet. The woman is making a shocked O with her mouth, but I think she's looking more at the bird than me.

I spin around to my left, briefly slip on an oily spot on the floor, and regain my balance. I see the man flailing in the corner. He is a short man, much shorter than me, but has the physical comportment of a tank, or maybe an aircraft carrier. He is wearing a black tank top that shows off his massive biceps and a barrel chest that's busting out of his shirt so much you can barely see his chin. He looks like one of those kangaroos that's always knocking out bushmen in the outback. He has a dazed look on his face that makes me think he might have a concussion, as well as a cut, with a considerable amount of blood, on his nose.

He is also still holding the gun. I instinctively move a step closer to him but keep my hands at my side.

"Holy shit!" Anderson exclaims, his own gun drawn, as he enters the apartment behind me. He regains his composure, looks at me, and looks at the man. He then looks back at me, confused.

"Get them out of here," I hiss at him, looking at the woman and her child. Anderson straightens up and focuses, happy to be told what to do. He runs to the kitchen, bends down, and effortlessly picks up the woman and her daughter in one arm. Their expressions of shock do not change. Her mouth is still making that O.

I turn to the man, who is now facing the opposite direction, toward the door that I just smashed into his forehead. He leans over and clumsily attempts to pick up the coatrack with his left hand and the birdcage with his right—particularly difficult because that's the hand with his gun. He stumbles, and both coatrack and birdcage fall back to the floor. I hear the bird squawking behind me.

Anderson, the two human beings cradled in his left arm looking like little patches on his enormous uniformed chest, stops to my left.

"He's gotta—"

"Go!" I blast the word right in his face. "Get them the fuck out of here." I have never screamed at him louder. I'm not sure I've ever screamed at anybody louder.

He looks to the man in the corner, who is starting, in his staggered way, to turn back around to me, and he raises both his eyebrows.

"FUCKING GO!!!" I shout with all my force. I can feel the vein in my forehead bulge. The little girl starts to cry. Anderson puts his right hand on her blond head and caresses it. Then, both of them tucked safely away, Barry Sanders streaking downfield, he powers out the front door. The wind caused by his sprint causes the open door to swing behind him, nearly closing it.

I turn to the man. He is alert, now, at last. He is still holding his gun, staring at me.

I ignore him and run to the door. Out of the corner of my eye, I see his arm lift.

But I do not open the door. I slam it shut.

I then turn around and face the man, who is still standing by the window. He looks outside and sees my partner bounding down the stairs with the two people he had been screaming at just a few minutes ago. He then looks back at me. He grips the gun at his side.

The pain in my skull is pulverizing. It feels like my eyeballs are about to shoot out of their sockets.

I stare at him, weapon still in my holster, feeling clear and certain. This is it. This is the one I was hoping for. It happened already. It happened just like that.

I put my hands out in front of me, palms out. I then close my right fist, and then point up my index finger.

We make eye contact.

"Wait," I say, and I turn back around to the door and, theatrically, with great purpose, lock the deadbolt. It makes a satisfying *click*.

I turn back to him. His weapon is pointed at my chest. He cocks his head to the left, confused again, a dog staring at a bee on a flower.

"That's better," I say, balling my fist again. I discover that I am smiling.

31.

I take a step toward him. I am powerful, I am strong, I am Zeus. I shall take these lightning bolts out of my brain and I will command them to rain down upon you with righteous fury. I can control all that is around me.

I can make him do what I have come here for him to do.

He is still holding his gun in his right hand, but he is not pointing it at me.

So I point my weapon at him.

"Huh?" he says, his face slack. This has all come on him very fast, but hey, join the party, pal.

He stares at my gun, then looks down at his own. His head moves back up, and he blinks dumbly and loudly, an old frog on a lily pad. He almost looks like he's going to burp, or throw up.

He then looks back at his gun again, and his eyes go wide. Here we go.

Then he throws the goddamn thing across the room.

"Augh!" he says, finally coming to. He puts both his hands in the air. Shit.

"I'm sorry, don't shoot! I forgot I had it in my hand and then you all just came in here! I wasn't gonna use it, I swear, I'm sorry, don't shoot, don't shoot, Officer, please don't shoot!"

He then, without prompting, bends down to his knees, takes his hands from out in front of him, puts them behind his head, interlocks them, and lies facedown on the ground. The guy knows how to get arrested, I'll give him that.

"Oh," I say. "Or you can do that." I sigh, then take out my cuffs, sit on his back, and place them on his wrists.

I start to say the *You have the right to remain silent* bit, but finally the big one comes and then I'm there on the floor right next to him.

32.

Our man is still lying face-first on the ground right next to me, hands cuffed behind him, with that same dumb look of wonder he had when I busted into the room in the first place. He hasn't tried to get away, and no one else has come in here. I closed my eyes to get through the lightning storm. I must not have been out as long as it felt like I was.

I stumble to my feet.

"Yeah, uh, you. . . . You have the right, um . . ." My head is still throbbing, and there's fog everywhere.

The man, chest parallel to the floor, looks behind him. "Hey, man, you OK?" he says. "Did you just pass out?"

"You have the right—"

"Lloyd!" Anderson's voice booms from behind the front door. "Lloyd, what's the situation in there?"

I find it much more difficult to lift my left hand than usual. "Yeah, uh, I got it, it's clear, come on in," I try to shout.

Anderson smashes open the front door, his weapon out in front of him. He sees me, sitting on this guy's back, with the cuffs on him. His mouth gapes open.

"Holy shit, Lloyd," he says, his eyes wide and a sudden huge grin on his face. "Way to fuckin' go, dude!" Anderson is lithe for his size, and before I know it, he slides next to me, lightly brushes me aside, grabs the man by the back of his shirt and lifts him two feet in the air.

"Hey, buddy, it's time to go," he says, setting him back down as the man struggles to get his footing. The man turns back to me, closes his eyes, opens them, shakes his head for a second, and then starts to say something. But Anderson taps his face gently—*Wake up, pal!*—and begins to drag him away before he can register much of anything.

"I'll get this turd back to the station," Anderson says as he steadies the man and starts to march him out the door. "Harrison'll give you a ride back and start the paperwork, cool?"

Before he takes the man through the doorway, he stops and turns to me.

"Seriously," he says, "that was badass." He then gives me a thumbs-up and takes the man away.

I look around the room. It's more ordered and put together than I thought it would be. It feels like we tore the place apart, but everything is in its right place. The guy's gun is sitting on the couch, comfortably, like it sits there all the time, like it's 7:00 p.m. and *Jeopardy!* is on. This whole thing took about forty-five seconds.

I gather my balance and walk toward the apartment door. I open it and turn to my right. The teenager is still there with his phone, his mouth agape. I give him a little nod and light wave and then, I don't know why—I guess I think I owe him something—I give him a little two-step and curtsy. I don't think my brain works anymore. He puts his fist in the air and says, "Woooo!" I walk toward him, and he steps out of the way, filming the whole thing.

I look over the stairwell, down to Harrison's cruiser below. There are three other cops now next to him, one guy I vaguely recognize, the other two I've never seen before. Though I'm having trouble seeing much of anything. There are more people down there too. The whole neighborhood is looking up at me.

I take hold of the railing on the stairwell and carefully walk down, step by wobbly step, an elderly man trying not to slip on the ice. I make it down and turn toward Harrison, who clears out a path for me.

I have to sit back down.

33.

"Can I sit in the back?" I ask Harrison. I want to lie down, but I won't. I just don't want to talk to him, or anybody else, right now.

"Sure thing," he says. "Hero gets to do whatever he wants." I get in the back of his cruiser, and, in the driver's seat, he eyes me in the rearview mirror. "Don't try anything funny back there, heh heh, or I'm gonna have to cuff ya," he says, and he gives me an A-OK sign, like a big dumb yokel. I work up all the energy I have to give him a wan smile.

And then we drive off.

The lightning bolts have faded a bit, just a dull ache now. I'm starting to figure out their patterns now. They're a little bit like contractions. They happen a little more often than they did a couple of weeks ago, they last a little bit longer, and the pain's a little more intense. But they do fade. For a little while. For long enough. For now.

I stare out the window.

Trial No. 1 in the Great Lloyd Brain Robbery Experiment is in the books. What have we learned?

- Just because someone has a gun does not mean they will use it to shoot a cop.
- This is true even if the cop is aggressive enough to encourage them to do so.
- I probably was a little *too* aggressive. I can't just start barging in on every domestic disturbance. It turned out that he didn't

have the gun on his wife and kid, but he could have, and I could have startled him into using it. I can, and should, be as reckless with myself as I need to be. But that may have put them in more danger than I meant to. The point is that this is only happening to *me*. Firmer incident rule from now on: if there's anybody else around other than the perp, this ain't the one.

- Having my partner stashing the mom and kid away helped. It allowed me a moment alone with the perp, gave me a second to assess the situation and see if I could goad it into something bigger. I wouldn't have been able to do that with Anderson in there. If I'm going to continue to keep this all secret from him—and I really have no choice—we need to make sure he's isolated from me during the most perilous moments, not just because then he'll be onto me, but also because, well, I don't want him getting himself killed just because I'm trying to get myself killed.

- I probably should have pushed more. It's hard to get a guy desperate enough to shoot a cop. I wonder if the right play is to make him physically scared for his life, almost make him convince himself this is self-defense. Should I have shot him in the leg? Or shot right next to his head or something? It's not like anyone's going to side with him if I end up dead. He was the one who caused the disturbance, so he's the one who will be blamed for my death. I just have to make sure he does it.

- Shit. That was a dark thought right there. Down this path lies madness. I don't want to turn someone into a killer who is not, in fact, a killer. It's one thing for me to get killed on the job. It's another thing to frame a guy for my death. If I'm going to goad someone into shooting me, it needs to be a push in a direction that he was already going. That is going to have to be the first step in this: assessing whether this is a real threat, or just something I'm trying to make into one.

- Look at me: the ethical self-murderer.
- Oh, along those lines: I know a lot of this is just a roll of the psychological dice, but considering the ever-fraught relationship between the police and the Black people who live in this city (and this country), the last thing in the world I need is to start a global incident. You know how in a movie in the 1980s, if someone was holding up a bank, the robbers were all Black and Latino, but now, in our more "enlightened" time, if you make the same scene, *none* of the robbers are Black or Latino? Part of this is that the filmmakers want to correct the mistakes of the past, but the other part is that, frankly, they just would rather stay out of the conversation entirely. Why racially code a scene if you don't have to? And that's what I'm doing here, really: I'm writing a scene. And I want to keep it as simple as possible: just a cop getting killed on the job, that's it, that's all, let's not make this anything larger than it has to be. I don't want this to turn into a story about policing, or inner-city politics, or immigration, or anything else it's not about. Put it this way: if I can avoid my death being used to scare old white people on Fox News, I'd like to do so.
- These are a whole bunch of rules for a guy who is running out of time.

But as I stare out the window while Harrison hums along with some old classic rock song on the radio that I don't recognize, bobbing his head side to side like he's got all the days in the world, all the time to do whatever he wants with this life, I find myself drifting toward something more surprising than any lesson that may be applicable to future suicidal endeavors. If I'm being honest, it's my central takeaway from what just happened. It's what I really can't stop thinking about it:

That felt good.
I felt strong.

I felt powerful.
I felt *feared*.
I liked it.

I don't know where it came from. I don't entirely understand who that person was back there.

But I definitely liked it.

So that's interesting.

34

Back at home, I sip a Buffalo Trace and stare at the television. I caught the end of a basketball game on TNT I couldn't follow and was too tired to find the remote to change the station.

My phone buzzes. It's three texts, right in a row, from Bishop. Bishop is not as obsessed with his phone as every other kid his age seems to be, but when he pays attention to it, he fires off texts in rapid succession about whatever he's obsessing over at that moment. The first text is a GIF of the soccer player Ronaldo whining over a call while an animated blue panda bear cries next to him, with the words WAH WAH WAAAAAA spark above him.

The second two texts:

FUNNY!

and:

ronaldo such a floppy weiner

I snort some of the Buffalo Trace out my nose, then drop the phone on the ground. I am too tired to pick it up. The GIF stares at me and continues to blink. I smile.

I could have died today. I *tried* to die today. But I look at my phone, and that goofy kid, probably lying in bed, scrolling through his phone, finding a funny picture and deciding he wants to share it with his dad—it makes me glad I survived today, that I'm here, tonight, right now, to see it, that that's what he's doing, not mourning, not crying about how his life has forever changed, just mindlessly texting his dad a funny soccer meme that he thought I might like.

I'm happy I'm alive. I really am.

I groan as I reach as far as I can to the floor to pick up the phone.

ahahaahaha

floppy weiner

good night bish

i love you

you floppy weiner

I do not know what tomorrow will bring. I don't know if that's the last thing he'll ever hear from me. But if it is? We could do a hell of a lot worse.

THE TEN GENTLE EDICTS OF LLOYD MCNEIL

Edict No. 6: Don't pretend you don't have to worry about money.

Ugh. I hate this one. I'm just gonna tell you that right out. This is a horrible lesson to leave for you, and part of me feels like I'm a terrible dad just for bringing it up. But it's true. I tried to pretend it wasn't true for a long time. But it is.

I do not know what you are going to want to do with your life. You're good at math, and your teacher says you are good at writing essays, though I don't know why you never want to show them to me. I feel kinda bad about that. I want to be the kind of dad you want to show your essays to. But either way: you're a smart kid. You know that. Everybody knows that. You can do whatever you want.

And I know the correct thing for me to do as a dad, the exact opposite thing from what my dad would have done, would be to tell you to follow your heart and your dreams. Be a poet. Go hike through the mountains. Find yourself. Whatever—as long as you are happy. That's what parents always say, right? *As long as you are happy.* And yes. I obviously want you to be happy. But the thing is, and again I feel like a terrible dad having to say this, but, well: to be happy requires having some money. Not a lot of money. But some. I'm sorry. I'm sorry.

This doesn't mean you have to be rich. Rich people are often assholes, because *all* they care about is money. Their lives have no other purpose, so they ignore everything else and think having money is enough. I know your mom and I didn't have much money for you, growing up, but trust me, you're a hell of a lot better off than if we had been rich. Rich kids have no idea how anything works, which makes them completely useless when they enter the real world. I worked a break-in at some Georgia Tech coed's fancy apartment a few years back. This nineteen-year-old college sophomore was living by herself in a place that's bigger than any house any cop I've met has ever lived in, all because her dad was a shitty dad but thought buying her a big pad for her to trash for four years would make up for it. I was asking her what was missing, mostly jewelry and computer stuff, and she told me that all the dresses she wore in the last week had been stolen too. Just as I was talking to her, a middle-aged Latina woman with her arms full of clothes let herself in through the front door. This girl saw the woman and screamed, "Hey, who are you? Oh my God, this woman stole them! There they are!" I mean, here's someone that her dad pays to do all her laundry, clean up after her, and generally make sure not one ounce of responsibility weighs on her pretty little head, and not only does she accuse this woman, a hardworking person just trying to get through their day, of stealing, *she doesn't even recognize her when she sees her.*

That's the world that guy has made for his daughter. That's not parenting. That's child abuse.

Fortunately, that was never a problem for you. Your mom and I tried to make it so you never had to *worry* about money. But obviously we are not rich. I'm a cop. She's a teacher. I'm still not exactly sure what Gary does. I honestly thought that would always be enough. We both have steady jobs. We both work hard at them. We both care about what we do. That's the mistake I made, I think. I thought simply having a job, and not spending more money than we had, would make it so we didn't have to worry about money, and you wouldn't have to either. That was stupid.

Because now here you are, five years away from college—which is basically the most expensive thing you and I are ever going to be involved with—and the only way you're going to go to any of the colleges you deserve to go to will be to go in debt for the rest of your life. We didn't save any money because we didn't have any money to save: we spent our money just living our life. The way the world is set up now, you have to be thinking about money *all the time*. There is never enough money. The only people who have enough money have always had enough money. They're the only ones who don't get to think about it.

If I had been a little more mindful of money when I was younger, maybe taken some more of those off-duty security jobs a lot of other guys on the force took, maybe invested in the market more, maybe we wouldn't be in this predicament. I'd be leaving you, but I'd be leaving you with something you can hold on to, something that can help. But I didn't think about it. So here we are: your dad has given you nothing but a good hairline and a weak chin.

You're going to have a kid of your own someday. And you're going to have this same problem. You'll want to say, "Do whatever you want," partly because you weren't able to, because you listened to your dad's dying edict of worrying about money. Which is just going to keep this whole cycle going and going and going. I'm sorry. I think this is my fault.

35.

I open my eyes, and there is light everywhere, and there is wind—so much wind, as if I'm in the jet blast of multiple aircraft firing away from me in every direction at once. My stomach lifts, up through my lungs toward my throat, and then it drops, and spins, and lifts again. I realize my mouth is open, and I try to close it, but I can't. I just sit there, mouth open, gawking, either in between breaths or unable to breathe at all. I gasp, and gag, and gawk.

My eyes begin to focus. Right. I'm in the car. I'm moving.

I look to my left. I see Mercedes-Benz Stadium, home of Atlanta United, *he's big, he's bad, he's a motherfucking wall*, flying past me in a mad blur. I feel my foot on the brake, but I am not stopping, or slowing down. I begin to rise out of my chair. My seat belt is still unfastened, and I can feel the top of my hair brush the ceiling of my car.

I grab the steering wheel. I turn it, but I do not swerve. I look out the window.

I'm airborne. That's what's happening here. I'm in the air.

36.

So here's how it happened. Here's how I got airborne.

It was a spur-of-the-moment sort of deal. These kind of have to be. As much as I'd love to be able to schedule potentially fatal conflicts, you have to take these things as they come. But you've gotta plunge in face-first when they do. You've gotta be all in.

I wasn't supposed to be in the office until around lunchtime. The plan was to take it easy. I was gonna get Bertha washed, grab a couple of fried chicken tacos from Taqueria del Sol, maybe sit in Piedmont Park for a while, text Bish some memes, clear my head while I still could. But on a whim I turned on the scanner in the back seat. We're not required to have those in our personal vehicles, but I always have mine in there, it's basically like turning on the news. And about halfway to the Auto Spa Bistro—Terrence always takes care of me over there—one of the new dispatchers popped up.

"We've got a 10851, auto theft reported. Twenty-twenty-one Toyota Highlander, light blue, license plate CVQ 1982, vehicle left the Publix in Atlantic Station roughly eleven ten, about four minutes ago. Victim called immediately, says she was loading groceries into her car when perp punched her, took her keys, and drove away. Victim claims her two-year-old is strapped in the car seat in the back of the vehicle. Repeat: 10851, light-blue 2021 Toyota Highlander, license plate CVQ 1982, near Atlantic Station."

It's the sort of call you don't need a death wish to respond to, and certainly not when you're only about a mile and a half away. A child helpless in the back of a moving vehicle brings back my recurring nightmare. When Bishop was about eighteen months old, I was in a hurry to get somewhere, I don't remember where. After I strapped him in the back, I put the car in reverse to pull out of the driveway and realized I'd forgotten my wallet.

I grumbled to myself, opened the car door, and ran back up to the house. As I was heading up the stairs to the front porch, I happened to look back at my car. It was rolling backward. I'd left it in reverse, and it was moving down my driveway, toward the sidewalk and out onto the street. With Bishop in the back seat. I screamed and sprinted to my car, reached the driver's-side door just as the car crossed the sidewalk, and grabbed the door handle. In my nightmares, still today, the door is locked, the keys are inside, and I can't do anything but watch. In the real world, the door opened, and I leaped in and slammed on the brakes with both feet as hard as I could. Bishop jolted forward in his seat. I turned to him, terrified.

He giggled. "Eeeee!" he said.

So when I heard this call, I didn't even bother radioing it in. I sat for a second. I looked down at my lap and then, studiously, demonstratively, like I was trying to mime the movement in a game of charades, unbuckled my seat belt.

"Won't be needing that," I said to myself, then floored it toward Atlantic Station. My one burning thought was a simple one.

Let's fucking go.

37.

I had to make a couple of guesses—do a little detectin'. If someone was stealing a car from a Publix, they'd been staking the place out for a while. You don't just wander around and suddenly swipe a Highlander on a whim. That meant they probably had a planned escape route, likely to I-85. You can get on it right there on Seventeenth Street and be off and running before anyone has a chance to stop you. All the local roads are residential, too stop-and-go; the freeway is your only real option. So: north or south? This is where I had to use that old cop standby: some wildly irresponsible profiling. The high-crime areas, the poorest areas, your College Park, your East Point, are definitely south of Atlantic Station, by the airport, winding in and around it like poisoned vines. That's where you'll find your quick-hit chop shops too, the ones that'll get you in and out fast after a smash-and-grab like that. It was certainly *possible* that the car had been boosted by some random teenager looking for a Thursday lunchtime joy ride, zipping out for a fun jaunt back to the suburbs. But probably not.

So: South 85. I turned onto the freeway off Courtland Street and began veering from lane to lane, looking for a blue Highlander. Bertha's got some pickup to it—Major McNeil and I souped it up big-time back in the day—and I sped through to and fro, finding nothing. Inevitably, as we got up to Fulton Street, by Turner Field and the State Capitol Building, we hit traffic: someone's always having an accident in Atlanta. I pulled all the way over to the shoulder, took out my little blue siren that I've had for two decades and used maybe twice, and put it on my hood as I breezed by all the stuck cars. It makes a funny little sound, like cop cars in the 1970s. I felt like T. J. Hooker.

I rolled my window down and scanned. The traffic jam was a lucky break: he couldn't have gotten ahead of it, which means he had to be in there somewhere. I slowed down on the shoulder to look closer at each lane of stopped traffic, and just as I was beginning to approach the accident that was blocking everyone, I felt a sudden SMASH to the front of my car.

Just ahead of me, two lanes to the left of the shoulder, wouldn't you know it, a blue Highlander, surely having just seen me creeping up on him, suddenly slammed into the car next to him, which then slammed into me on the shoulder.

There was a wailing scrape and squawk. You forget how awful it sounds when one piece of metal meets another piece of metal at high velocity. And then the Highlander floored it up the shoulder and toward the GA 366 exit.

The poor woman whose car just smashed into me, her eyes met mine, and she made a silent O with her mouth.

I waved my arms to her through the rolled-down window. "Back up!" I yelled. It took her a second, but she got there, only scraping the stuck car behind her a bit, not bad, probably not even worth calling that guy's insurance over. And then I was past her, and then I was right behind him.

I could not see the car-seat back there. I looked. I was grateful not to.

Screeching and briefly bumping against the concrete embankment, the Highlander zoomed off the exit and flew through a red light, barely missing a kid on a scooter and a sturdy old Buick that would have folded in that Highlander like an accordion. Siren blaring, I followed, and we both blasted through another red light before, just past a Dunkin' Donuts on his left, he made a sudden, insane U-turn that he barely even slowed down for. His tires wailed, sparks scattered in all directions, and the Highlander nearly tipped over before smashing its back end into a lamppost.

Then the car settled, straightened, and headed straight for me.

If the kid hadn't been in the car, I could have taken care of all this right then and there.

I am, after all, not a person you want to play chicken with these days.

I couldn't risk it, though. I slammed on my brakes and, as he barreled toward me, shoved my car in reverse and tried to spin out of his way. I saw him, briefly, staring at me as he approached. He did not have a mad, wild look in his eye. He didn't look like he wanted to kill me. He looked scared as shit. He looked like he hadn't signed up for any of this.

And then he rammed the front of my car, careening me into a mercifully empty bus stop. I paused for a moment and felt the rumblings of another lightning storm approaching. But there was no time for that. I saw him speed toward the I-85 North on-ramp. I smashed the gas pedal.

I was having fun. It was true. This was the sort of thing I probably should have been doing years ago.

38.

hit a bird. I remember that part now—I'd forgotten about it. I was chasing the Highlander back up I-85 North, wildly jumping from lane to lane, trying to follow his increasingly desperate maneuvers without pancaking multiple people in their Teslas. I wonder how the onboard technology in those handle a high-speed chase. I can't see AI pulling this off.

I'd gotten a little space in front of me in the far right lane, with a straight shot between me and the Highlander, when SPLAT, the bird smacked right against Bertha's passenger-side windshield. It went flat when it hit, with its wings spread out, like a cartoon; you almost expected it to slowly slide down the glass and a little thought bubble that read OOF to pop out of its head. It didn't, though. It just bounced off and went rolling over the top of the car, leaving a little crack in its wake. I didn't register it at the time. I just sped up.

The Highlander veered over to the shoulder again, leaving a trail of smoke behind it. He'd blown a tire, and now he was starting to swerve dangerously, to the point that I thought he might flip over. I was able to pull up directly behind him, and I waved my arm out my window. I didn't have an intercom with me, but I have to say, I was still pretty damn loud.

"PULL THE FUCK OVER!" I yelled, pointing at the siren and honking my horn. Bertha makes the meekest little horn sound, like one of those Fisher-Price things you put on your kid's high chair. I wondered if the kid in the back seat had one.

I briefly saw the man in his side-view mirror, and you could tell, for that split second, that he was considering it. But then more screeching, and more smoke, and he pulled away from me toward that exit. He was going too fast, and wobbling, and he barely slowed down as he attempted a hard left off the exit, squealing and skidding nearly to a stop in the middle of the intersection. I tried to pull in front of him to cut him off, but he stabilized in time and tore off again, turning right onto a side street—I think it was Pryor.

I turned right and caught back up with him on a four-lane residential street, and he nearly collided with a Ryder truck pulled over to the left. He slammed left again, then another right, but I stayed on him, goddamn right I did, and then somehow we were back on I-85 North again, free of traffic but still going the opposite direction to where he presumably wanted to end up. He clipped a Volkswagen Jetta, sending it spinning in front of me, but I dodged him and followed him off the Memorial Drive express exit. Bertha was holding up, in a lot better shape than the Highlander. Hopefully he'd break down before the engine exploded and killed both of them in there.

As we both pulled off the exit, we ran into more Atlanta traffic, and the Highlander stopped. I thought that was going to be it. There were rows and rows of cars ahead of him, no logical way to turn around, no place to go forward. I glanced to either side. There was a Mexican restaurant I recognized—No Mas! Cantina, I go there with Bishop before United games a lot, it's a great place to park and just walk over to the stadium—to our left. To the right, an old apartment building. He was stuck. And so was I—right behind him.

"GET OUT OF THE CAR!" I yelled.

He turned his head toward me. We made eye contact. He was lost,

I saw—trapped, without entirely understanding how he'd found himself here. He seemed to be pleading.

I did not know you would follow me this far. I just want to go home.

I looked to my left. Several people eating outside had noticed us and were filming me with their phones. I caught the eyeline view of one. I waved and smiled. Why not?

I grabbed my revolver, opened my door, and began to step out of the car. In his sideview mirror, I saw his eyes widen. He turned back forward. And he floored it.

A horrible sound of burning rubber and mangled steel, smoke billowing everywhere, multiple drivers screaming. The car in front of him pushed out ahead, like a blocker, as he rammed it, and then it rammed the car in front of it, and then everyone was hitting the gas just to get out of his way.

"Fuck!" I yowled, got back in Bertha, and floored it, hoping to stay in the path the Highlander was clearing. Two cars spun out in front of me, and after he got past them, I sped up and split them. The Highlander bounced madly, like a bicycle going down a flight of stairs, and hit a hard right.

I made the same right and hit the gas as hard as I could. I could no longer see him, I realized. He had disappeared.

Then everything went black.

39.

A nd here we are. In the air. This is where I left you.

There's a little parking garage for the employees of Mercedes-Benz Stadium and State Farm Arena, where the Atlanta Hawks play, deep underneath the stadium. It's also where the team buses unload all their equipment, and where all the rock bands pull in from the road and unpack all their gear. It's convenient because it allows all that to happen out of sight from everything up above, away from the traffic. If you don't happen to be looking down from the main road that takes you past the Benz, you wouldn't even know it was there. But if you're walking to the game, you can look down and see where it is. When Taylor Swift played here a few years ago, fans lined up on the overpass, looking down toward the roadies coming off the bus, trying to capture a peek of their pop star hero, seventy-five feet below. That's how far down it is.

As I open my eyes, I've fallen about thirty. These other forty-five are going to be a bitch.

I brace. I have time to brace. Even when you are trying to kill yourself, your body can't help but brace.

40.

My head hits the roof of the car, and I feel my legs float out from under me. I come crashing down, and the gearshift rips into my right side. I bounce up again, not as high this time, and come down in the passenger seat, landing in a normal seated position.

The car careens around me, like I'm the center around which it must pivot.

I watch, helpless, almost bemused, as Bertha does a series of slowing spins. I notice we are approaching the ticket booth for the parking area. An old man is sitting there, looking away at something else. Bertha is headed straight for him. Still in my upright seated position, I wince and prepare for impact.

Then there is another smash behind me, and Bertha is spinning the other direction, faster. I bang my forehead against the glove compartment. Bertha slows. My face feels wet, and cold air blasts out of the dashboard. It feels nice.

Bertha makes one last sad little *whiirrrr*, hits with a little hop, and comes to a stop right in front of the ticket booth.

I turn my head slowly toward the window and see the old man, about ten feet away from me. He puts up his hand.

Hello.

"Hello," I say back, I think.

41.

I look around the car. Everything is in a different place than it was when I left this morning.

"Police officer!" I shout to the old man, though my mouth feels like it's full of cough syrup. "I'm a police officer. Did you see the other car?" That kid. That kid!

Wordlessly, he points to his left, about forty feet away, on the wall away from the parking garage, where the buses usually park before they start unloading. The Highlander is upside down, and it is on fire.

"Shit!" I say, and try to open Bertha's door, but it's stuck. I start to lift myself through the open window, but my stomach tears and groans; I hit that stick shift hard. But that kid. I push up and crawl out through the window, landing on the asphalt with a wet thud. The old man takes my arm and settles me. I turn and run to the Highlander.

The driver—we were just looking at each other about ninety seconds ago—is hanging halfway out his window. His eyes are closed, and there's a little hole in his left cheek. Because he hadn't planned on dying today, he's still strapped in. I lean my head in the open window and look to the back seat, hoping the kid is still there in the seat, maybe hanging upside down, maybe still alive.

But there's nothing back there. No toddler, no car seat. I see a carton of severely mangled eggs, several packages of diapers, and a bag of Doritos. It smells of gasoline and milk. There is no kid.

I turn back to the driver and unbuckle him. His body is limp, broken, but I have to get him out of this car. I put his arms around my neck, turn around, and drag him out. The old man is waiting for me, and he takes his left hand and drags him a little farther away from the Highlander. We drop him on the ground.

I turn him over and look at him. He's not moving. I look at his torso and discover that I can see his part of his rib cage. I put my head to his chest. I cannot hear his heart.

Jesus Christ.

I rip off the rest of his shirt and begin chest compressions. If I crack a rib, I crack a rib: I gotta get his heart going again. They teach you to do it to the rhythm of "Staying Alive." I remember that.

ah
ah
ah
ah
stayin' alive
stayin' alive
ah
ah
ah
ah
stayin' alive
stayin' alive

I do this for about twenty seconds, or maybe twenty minutes, I have no idea, and I think I get a heartbeat, but I can't tell, and a couple of lightning bolts hit, but I keep going, and then there is an ambulance, and a paramedic, and he pushes me out of the way and goes to work on the man himself. A few feet over, another paramedic shines a light in my eyes, but I wave him away.

I lean back and roll over, facing the old man, who is still there. There are now two people on each side of him. Three of them are pointing their phones at me. The other is looking up, filming where I just was, where we all fell from. The old man looks just at me. He doesn't move. He just stares. I guess this is nothing new for the ticket agent at the Mercedes-Benz Stadium luxury parking area.

I roll over and lay myself down. My face lands lightly on the asphalt. It is cold. It feels nice.

42.

I bet old Major McNeil never kicked in a door and dared a guy to shoot him. (Did he?) I bet old Major McNeil never straight-up ramped his car over an embankment, falling seventy-five feet and crashing in the parking lot next to the Falcons bus, all in pursuit of a suspect. My dad was a straight-arrow, textbook cop in all the good ways and also all the bad ones, but he valued his life. There was never a situation he walked into that he didn't plan on walking out of. He always planned on making it back home.

"He always planned on making it back home," I apparently just said out loud.

"What's that?" asks the paramedic wrapping my midsection in gauze.

"Oh, nothing," I say, remembering he's here. The driver's eyes were briefly open when I got him out of the car, but the lights were out, nobody was home.

"The man in the car," I say, running out of breath before I can finish the words.

"They just got him out of here," he says. "Don't know if he's going to make it, but he was alive when they put him in the van."

The lights were out.

"You really are a lucky man, Mr. . . ."

"McNeil," I say, and I straighten up, firm enough that I feel a pull in my rib cage. "*Detective* McNeil."

"Yes, sir, sorry, Detective," he says. He looks above him, at the bridge above us and the mass of twisted metal where the barrier I just went flying through used to be. "I mean, that's quite the fall. I can't believe you're not . . ."

"Him?" I say, pointing to the ambulance carrying off the man I've been chasing for the last fifteen minutes, the guy whose cheek was already cold, the guy who made eye contact with me just about eight hundred seconds ago, as it turns and pulls away.

"Well, yeah," he says. "Other than your ribs, which sure just seem bruised to me, though we'll get an X-ray to know for sure, you don't have a scratch on you." He looks over to my car. "I mean, even your car is still running."

It's gonna take a lot more than a plummet off a bridge to take out Big Bertha. She'll survive nuclear war. She's still got a full tank of gas too. She's ready to get moving. So am I. I want out of here.

"Well, that's me," I say as I rub my tongue across a tooth that has been *this* close to falling out all week. "I'm just a lucky fella that way."

I begin to stand up. The world whirs, but just for a second. I steady myself.

"Whoa there," the medic says, and I realize I haven't asked him his name, and I feel kind of rude about it, but then again, it doesn't matter, I always worry too much about stuff like that. "Maybe you should take it easy."

"I thought you said I was fine," I say, brushing some pebbles off my left pant leg and trying to stifle a groan. The ribs do hurt, quite a bit, all told. "I gotta go talk to the officer on scene over there, and then I'm getting the hell out of here."

The medic looks at me like I've got donkey ears, but shrugs. He doesn't get paid enough to fight with a cop. He packs up all his gear in a duffle bag and throws it in the back of his ambulance. There's probably more he could do for me, but there also isn't much of a point. I didn't see a tool in that bag that said "Excise brain tumor." He can go help an old lady who fell down. I'm all spoken for.

"Be careful over there," he says. "There's a crowd now."

I limp my way over to the responding officer, a young guy named Jeff, Officer Ripps. I've seen him around a couple of times, but I don't know him well. I'm not the sort of guy the young cops usually hang around with much. They all look like they feel bad for me all the time, like they're seeing what they'll look like in twenty-five years if everything goes wrong for them.

But Ripps has a huge smile on his face.

"Holy fuck, dude," he says, taking off his hat and wiping his forehead with his sleeve. "You're an animal."

He turns to one of the bystanders who is standing too close to us. "Hey, clear out, everybody clear y'all's ass out," he says. "I'll break that phone in half if you don't get your shit back. Give the man some space, for Christ's sake."

I wave him off. "It's fine," I say.

"It ain't fine," he says. "You're a goddamn hero, these vultures need to show some respect."

I chuckle. "All in a day's work, right?"

"Yeah, a day's work for fuckin' Rambo," he says. "Christ, you wrecked this goddamn place. You weren't letting this sumbitch get away, that's for sure."

"I thought he had a kid back there," I say, and hey, oh shit, now that I just brought it up, I *did* think he had a kid back there. "Didn't the dispatcher say he had a kid back there?"

Ripps spits off to his right. I think he's got chaw in his mouth, disgusting. Some of these South Georgia boys don't quite fit right in the big city.

"Guy dropped him off, can you believe that shit?" he says. "Apparently he got just down the road before he realized there was a kid in the back. He must have pulled over, got out of the car, put the kid on the street corner, and then took back off. We got a call about ten minutes after the mom hit nine-one-one from someone in an apartment complex up there, saying there was a baby on the street. We picked him up and got him back to his mom right quick. I think he slept through the whole thing."

I blink loudly. There was never a kid in the car at all. This whole thing was just about some lady's old Highlander and her groceries. The guy I was just chasing, the guy whose lights were out, he saw the kid, stopped the car, and took the kid out.

I click my tongue.

"Well, that's good," I say, trying to sound casual and cool. "That's a relief. I was worried when I couldn't find him in there."

"That explains why you tore after that guy like a house afire," he says, snorting a little after every few words, like it reloads his brain or something. "But seriously, man, that's a wild-ass chase," he says, looking at Bertha. "I can't believe, uh, everything's not on fire. Including you. Christ, is your car still running?"

"Big Bertha is quite a vehicle," I say, and another pain in my side makes me wince. "So, are we all set here?"

"What's that?"

"Can I go? Do you have all you need?"

I am not sure why I am so desperate to get out of here, but I am.

"Heh, well, I have to file a report, but I can get a statement from you later, 'suppose," he says, clicking and unclicking his pen on his chin. "But, uh, you sure you're all right? It's really high up there."

"I'm fine," I say, and I catch a tone of irritation in my voice. I soften. "Really, I'm fine."

His eyes widen, and his mouth opens to reveal a few missing chompers on the left side of his mouth. This guy definitely grew up with a car sitting on cinder blocks on his front lawn. "That's so bad-ass!" he says. "You're like the Terminator. *I'll be back!*"

I nod limply at him and turn to walk to Big Bertha.

"*Hasta la vista*, killer," he says, and it's all I can do not to throw up right there.

43.

He's gonna live. I got the full report when I got back to the office. He hasn't woken up yet. But he's alive.

He has a story, like we all do. He is the father of three little girls. It isn't the first car he's boosted, but he is lousy at it. He got busted a few months ago outside a chop shop notorious for being amenable to car thieves. We've always got somebody casing that place. He swiped an old Buick from one of the knockoff parking garages around the airport, one of those cheap jobs that only charge you ten bucks a day but tend to forget to lock the gates overnight when it's financially convenient to do so. He didn't even think to take the plates off the thing, total amateur hour, and it popped up hot the second our guy traced them. It had to have been the easiest bust we'd made all day.

He posted bond the next day, probably put up by one of the guys who run the rings down there in College Park. They find newbies like him, men desperate for cash however they can get it, and promise them more work if they give up a portion of whatever they get when they sell off whatever they stole, like a work-for-hire program. It always ends up being a lot more work than hire. What an easy mark he must have been. He was obviously shitty at stealing cars. Every time he got lucky and pulled one off, they would shake him down for cash, and before the bill of more stable employment came due, he'd get tagged and they could walk away clean, with no further responsibility. A thing people don't realize about criminals is that they scam other criminals before they scam any of us. Criminals are a lot less likely to press charges, they tend to carry a lot more cash than we do, and, well, they're usually not very smart. Whole thing's a pyramid scheme.

He came over from Puerto Rico in 2017. His brother lived here—still does, works as a bouncer at one of the strip clubs out near Vine City, the ones that look like anonymous warehouses, the ones powerful and infamous enough that they don't have any need to advertise, everybody just knows to go there. You gotta be a big dude to run security at a place like that. He'd have to be a lot bigger than his little brother. Little brother didn't seem very big at all, smaller than me even. I wonder if his big brother is protective of him. I bet he is.

Two of the girls, both under the age of five, have the same mom; the mom of the other, just born earlier this year, is still a teenager. He isn't married to either one of them. I don't know how much time he's spent with those girls. That's a lot of kids to have in a short amount of time. The two older girls are listed as living at his address, though I wonder if that's a school district thing; there apparently wasn't very much kid stuff found at his apartment, just an old pack-and-play and some diapers, no kid's room or anything like that. But they do use his address. He is obviously a part of their lives. It doesn't really matter how good or bad of a dad he is. There are three little girls who, if this had gone down just slightly differently, were never going to know their father. Maybe he'd have been for them what they needed him to be. Maybe he already was. I have no idea. How could I know? I only met the guy once.

His name is Jose Manuel Gutierrez. I met him when I was trying to kill myself. We made eye contact. He looked scared. I bet I looked scared too. I hope he makes it. For those girls. For himself. For all of it.

I do not know if I am helping or hurting. No time to worry about that now, though. I can only hope it all gets sorted out in the next life.

44.

Bishop will not stop hugging me. He's been hugging me a lot less since he started middle school. An enterprising therapist should specialize in helping parents cope with how their kids stop hugging them once they get into middle school, when it becomes uncool to show affection to their family, when the last thing they want is to admit that they need their parents, or ever did. We spend the first decade-plus of our kids' lives with them grabbing us constantly, holding on for dear life, and then one day it just stops. They go from asking you nonstop questions from the back seat to staring at their phone as if you are not there at all—like *that*. You understand. It's what growing up is. It's how this is supposed to work. But you miss the hugs. They'll never come back, not the way they once were. They're gone.

Unless, that is, you fling yourself and your car seventy-five feet off an embankment and somehow survive. Then your son won't stop hugging you. I wouldn't necessarily recommend this specific strategy to bring back those elusive embraces, particularly because every time he squeezes, it feels like my lungs are going to pop. But it's not an unwelcome by-product.

"I think he is happy to see you," Jessica says when Bishop leaps over the edge of the sofa and puts his arms around me again. "I guess we all should be." She looks worried, but also has a wry grin on her face. She doesn't see Bishop like this very much anymore either.

"Jesus, Dad, are you OK?" Bish says, face burrowed into my shoulder.

"I'm all right," I say. "Just normal cop stuff, I swear."

He looks up at me. "C'mon, Dad," he says. "Somebody almost died!"

Indeed, someone almost did.

These two came by as soon as they heard. I'm happy to see them, but I'd rather they have not heard. Big Bertha took me home straight from the Mercedes-Benz garage, like it was nothing, I was able to jam open the door, and after it locked back into place, it was like she hadn't gone through a thing. I noticed a little rattle on the drive home and made a note to check that out later—a little nick in her ribs, probably, kinda like mine, nothing a little oil or bourbon won't fix. She pulled into the carport just fine and deposited me at the front door just like I needed her to. I opened the door, face-planted on the couch, and slept until Jessica and Bishop started banging on the door about half an hour later. I needed a lot more sleep than that. But I did not mind the interruption.

After all, I didn't expect to see either one of them again. I'll take the bonus time.

"I shouldn't have to get a call from your partner to find out about you nearly getting yourself killed," Jessica says as she takes a seat on the opposite end of the couch. Bishop is now lying face up, head on my knee, like he's seven years old again. He puts his feet in Jessica's lap. It has been many years since we have been together like this.

I groan, but in a cartoonish, those-darn-partners way. "He knows he's not supposed to bother you guys with stuff like this," I say.

Bishop punches my left leg. "I'd beat his ass if he hadn't, Dad," he says, flexing his arm. "He's not so tough."

Jessica massages Bishop's ankle, and he starts to giggle.

"So, are you going to tell us what happened?" she asks.

It occurs to me that neither one of them even knows about the man and his family in the Bedford Pine apartment complex. Maybe that story can be left for another day. Though I have no idea when. Maybe Anderson can tell them that one too.

To see Bishop like this—so terrified that he almost lost me—and to know what is yet to come for him breaks me in half. Anderson will have to tell him so much.

I *pshaw* at her, like this is all no big deal, like this sort of thing has always happened to me, like it's just normal cop stuff. I know she knows better. But Bishop doesn't.

"Oh," I say, waving my hand in the air like I'm swatting a loose fly, "the guy stole a car, and I was in the area, and I was on my way to the precinct anyway, so I decided to pursue him."

"In Bertha?" she asks.

"Well, I couldn't exactly go switch out cars at the station."

"You couldn't call for backup? One of those young kids could have at least used a city car," she says. "You decided to just cowboy it?"

"Cowboy it?" Bishop chimes in. "Dad, did you put on a hat?"

"Giddyup," I say, playing along but not exactly loving play-acting the outlaw right this moment. There was a hole in his cheek. "Make my day."

Jessica tries to smile but clearly does not feel like smiling. She looks stricken.

"So?" she says. "When did you become so . . . aggressive?"

I wave my hand in the air again, this time at her, she's the fly, shoo fly.

"It really is standard procedure," I say, lying, obviously.

"Uh-huh," she says, narrowing her eyes at me with a skeptical twinkle in her eye, a librarian peering down her glasses at a whispering teenager, the way she used to, back when it was sort of lovable that there were certain things I didn't want to talk about, before it became so constant and distancing, so *alone*, that she couldn't be around it anymore and feel like she was in any way alive and breathing. "The Atlanta Police Department is famous for encouraging its officers to go flying off bridges, in their personal vehicles, in pursuit of petty car thieves. What section of the handbook is that in exactly?"

I start to say something, but Bishop interrupts.

"Mom," he says, but not in the whiny teenager way, more in a soothing tone, like he's in the middle of something special and rare and doesn't want it spoiled. "Leave him alone. He was just doing his job. Right, Dad?"

I look down at him. He has a row of whiteheads running down his left nostril, like a tiny inlet on a map, and he's fiddling the rubber bands of his Invisalign with his tongue. He's greasy and sloppy and appears to have not washed or brushed his hair in a week. He's beautiful, he's beautiful, he's just fucking perfect.

I have to look away from him so that I do not collapse within myself.

"That's right, Bish," I say, looking at the door. "Just your old man doing his job." I turn back to him, put my hand on his head, and start to brush his hair with my fingers. It's so oily I have to wipe my hand off on the couch. "But wow, you need a shower, gross."

He sticks his tongue out at me, then looks very sad. He closes his eyes and puts his head back on my knee. "I'm glad you're OK, Dad," he says.

I cannot save him from what is coming next. I see him, head on my knee, and I wish I could prepare him. But I cannot. So I just brush my fingers through that oily hair and listen to him breathe.

"I am too," I say, and I am.

45.

"What is Argentina?"

Jessica turns to Bishop and punches him in the arm. "How in the world do you know that?" she asks. "I can't get you to make your bed. You know the country that Eva Perón was from?"

"Boca Juniors," he says, smiling. "They're the soccer team in Buenos Aires. She was their most famous fan. Right, Dad?"

I can barely keep my eyes open, and I'm starting to get a scrambling sensation in my inner ear, and I had a moment a few minutes ago where I got confused and thought Jessica was my aunt Brenda, but, hours later, I think hours later, it might have just been a couple of minutes, Bishop and Jessica are still here, and I am grateful that they are. Even if I can't barely pay attention to them. I do not know if I will ever be able to get up from this couch. Perhaps I can sink into it, and collapse within it, and never return. There has to be some way to sell that as a police-related, on-the-job fatality, like I collapsed under the stress of today's incident, like I just withered away because of it, please deposit the money directly in Bishop's account, I have the bank statement around here somewhere, let me find it, I was just looking at it, they're still here, that's them right over there, that's *Jeopardy!* on the television, though that's not Alex Trebek, unless he just looks crazy different after shaving his mustache.

I nod to Bishop, or I sort of nod—my head rolls around, kind of sags, really, like a sad spinning top, wobbling and shivering as it winds down and slowly stops moving. I pull it up and lift an eyebrow. "Eh," I say, and the effort almost makes me fall over, back into the couch cushions, into oblivion.

Jessica sees this, and then she's next to me. She puts the back of her palm on my forehead, like she's checking for a fever. She puts her face close to mine, and I can almost see the woman who once loved me, or maybe it's Aunt Brenda, there is really no way to be sure.

Her eyes meet mine.

I know you are not OK. You can try to hide it from him. But I know.

I try to give her a reassuring grin, but my face just sort of falls. I'm worried my tongue has fallen out of my mouth.

She pats my face, then turns to Bishop on the other end of the couch.

"Bish, I think it's time to let your father rest," she says.

"What is . . . Tecate?"

"Bish . . ."

"Damn it, I knew that wasn't right," he says. "Quick, Mom, what's another South American beer?"

"Bish, it's time to go, I think, probably now," she says, more urgent, in a way that makes me wonder if my tongue really is hanging out.

"What is Red Stripe?" he yells at the television screen. "No, wait, that's Jamaica."

"Bish!" she says. "We have to go!"

He looks at her, and then over at me, slumping, bit by bit, into wherever the crack of the couch will take me. I bet there's a lot of plastic takeout forks down there.

"Oh, sorry," he says, and straightens up. He looks at me with worry and confusion, but also relief: today scared him. Poor kid doesn't know the half of it.

Maybe this is the last time. It wasn't before, but maybe it is now.

He leans down to me. "Yeah, Dad, get some rest," he says, though the words are starting to jumble a little bit as he says them, I don't know if that's him or if that's me.

"And I'll see you this weekend?" he says. "It's Orlando, I hate those guys, we gotta beat their ass."

I lift my hand and cannot tell if I'm looking at him. I lean toward him.

"Quilmes," I whisper.

"What's that?" he says, worried, even leaning back a little. Jessica once told me that, about two years before her dad died, she went to visit him one day and realized, seemingly overnight, that he had gotten old. He went from being her dad, the rock, the slab of granite, to being an old man, instantly, the snap of a finger. I wonder if Bishop is looking at me like that right now.

"Quilmes," I say, a little louder, really as loud as I can. "The Argentine beer from that last question. It's Quilmes."

"That's right!" he says. "Thanks, Dad!" My trivia bona fides have cheered him. His pops has a little life in him yet.

I start to get up, but Jessica puts her hand on my shoulder.

"Rest, Lloyd," she says. She kisses her finger and places it on my forehead. "Rest."

I watch them walk out the door, and it's not a big dramatic moment, it is not an emotional goodbye, they are just gone, and then my head is in the cushion and it's fine and it all goes dark and it sure was nice for Aunt Brenda and her son to come visit.

46.

It would take more years of therapy than I have time left on this planet to unravel how many peculiarities and quirks I will never shake because I grew up with the father that I did—and this would be true, so you know, even if there weren't an *Evil Dead* tree eating my brain—but there's at least one seed Major McNeil planted in my subconscious mind that I'm forever grateful for: I'm always on time. "People who are late always think they're charming, or eccentric, or somehow interesting because they are never on time for anything," he told me once, after he made me stay home from a planned night out with a friend of mine because the friend was fifteen minutes late to pick me up. "They're not any of those things. They're just assholes." I can still hear his words in my head today: *They think their time is more valuable than yours. Prove them right by making them spend it by themselves.* I haven't always agreed with my father over the years, but I agree with him on that. I showed up twenty minutes early for my first date with Jessica. I knew we might be a good match when she was already there too.

I learned my lesson from Dad. In twenty-three years of working for the Atlanta Police Department, I have been late to work twice. The first was when we thought Jessica was going into labor with Bishop, which turned out to be a fakeout, but which forced me to arrive at the office exactly seventeen minutes late. The other time was today. I slept through my alarm, which had been blaring for nearly two hours. In my dream, I was at a rave, and it was a techno beat, and I was standing in the back of the club watching everyone jump up and down as my head throbbed. But it wasn't a rave. It was just my stupid alarm. I woke up, saw the clock, and leaped off the coach like it was spring-loaded. I found it encouraging that I had such pep in my step.

The disoriented effort to scramble to the office on time—Bertha was cruising like yesterday never happened, and I got halfway to the precinct before I realized I'd forgotten my belt and gun—ended up being wasted entirely. Sergeant Ellis had been in a commissioner's meeting all morning, Anderson got tired of waiting around for me after an hour and just went to the gym, and no one else noticed at all. I sneaked in there like a teenager crawling in the window after curfew, and nobody gave two shits either way. Yet another way this place stopped being Major McNeil's years ago.

But if I had thought I was going to get away with blending into the architecture, I was extremely mistaken.

"Hey, look, it's Superman!" Coming out of the bathroom, Officer Perkins announces my presence to the whole office. "It's Lloyd McNeil, one-man war on crime over there." He begins to clap sarcastically, but he's got a look on his face I have not seen from him before: sincerity.

Officer Jesse, another new kid I don't know very well, turns in my direction, stands up, and walks toward me alongside Perkins.

"That was badass yesterday," she says. "That took some serious fucking balls."

"*Serious* fucking balls, bro," Perkins says, and he really does seem to mean it.

"Well," I say, not feeling (or, surely, looking) like much of a superhero, but not actually hating all this, "my balls are well known for their seriousness of purpose."

A voice booms from behind me. "Yeah, my balls make too many jokes." Anderson, freshly showered and nearly busting out of his uniform as always. "I'm glad to have a partner whose balls take life seriously." He smacks me on the back, and it hurts, but it feels good.

"Hey, partner, sorry I was late," I say.

He sits on the desk next to me, and it buckles for a second before settling under his weight, for now. "I don't think anyone's gonna give you any shit for sleeping in after yesterday," he says, and while there is bravado and pride in his voice, I see a flicker of worry in his eyes. "You all right? That was wild."

"Fuck yeah it was wild," Officer Jesse says. She's eating an apple and flicking specks of it all over her uniform. These new kids can't keep anything clean. She looks around her at the flock of cops gathering around my desk. "Do you guys realize how far that fall is? My God!"

You can wake up in the middle of that fall, that's how far that fall is.

Another kid, so young he reminds me of one of Bishop's friends from school, takes out his phone. His badge reads BURCH, so I guess his name is Burch.

"People are losing their minds about this online," he says, pointing at some blurry video I can't make out. "You're quite the celebrity. 'Happycop' is the hashtag. I guess they think you're happy. It's pretty dope. I think you're still trending."

I don't know what any of those things mean, but I smile and pretend like I do. *Happycop.* Huh. "I was just doing what any of you would do, you all know that."

"Fuck that," Perkins says. "I'da let the shitbird just keep the car."

"Well, that's why you're a pussy, Perkins." Anderson turns to me, only slightly grinning. "And here you are, still standing, Maybe you are Superman."

I pat my ribs, which flare in pain every time I move. I meant to change the wrap on them before I left home, but I was in too much of a hurry. "I sure don't feel super," I say, but I laugh to let them know everything's fine here. "But Bertha took the worst of it." And all told: I don't feel too bad for a guy who's dying. Even my brain feels fine this morning. But I remain so, so tired.

"Well, I'd say the other guy took the worst of it," Perkins says, and I think of him again. Perkins has an uncanny ability to ruin the vibe. I catch myself wondering what he'd look like with a hole in his cheek.

Anderson, sensing my sudden discomfort, takes the opportunity to pivot and bring us all back. "Well, we're all just glad you're OK, partner," he says, putting his hands out in front of him, letting the gang know the show's over, we all gotta get back to work now. "I think we've all learned that if anybody ever needs a lift home, definitely don't call McNeil, right?"

The group laughs. The kid is good, he really is gonna run this place someday.

"You ready to go hit patrol?" he says to me, patting me on the shoulder. "Time to go keep the streets safe." He turns to me. "But this time, pal: I'm driving."

ctually, *I'm* driving," I say, and Anderson tosses me the keys.

"You got it, boss," he says as we get in the car. "I can stretch my legs better over here anyway."

Anderson's jovial attitude in the office has faded. He is looking at me in a way similar to how Jessica was looking at me yesterday, and Sergeant Ellis was the day before: like he knows something's up. He's willing to give me my space for a while. But only for a while.

"So," he says, massaging his left hamstring, which is threatening to bust out of his uniform pants; it must have been leg day. "What *was* that all about?"

I glance out the window and pretend not to hear him.

I turn left past the 7 Stages Theatre, where Bishop and a buddy of his dragged me last year to a terrible supposed comedy show, and then right past Hattie B's Hot Chicken, where we went afterward and made the whole night worth it. Those nights were always worth it.

"So, as I was saying," Anderson says, clearing his throat and coughing lightly, something he does when he's about to talk about his feelings but wants to make it clear he's still tough. "What exactly happened yesterday? Since when did you just up and take off after suspects?"

"Oh, it wasn't—"

"Don't bullshit me, 'Happycop,'" he says, and he means it: there is real concern in his voice, and he's forceful enough to make it clear he's not going to let it go. "That might work with an idiot like Perkins. Not me."

I pause.

There is a brief moment when I want to just tell him. Just let it all out. Unburden myself. It has been hard—harder than I thought it would be—to keep this in, to not have anyone to talk through all this with. I have been having doubts. Am I doing the right thing? Is this really helping Bishop? Am I really helping anyone? Is Jose Manuel Gutierrez awake right now, with his daughters, if I just roll over and die like I'm supposed to? But then again: Maybe that asshole at the Bedford Pine Apartments shoots his wife and kids if I don't break that door down? And maybe it doesn't matter? What I'm doing, in the end, doesn't have anything to do with either one of them. I'm doing this for Bishop.

But also: I am doing this for me. I cannot lie: it has made me feel strong. It felt *awesome* kicking down that door and seeing the look in that guy's eyes. It was thrilling to tear ass after that Highlander, jumping curbs, spinning out, and, yeah, ramping off that overpass. When I landed? And I was still alive? I know this isn't going to make a lot of sense coming from a guy dying from a brain tumor, but that made me feel indestructible. *I am indestructible.*

I did feel like Superman. I felt like Rambo. I felt like I could fight the world. I *wanted* to fight the world.

It felt good. It felt great. It felt, maybe for the first time in my life, that I was really me. Happycop. (Why Happycop?)

I feel like that now. I do. I cannot lie. I do not know if it is right, or just, or fair, to feel this way. That does not change the fact that it's how I feel.

And I also have to remember that I don't even know to trust how I feel right now. The lightning bolts aren't the problem anymore. It's the waking up in the middle of the kitchen with my hat in the microwave. It's my dead old Aunt Brenda sitting next to me on the couch. It's that other night, when I suddenly found myself standing up in the corner of the bathroom, facing the wall, *Blair Witch* style, resting my forehead on the cold tile, it felt so wet and calming. I didn't know how I'd gotten there, or why I was there, or what I'd been doing before I opened my eyes and found myself there. It's just where I was.

That's going to keep happening.

How much longer am I going to be me?

It would be such a relief to say this out loud.

But I can't, of course. Because then I would have to tell him why I'm doing this. Which makes him an accomplice. Or, more likely, it forces him to turn me in. He is a good cop, after all. He'd just be doing his job. I would expect nothing else. I'd even be proud of him.

No. I can say nothing. Obviously. I'm sorry, partner. You deserve more than I can give you.

"I was just in the right place at the right time," I say, trying to sound scoffing and tough. "I thought there was a baby in the car. Any cop would have done the same thing."

"I doubt that," he says, "and I'm sure as shit certain that you wouldn't have."

I smile. "And yet I did," I say. "Maybe I've got more tricks up my sleeve than you thought, partner."

"You did," he says, clicking his pen on and off in his left hand, something I've seen him do during interviews with witnesses or suspects when I know he doesn't believe a word they're saying. "Just like you busted into that guy's house out of nowhere."

"Yep, I did that too," I say, straightening up, hoping I can strong-arm this into being over. "This is the job you signed up for, kid. If you're not ready to take risks, you're not going to make a very good cop."

"Uh-huh, thanks, Obi-Wan," he says, smirking. "King Kong's ain't got shit on you."

"You're mixing up your movie references."

"Look, I'll let this go because you clearly don't want to get into it," he says. "But don't take me for a moron either. This is very un-Lloyd behavior."

"Thank you," I say, as static comes on the radio. "I'll take that as a compliment."

We drive for another hour, stopping for coffee (of course) and pulling over a guy with expired tags, not doing much of anything. At one point, Anderson even asks if I'll take him by the overpass by Mercedes-Benz so he can see just how far I really fell. I make up an excuse. I'm not ready to go back there yet. My ribs hurt.

It's an uneventful day. I don't have much time left for uneventful days.

THE TEN GENTLE EDICTS OF LLOYD MCNEIL

Edict No. 7: Do not forgive us for what we have done.

Your mom made me read a book a few years ago, said it was the most important book I could possibly read as a father, which probably should have made me read it quicker than I did. Sorry about that, Bish, just not really a book guy.

You know this book, because last year, you told me one of your teachers told you to read it, though I don't think you ever did. It's called *The Uninhabitable Earth*. Remember that one? I put it in your room, though it's probably buried by a dozen pizza boxes by now. It's by a science writer for the *New York Times*, I think it was the *New York Times*, who has been reporting on the climate crisis for years now. It is, even allowing for the fact that I've maybe read five or six books since you were born and half of them were about cars, the scariest book I've ever read.

Basically: We can't live here much longer. We've destroyed the planet. Well, we haven't destroyed the planet. We've just made it so humans can't live here that much longer.

I shouldn't say "we." It's not you, Bish. It's us. It's me. It's your grandfather, and his father before him, and also the Chinese, I think—the book says they're a big part of this too. It's all the factories and aerosol cans and coal-burning planets and air conditioners and Humvees and everything else all of us who came before you did to ruin this world for you before you were even born. The bare minimum of what we were supposed to do for you is give you a place to live. And we couldn't even do that.

Do you know what my primary chore was when I was a kid? The job I had to get done every single day before my dad got home from work? It was burning the trash. This was a freaking awesome job to get to do every day, Bish, I have to say. *Hey, eleven-year-old boy, here is a big bag of junk. Please take it out to the backyard, put it in a barrel, and set it on fire. Oh, and make sure you sit there and watch all of it burn.* Recycling? I had no idea what recycling was. You just put everything in the barrel and set it all ablaze. I watched Coke cans burn. I watched your grandmother's empty hairspray canisters burn. (They would always explode real loud, it was awesome.) I watched plastic bags from the supermarket burn. Bish, I watched *styrofoam* burn. Styrofoam burns in an awfully satisfying fashion, I have to say. It sort of implodes, spiraling into a little black hole, before collapsing inward in puffs of toxic smoke. It makes a *lot* of smoke, thick, dark smoke, though it has an oddly pleasant smell, even a little citrusy, like someone seared the orange for the old-fashioned too long. I used to sit back there and inhale it, cough, and inhale it again. It's apparently carcinogenic. I'm going to try not to think about that too much.

The point is, that's how little we thought about the world around us, and what we were all doing to it, as recently as thirty years ago. You just burned whatever you wanted to, and whatever you burned went into the air, and as far as we were concerned, that meant it disappeared, that it was gone forever. We were so entranced and excited by all the new stuff that was in the world, all that we were discovering, the computers, the phones, the internet, the big trucks, all the cool shit that we could suddenly do, that we thought there wouldn't be a bill to come due, that the future was just limitless—really, that we were indestructible.

We were not, it turns out, indestructible.

None of us are. We know that now, but it's probably too late. That's what the book is about. It's about how all the stuff we thought we could stave off, that we could push off until someone came up with some magical solution for, is not only a lot closer than we thought, it's already here. You see it, you know it. The heat, it's always so goddamn hot, it was never this hot when I was a kid. The tornadoes, the hurricanes, the earthquakes, all the extreme things that used to be rare but now feel like they're happening everywhere, every day. The fires, the smoke . . . the smoke! Remember when they couldn't play that MLS game because there was too much smoke in the air, even though nothing nearby was on fire? That's scary shit. There are so many fires that we can't even contain the smoke, let alone the fire.

And the worst part about it—and this is why the book is truly terrifying, Bish—is that this is as good as it's ever going to get. I always joke with the guys on the force about this whenever they complain about how hot it is in, like, March, or October. I tell them, "Yep, and this is the coolest it will ever be on this day, the rest of your life. Appreciate this!" They hate it when I do that. But it's true! It's just going to get worse. It will be a little hotter, with a little scarier storms, next year, and then hotter and more, and scarier, storms, and then we'll be nostalgic for when there were days when it *didn't* storm, and then it's going to be so hot and terrible that no one is going to be able to live here at all. That's what we've done. That's the world we've handed to you.

Because this won't be a problem for me, or your mom: we'll be long gone before it gets truly unlivable. But you? And your friends? And, Jesus Christ, your kids? Where are they going to go? Because they sure aren't going to be able to live here.

When your grandfather was a kid, his dad told him the only thing a man did that truly mattered in this world was making his kids' lives better than his was. That was the job. You work hard, you put up with the bullshit that you have to put up with, you make every sacrifice you can, so your kid doesn't have to. Did you know your great-great-grandfather was a coal miner? He worked the Durham coal mines up in northwest Georgia, just across the state border from Chattanooga. He died of cancer when he was forty-three years old—my dad never even got to meet him. He worked down there, breathing in all that horribleness, so his kid could get a better job, so he could live past forty-three. And he did. He became a cop. Which, for all its problems, sure is better than working in a coal mine. And because he became a cop, my dad became a cop too. Which meant that's what I did.

I don't want you to have to be a cop, or a coal miner, or anything that's not what you want to do. Your life is yours. It was my job to give you the opportunity to choose your life, to not feel like you must somehow honor mine. That's one of the biggest mistakes I made. I became a cop because my dad expected me to, not because I wanted to. It messed me up. I know that now. I know it like I know that blowing up hairspray canisters is bad. My job has been to bring you in the world, to keep you safe, to make sure you've got food in your belly and a roof over your head and to otherwise stay out of your way. You don't need my burdens on you. You don't need to live in response to my mistakes.

I hope I have done this. I have tried very hard to do this. But what I know now, what we all know now, is that in the end none of it may end up mattering. Because all the things I tried to do, all the things my great-great-grandfather tried to do, all the things, God bless him, even your grandfather, for all his faults, tried to do, none of it is going to make a lick of difference. Raise you, support you, keep you safe, build a foundation for you, the same way you'll try to do the same thing for your kids, and them for theirs, the paying it forward, the trying to make it all a little bit better than it was before . . . what was the point of any of it if *there's no goddamn place for you to live?*

That's what the book got in my head, Bish. All we care about, all we value, all we try to pass along, all we try to fix, all we try to improve, all we want for the people that we love . . . it all is just going to go up in fire. It was all pointless. We destroyed it all. For some Styrofoam. For a big stupid fucking truck.

I am sorry. For all of us. I don't have any advice here, no edicts that will help you, nothing that can make any of this better. Maybe just get on the first rocket ship to Mars when you have the chance? That's all I got. That's all I can give you.

All I ever wanted to do was protect you. But I can't. No one can. I am sorry we have done this. Let your vengeance rain upon us, in this life or the next.

48.

We're just about to turn back to the precinct when a muffled voice comes through the transponder. Both Anderson and I reach for the radio to turn it up. He playfully slaps my hand away.

The dispatcher clicks on and off a few times—they never can get that right the first time. She finally crackles through.

"We've got reports of shots fired off the Georgia State campus, an apartment building about three blocks away from the GSU Sports Arena. No injuries yet, but the caller says there's a white man with a gun on the roof of her building. Looking for closest responding officer."

I look at Anderson. He looks at me.

I punch him in the shoulder.

"King Kong ain't got shit on me," I say.

"Fuck," he says, taking a deep breath. "All right. Let's go."

49.

The scene outside the GSU Sports Arena is already chaos when we arrive. There are a couple patrolmen here, trying to clear out the street and cordon off the perimeter, and they're not having much luck. One of the many ways this job has changed in the last decade or so revolves around active shooter situations—how much training they give us for them, how much they inhabit the popular imagination. Growing up, when I heard a car backfiring, I knew it was a car backfiring. Now everybody assumes it's somebody firing a gun. I suppose it's a fair assumption. Only old cars backfire anymore. The guns are a lot newer. The average American thinks they're all we deal with, but all told, I'd say we get about one or two a year. Which is a lot! That's about one or two more a year than we had when I started out.

By the time Anderson and I pull in, the streets are full of students looking up at the roof of the Georgia State Urban Life Building, right across from the arena where Bishop and I used to watch Panthers games, that's the building where we parked, back when they were good, back before soccer took over both our lives. We park in front of the arena, right under the I-85 overpass, and one of the patrolmen runs up to me.

"Hey, I'm Officer Kuhns, you guys got here fast," he says. He's young and sweaty and has a thin line of whitehead zits across his chin, like a strap.

"McNeil," I say, with a now-common authority in my voice that I'm beginning to enjoy. "This is Special Officer Anderson. You gotta get this street cleared out."

"I know, I can't get them to move, they're all students, they keep pointing their phones where the guy was," he says. "People are nuts."

"Yeah, that'll happen," I say. "Just do your best. He still on the roof?"

"I don't know, we just got here ourselves. Security guard said there haven't been any shots in five minutes, but he hasn't seen anybody come down."

Anderson comes around to my side of the car. There is always a moment when cops who don't know him take a tiny step back at first sight of this sudden mountain, like they weren't expecting to have the sun blocked out like that.

"I'll call for backup," he says, but I think I'll let him wait for reinforcements. I might not get a better chance than this.

"Cool," I say, already turning to head into the building. "I'm gonna get the lay of the land."

Anderson takes my arm. He has a look of exasperation.

"Wait, what?" He's lowered his voice, not wanting to contradict his partner in front of this kid, but also, *Wait, what?*

I turn back to Kuhns. "Just clear these idiots out of here, OK?" The kid shrugs and dutifully turns back to the crowd, where I see him talk to the back of a student's phone for about ten seconds to no effect, before finally just tapping him on the forehead so he can tell him to move. People have gone nuts.

"So what are we—"

I hear Anderson's voice behind me, but I'm already on the move.

"Yo, Lloyd! What the fuck?" he booms.

I turn around, now running backward. "Watch the back exit, the south one," I yell. "Radio me if he tries to sneak out. If another cop comes, have him cover this door. I'm gonna go find this guy."

"Jesus, Lloyd, what the hell is wrong with you?"

I stop. I smile.

"What do you want from me?" I say. "I'm motherfucking Rambo."

And you know what? I am.

50.

The building is evacuated, anyway, which is a relief—if a decade of shooting drills in elementary schools have taught these kids anything, it's to get the hell out of the building, at the very least. A classroom around the corner from the front door is already empty, even though there was clearly just a class in there. A movie strip about measles is playing from an overhead projector. It looks interesting—there's a lot of people who don't know about measles.

I look around the room. There's a desk in the corner—that'll work. I drag it out of the classroom and cram it up against the door I just came in. I've got Anderson guarding the other exit; if anyone tries to get out, that'll at least slow them down. For good measure, I find another one in the adjacent classroom, and after a couple of minutes of straining, I put it on top of the first. All I need now is a guard dog. If only this were the vet med building.

I turn the corner toward the stairs. There's a quiet alarm *bloop blooping*, a silly alarm, like a bird squawking at itself in a mirror—it's a very unalarming alarm. A blue light flashes every couple of seconds, and every thirty seconds an automated voice reminds the students and faculty of Georgia State University to please evacuate the building in orderly fashion and await further instruction.

I take out my gun. Up the stairs.

This, it occurs to me as I clear another classroom—nobody in there, nobody home—is my ideal scenario, if I can play it right. There's no one in this building but me, and very likely a guy with a gun. I've got my partner guarding an entryway, ensuring that no one can come and get in our way. There'll be no witnesses to anything that might go down, which means I can push this in whatever direction I need it to go without anybody someday testifying in a way that my insurance can use as an excuse not to pay up. And, perhaps best of all, we are dealing with, fair to say, a somewhat unstable person here. I do not know why this person took a gun to the rooftop of the GSU Urban Life Building. I do not know what drove him to this point. I do not know what went wrong with his life to make him do something like this.

None of that matters today. Not to me. Not right now. All that matters is that he's capable of anything. And I can find some real use for a guy who's capable of anything.

I turn onto the last set of stairs before the fire escape. I'm one floor from the roof. The building remains cleared. The lights are still flashing. The alarm is still *bloop bloop*ing. I slip for a moment; the floor is oddly wet in spots. I check another classroom—the last one, it seems. Zilch.

I secure my footing. I can feel a dim thud approaching from the back of my skull. I walk toward the fire escape and see an entry on my left to a hallway I hadn't seen. I turn the corner.

There he is.

He is facing away from me. His back is broad, muscular, slightly rippling out of his shirt; he's not Anderson Big, but he's plenty big, hulking, even. He has long hair that flows down past his shoulders. He is wearing tactical gear, but cheap—the kind you can buy on Amazon if you want to look tough, the kind that serves no real purpose, basically just black cargo pants. He's wearing brown boots, and I'm amused to find myself a little disappointed that he didn't think, on a day as big for him as this one, to find boots that matched his pants. He has a strap around his neck—it's supposed to go around his whole body, but he's too big, and the strap is cheap too, so it just sort of clips around his neck, like he's in danger of being strangled by it. But the strap is strong enough to hold the semiautomatic rifle he's cradling in his arms. That doesn't look cheap. That looks like a finely crafted piece of American machinery right there.

He's perfect. My God. He's so perfect.

It is as if he were put on this earth just for me, at this moment. If you were to construct the platonic ideal scenario for how this journey was going to end, this would be it. He's right there. He's lost. He's alone. He's scared. He's got a killing machine in his huge hands. And he's got a cop standing right behind him, just desperate for him to use it. We were destined to meet. This is where this was going all along.

I stand up straight. I am ready for my close-up.

It occurs to me to say a little prayer. I do not know why. It just does.

Lord—

I am not sure what I am supposed to call you, but I do not even know if you are real, so you will have to forgive the lack of formalities. If I get to meet you in a few minutes, I promise I will apologize.

Now that we are here, I just ask that you, or whoever, please keep Bishop safe and happy, let him be the beautiful kid that he is, let him grow up into the special person I and everyone who has ever met him knows that he will become. That I will not get to see it happen is the greatest tragedy of my life. But I know it is coming. I know who he is. You must know too.

I wish it had not gone like this. I do not believe that I or Bishop deserve this. But deserve has nothing to do with it. Just please keep him safe. That's all I ask. I know this is cheating. I know I can't just show up at the end like this and start asking for stuff. But I'm going to cover all my bases anyway. I'm here, after all. I finally made it.

OK. That's all I had to say. That's the only thing that's important. I don't know what comes next. But I'm ready.

I'm ready.

Amen

51.

'm ready.

I position myself about ten feet behind the shooter. I take out my weapon and unclick the safety. I must be careful here. I don't want to accidentally shoot him before he shoots me. But I also don't want to let him get away so he can shoot somebody else. After all, I can stop him, you know, *while I'm here.* My plan is to make sure he sees me pointing the gun at him, so he can fire back at me in self-defense, and then be ready to fire right after he does. If he clocks me right in the head, well, it'll be too late for anything after that, I gave it the old college try. But if he gut-shoots me, maybe I can wing him, or get his knee or something. This might not be the best plan. Give me a break. This is all happening very fast.

I get myself in shooting position, feet secured, weight centered, arms locked, finger on the trigger. They teach you not to scare a guy when you've got a bead on him, that it just accelerates the situation, that it increases the possibility of violence. You're supposed to be calm, to de-escalate. But we're going off book here. I won't get a better opportunity than this.

I whisper one last word, to myself, just so I have it.

"Bish."

I love ya, kid. This world is going to be yours.

Out of the corner of my eye, I see a bird in the corner of an adjacent classroom. It is lightly hopping in one place, its beak bobbing up and down. It looks at me and cocks its head to the left.

I clear my throat as quietly as possible. Then, I scream:

"FREEZE!!!!!!!!!!!"

It happens so slowly I can see his skin ripple. The man swings around, weapon in hand, finger on trigger. His hair swirls around him dramatically, like he's in a shampoo commercial—he's got pretty hair. He's not snarling, though, and as he turns, his eyes go wide, his mouth breaks into that O shape, his head snaps back like he's been slapped. My jump scare has been successful.

And he points the rifle at me. And fires. And then he fires again. And then he fires again.

Pop pop pop. Rat-a-tat-tat.

I pull the trigger instinctively, and see a window behind him shatter. He turns to it, leaps in the air slightly, and then sprints down the stairs.

It occurs to me that I am still standing. I turn around. There are three bullet holes in the old drywall of the GSU Urban Life Building. A puff of smoke curls outside one of them, tauntingly, almost seductively.

You have got to be shitting me.

I shake my head clear. I run after him down the stairs.

52

I am not fast. But I can get flying down stairs like nobody's business. Four at a time, baby, I'm like a cross country skier.

I turn the corner at the top of the stairs and catch a glimpse of him at the bottom. He grabs the railing to spin him around faster, and his hair whips behind him, like the rally towels we used to wave at Braves games. Down down down.

He spins around another set of stairs, and I'm gaining.

Then I hear another gunshot beneath me. There's a *wheeeewsh*, a crack appears in the wall next to him, and he hits the ground and skids across the floor. I think he's hit, so I run up to him, my arms splayed, pinwheeling. I've holstered my weapon, and I'm not exactly sure what I'm supposed to do with my hands.

He pops back up and starts to pull his rifle toward me. I think he plans on shooting me in the face right here, but I'm moving too fast toward him, and before he can get his hand on the trigger he instead deposits the end of his rifle right in my nose. I smash into it at full speed, and everything goes white for a second.

I slide around his ankles, sort of a spin-the-bottle-type thing, and collide with the wall next to him, ribs-first.

"*Ooooph,*" I say, or something like it, as a puff of air comes rushing out of me. I am lying at his feet. I am at his mercy. May he please not show me mercy.

I can feel him standing over me. I don't look up at him. I look down.

I hope my looking down will make it easier for him.

He pauses. I can hear his breath above me. I close my eyes.

Bish.

And then, a shot.

The man, still above me, groans. I feel a wet splash against my face.

"Put the fucking gun down!"

Anderson is standing about six feet below us, at the bottom of the stairs. I look down at him. He's young, earnest, sincere, but don't let it get twisted: he's still a monster of a man, and he is furious. He looks like a killer. He looks like an avenging angel. He looks like the man who is gonna cut the devil's goddamn throat.

"Now!" he barks, the authority of the Old Testament behind him.

The man looks down at his leg, which now has a hole in it with smoke coming out. His face is a howl of pain and confusion. He turns his gun away from me and toward Anderson, finger on the trigger.

Another shot rings out, another thundering *pop*. It hits the man's shoulder and he's flung backward, briefly stepping on my throbbing ribs, and begins to fall. As he falls, there are a series of eruptions from his gun, *whamp whamp whamp whamp* in rapid succession, in the general direction of Anderson. I see Anderson dive for cover on the other side of the stairs, away from the trestle, around the corner. I can't tell if he was hit. I can't tell much of anything.

The man wobbles above me and regathers his balance. He teeters for a moment, then straightens. He looks down at me, blankly, like he can't see me anymore.

Then he turns and throws himself down the stairs.

This fucking guy.

close my eyes again. The room smells burnt. I cough.

I pull myself up, still alive, somehow, indestructible despite all my best efforts.

"Anderson! You OK down there?"

I hear shuffling.

"All good!"

I fly down the steps again and stop next to him. I extend my hand and am surprised to find myself smiling, after all of it.

"I think he went THATAWAY," I say, pointing my thumb cartoonishly down the stairs. I start to pull him up, but he moans.

"Aw, shit, I think I'm hit," he says.

"Fuck," I say. "Where?"

"Uh . . ." He sounds woozy. "I don't know?"

I ease him back down to a seated position and begin to pat him down, looking for the wound. His eyes are darting around, but there's no blood on him, and he's alive, so I go from the chest down. I tap on his chest, then his ribs, then his left shoulder, then his right, then his left thigh, then his rig—

"Awww, SHIT!" he bellows.

"Hey, I think I found it." I take out a handkerchief I always carry with me—Major McNeil taught me to do that. I press it on his leg.

"You're fine, it's just your quad, it's not bleeding too bad," I say, like

I'm a doctor or something, like I have any idea what I'm talking about. I take his left hand and place it on the handkerchief.

"Good thing you never miss leg day," I say. "Press down, OK? I'll be right back."

"Wait," he says, his eyes now focused on me. "Where are you going?"

I smile again. I cannot stop smiling—I think I might be going insane.

"I'm gonna go get this guy," I say. "Obviously."

A slight grin comes across his face, but then he grimaces as he puts his hand on his leg.

"Jesus, Lloyd," he says. "You really are fucking Rambo."

I blow him a kiss, because why not at this point? And I turn around and tear ass down the stairs, because I am Rambo.

Down one set of stairs. Nothing.

Down another. Nothing.

Down to the ground floor. Nothing. I see the door I came in, open, but slowly closing. I'm right behind him.

I sprint toward the door and push it open.

I look to my left. There are some sirens in the distance, but all I see is a kid with his phone out in front of him. I start to tell him to get out of here, but then I see his eyes widen.

"Dude," he says, no alarm in his voice, just calm, chill, wholly disconnected awareness that something is about to happen.

I turn around.

The man is ten feet away from me. He is resting against the corner of the GSU Urban Life Building, his back against the wall, a pool of blood accumulating at his feet. For the first time, he doesn't look shocked, or scared, or bewildered. He is staring at me with murder in his eyes. He has had enough.

He aims the gun at me.

I look at him. I wonder if he sees my relief. I hope so.

Once again, I close my eyes, and I think of Bishop, and the world that awaits him. I can see him. I am picking him up under his armpits, I am lifting him to the skies, *goalllll, goalllll, vamos vamos vamos ATL.* We did it, kid. We did it.

I inhale, ready.

I hear a shot, then a dull thwack, and then a duller thump.

I open my eyes. I have always been curious what comes next.

He is lying on the ground.

Standing over him is a girl. She is young. She is wearing a Georgia State varsity jacket. She is holding her phone over him.

"Yeah, motherfucker, take *that*, you fucking fuck!" she bellows.

To her right, a friend is filming her.

A cadre of police officers run up to the man, weapons drawn, and shove the two women out of the way, a little rougher than they probably should have, but, to be fair, the officers did just shoot a guy. They surround him, their voices booming as one.

The girl turns and runs up to me.

"Oh my God, are you OK?" she says. She sounds *thrilled*. She sounds like she might just start flapping her arms and flying away.

"Eh?" I say, I think.

Her friend comes up to us and points his phone at me.

"It's Happycop!!" I hear him say. "Yo, man, Happycop!"

The girl puts two fingers up in the air and points them at her friend.

"Happycop saves the day again!" she says, leans down, and strategically places us both in the shot. She turns to me.

"You saved us," she says, brushing her hair out of her right eye. "You're Happycop. It's what you do!" She then gives me a peck on the cheek.

"Eh?" I say, again.

"Thank you," she says. And then she jumps up and raises her fist in the hair. "Happycop!"

I close my eyes again. It is time to rest.

ENTHUSIASTIC!

THE TEN GENTLE EDICTS OF LLOYD MCNEIL

Edict No. 8: Do not be afraid to be surprised by pain.

When you were about eight years old, I had you for a weekend when your mother and Gary were off at a music festival. You might remember this? It wasn't that long ago. But five years is a lot longer for you than it is for me. When you get old, all the years start to smush together. One year becomes two, which becomes four, which becomes eight. You blink, and *woosh*, there goes five years. But for you, jeez, five years is more than a third of your life. You may as well have been a different person entirely.

You'll probably remember this, though, because this was the weekend when you were sick. So sick. Jessica and Gary dropped you off on Thursday night, early, so they could catch their flight, and we ordered in Mexican food and stayed up late watching *Ghostbusters*. Remember that? You didn't like it nearly as much as I thought you were going to. I think the marshmallow man might have scared you. We ate chimichangas and drank Cokes and you said you wanted to sleep on the couch and I let you because I knew Mom would have made you go to bed and I wanted you to feel like you could get away with stuff at my house that you couldn't get away with over there. I just wanted you to like me.

You woke me up around three. "Dad, my stomach hurts," you said, and before I'd had time to wipe the gunk out of my eyes, you vomited all over the floor. I took you to the bathroom, and you went a few more times, and then I got you a wet rag for your head and tucked you into bed next to me. I stayed up all night with you. You'd fall asleep for a bit, then wake up suddenly and sprint to the toilet, then go back to bed and then do it all again an hour later. You were eight. You were so small.

What I remember, though, is not how sick you were. I remember how *sad* you were. The look you had on your face was not one of agony, or pain, or even nausea. You looked *stricken*. You looked like someone had stolen your dog. And not just that. You were, more than anything, stunned. You could not believe that this was happening to you.

The feeling a parent gets when they see that their child is suffering and they know they can do nothing to help them is the worst feeling in the world. You feel helpless, pathetic—pointless. And I remember that sensation, how awful it was to know that I could not protect you from this sickness, that you were puking your guts out and there was nothing I could do to stop it.

But you know what? I also remember feeling like a good parent, like we'd done a good job. Seeing the way you reacted to being sick made me proud.

Because it was good that you were surprised. That look you had, the way your eyes went wide, asking *Why, why do I feel like this?* meant that illness, sorrow, discomfort, pain, suffering . . . what you were going through . . . was an aberration. Your sickness was a deviation from the norm—it was something new. You were sad that you were sick. But the sadness came not from how you felt but instead from the fact that the sickness existed in the first place. It was as if you had no idea that human beings could feel this way.

There is a school of thought, Bish, an older one, one that my dad believed in, and his dad did, and surely his dad did too, that parents are supposed to toughen up their kids. That their primary job is to make sure kids know how difficult the real world is, how harsh it can be, how they need to be prepared for it. Pain is coming for you, for all of us—a parents' job, in this thinking, is to get them ready for it. Looking at you, so confused by what was going on inside your body, it was obvious that you were not ready for it. My dad would have been appalled. But it made me happy. It made me feel like you were living a good life: like you were happy. You did not react to being sick with rueful resignation, rolling your eyes like you knew this was coming, of course it was coming, this sort of bad stuff happens to you all the time. You saw it as *different*. You saw it as abnormal. You saw it as flying in the face of what the world is supposed to be.

When adults get sick, we get angry. Illness is something in the way of all the things we have to do, something that will slow us down, just more crap we have to deal with. This is also because we have all been sick before, because we know the world is hard, because we know we're going to someday get sick again, and someday we will even die. This makes us fight back against it, try to fight through it, which just makes us even sicker. We are too familiar with sickness. We think about it all the time. But it doesn't make us any more ready to deal with it.

That's not what you did. You saw the sickness for what it was—abnormal. The normal world, where you would run outside and play and pet dogs you met on the street and let the ice cream you're eating roll down your cheek and stay up late jumping on the bed, that was what life was to you. The sickness was an invasion of that, but it was also something to be expelled to get back to life as it is meant to be. You didn't pretend you weren't sick. You just took your medicine, closed your eyes, and went to sleep until you felt better. Before you knew it, you were.

I know people who walk around all day waiting to get sick, or waiting for something bad to happen, for the piano to fall on their head. They believe it is wise, even healthy, to expect the worst out of the world, to always expect misery, as if that will make it easier for them when it comes. They think sickness is what life is. They allow themselves to be sick even when they are not, in fact, sick. They wait for something bad to happen. They never really live.

Not you. Sickness made you sad. So you went about getting better. And then you were. This is my lesson to you, as sickness roils my body and my mind, as a poison inside me eats away at everything I've ever been. Know, remember, that this is not what life is. The real me is the one who stayed up eating takeout and watching movies and lying on the couch. That's what's normal. When sickness comes, when sadness comes, when pain comes, accept them as what they are: a perversion of life, not an expression of it.

That look on your face was not a look of pain. It was a look of hope. It was a look that knows life isn't supposed to be like this.

Hold on to it. Because it isn't.

54

So," he says, "you're still here. Great."

Dr. Lipsey eyes me as I sit on an examining table, in a hospital gown, for reasons not entirely clear. If I'm being honest with you, I don't entirely remember changing into it. I came here in regular clothes, and then I met with his assistant, and then I was in here, and then I felt cold and realized it was because my bare ass was flapping behind me in these scrubs. (How do people keep these things tied, by the way?) This is the sort of thing to which I am starting to get acclimated, the sudden snapping to as I absorb a brand-new reality, *Oh, I'm in the shower right now, I wonder how that happened?* These have a certain predictable rhythm by this point, and they're only confusing for a moment before I adjust.

It's not like one second I'm brushing my teeth and the next I'm running from a tiger. It's not *Memento*. It's more like a movie where a jump cut is inserted to speed you past the boring stuff. You don't need to watch the guy's entire elevator ride. You see him get in the elevator, then you cut to him getting off, the audience gets the point, no one is confused about what happened. That's how it feels. I'm walking into an office, I'm signing in with the receptionist, I'm looking at my phone in the waiting room, then WHOOSH JUMP CUT I'm here in scrubs with Dr. Lipsey looking irritated with me. It takes me a second to solve the mystery of what I just jump-cut past, but once I walk it back, it's not too hard to retrace my steps. So far, anyway.

"Sorry to disappoint you," I say, trying to smile.

"Well, you're not forgiven," he says, more with exasperation than anger. "Christ, Lloyd, what the hell? I mean, fuck me, man . . . you're messing up the whole plan. It turns out you're pretty shitty at dying!"

"I am doing my best," I say. "It turns out to be kind of difficult."

"Apparently!" he says, his eyes bugging out for a moment as he waves his hand in the air. He's amusingly deranged—he's giving off a real Doc Brown vibe. "And not only are you shitty at dying, you're super, *super* loud about it!"

Oh yes, that. "Yeah, I didn't really . . ."

"You didn't what, Lloyd?" he says, shaking his head violently as his voice rises. He's not very good at being angry. He's a little brother stomping his feet and demanding his toy back. "You didn't mean to become a fucking meme? Because that's what you are. You're a fucking meme!"

"I wouldn't go so far as to say—"

"Oh, you wouldn't?" He takes out his phone. "Look at this! Look at what my girlfriend showed me when I woke up this morning. She says everybody at her school has been sharing this like crazy."

I look at his phone. It's a video, one that begins with me, in full uniform, smiling and waving, saying, "Hi, I'm Lloyd!" with the hashtag #happycop superimposed below me. "Good to see you, fellow citizen!" I say, as I do. "Just your friendly neighborhood public servant, here to keep the peace." More words pop up underneath the hashtag—WAIT FOR IT . . .—as the quiet opening strings of System of a Down's "War?" begin to play.

The video then cuts to a shot from ground level, outside the Bedford Pine Apartments, looking up at me as I kick open the door to that man's apartment. As soon as I do, the heavy metal guitar kicks in, and Serj Tankian begins to scream "WE WILL FIGHT THE HEATHENS!" and they show me kicking the door in over and over on a loop, and the song screams "YOU MUST ENTER A ROOM TO DESTROY IT!" and then we cut again to me coming down the stairs, bloody but still smiling and waving. I don't really remember doing that part, but, well, there I am. Then the video freeze frames on my grinning face. #HAPPYCOP DESTROYYYYYY!!!! blinks, strobe-like, all across the screen, as Tankian roars like he's on fire and GIFs of little bunny rabbits headbanging while playing electric guitars pop up in every corner.

"Whoa," I say.

"Oh, that ain't the half of it," he says. "Look at this one."

He waves his finger up the screen, and now it's a shot of Big Bertha going flying over the railing outside the stadium. I hit that thing faster than I realized. I ramped the thing like a motorcycle daredevil zooming over the Grand Canyon, fully airborne. This time I freeze-frame, still in the air, as Metallica's "Battery" starts playing. On one side of the screen a GIF of Deadpool dancing pops up; on the other, Macaulay Culkin from *Home Alone* putting his hands on his face. Then they repeat the launch several times, reversing it, rolling it back, and then Bertha goes flying down into the gulch. There's then a cut to an ambulance leaving the scene, presumably with poor Jose Manuel Gutierrez in there, and a jail cell image appears over it, with Charlie from *It's Always Sunny in Philadelphia* pointing at the viewer, saying "Ya Busted." Then the same image of me from the last video returns, the freeze-frame of my grinning face. And again: #HAPPYCOP DESTROYYYYYY!!!! The headbanging bunnies are back too.

"Or, jeez, look at—"

"I got it, I got it," I say, lowering the phone. "You know I didn't make those, right? I wouldn't even know how to make one of those."

"Who gives a shit if you made them?" he says, and he's so exasperated Doc Brown now that I half expect him to say *Great Scott!* "These things are everywhere! Look at this one! It has four hundred thousand views!"

"Is that a lot?"

"Well, I guess I don't know if that's a lot or not, but shit, it sure seems like a lot!" he shouts. "More to the point, that's your face all over *everywhere*. And, and I don't know why I need to remind you of this—I would have thought it'd be constantly on your mind—that face is attached to someone I'm currently committing insurance fraud with. You're keeping a pretty high fucking profile for someone who is supposed to be dead by now, Lloyd!"

I didn't know it got this big—assuming four hundred thousand views on TikTok is big?—but it has been tough not to notice that *something* has been going on. After the GSU incident, I went with Anderson to the hospital, where I got some stitches in my nose and lip. Anderson was lucky: the bullet went right through. They found it in the stairwell, and he says he wants to keep it. "My first gunshot," he said, and he tried to make it sound like he was all right with it, like he could pretend it was some sort of rite of passage. He better get over that soon, or this job's gonna eat him alive. He's gotta process this shit at some point.

But he's fine. They booked the guy, we filled out our papers, we both got the hell out of there before anyone even knew we were there. Anderson even drove me home. "Sleep, killer," he said, but he sounded even more tired than I was.

I nevertheless went straight home and slept for twelve hours, and when I woke up, I had exactly 327 text messages from 113 different numbers. I wasn't aware 113 people even had my number. Some were from the guys at the station, some were from old high school buddies, a lot were from reporters trying to get my story, whatever my story was. But the only ones I cared about were the four I got from Bishop:

DAD?

IS THIS YOU? (with another #happycop video)

WTF?

ARE YOU OUT OF YOUR MIND DAD?

I've told him not to use all caps, that it makes him look like he's shouting. Though he probably was shouting. I texted him back, and no one else:

lol

dont trust the internet bish

im fine

Then . . . I guess I came in here? Did I call? Did I make an appointment? Or did I just show up? I don't remember. I just know I'm here now.

Dr. Lipsey snaps his fingers in my face.

"Jesus, Lloyd, we lost you there for a second," he says.

"Sorry," I say.

"It's OK," he says, his voice softening. "I bet that has been happening a lot."

"Man, you have no idea," I say. "To be honest, I'm actually a little confused how I got here."

"Well, that's great," he says. "You definitely are someone who should be driving a car through the streets of Atlanta. Remind me to check and make sure you're not parked in the lobby. You didn't run over my secretary, did you?"

"I don't think so," I say, and I begin to feel woozy. Dr. Lipsey sees this and gently puts his hand on my back and guides me into a prone position on his examining table. The paper roll atop the plastic feels cool and clean. I might take a nap, that sounds nice.

"Relax, man, here's some water," he says, handing me a cup and guiding the table up so I'm in a seated position. I drink it and feel myself coming back. I look at him.

"Thank you," I say.

"You're welcome," he says. "So, uh, how long has that been going on? You not realizing how you got places?"

"A couple of weeks, I think?" I say, but I'm not entirely sure. "I'm not entirely sure."

"I guess you wouldn't be," he says. "This thing manifests itself in a lot of ways. Temporal disorientation is definitely one of them. How have your moods been? Any violent outbursts?"

"No," I say, and I'm pretty sure that's right, though it should be noted that I have been shooting my gun more than usual.

"Other than kicking in doors and driving cars off cliffs, of course," he says.

"All in a day's work," I say, but I think I'm all out of jokes for the moment. I drop the water and lean back against the table.

"Also, it, uh, looks like you broke your nose?"

"That's another job hazard," I say. "But it's fine." Sure. Maybe it's fine. Like I care about my nose right now.

Dr. Lipsey sighs. "This is going to get worse," he says, "and fast. You know that, right?"

I look at him. "I'm fully aware," I say. "The other day I put my hat in the microwave."

"What?"

"You should try it, they taste incredible."

"Wait, Lloyd, are you—"

"I'm kidding," I say. I guess I had one joke left. "I have not tried to eat any of my clothing. Yet."

"Well, that's good."

My eyes focus, and my head clears for a second. That doesn't happen as quickly as I'd like it to of late, and I find myself trying to take advantage of the situation when it arises.

"So how much time do you think I have left?" I ask. Seems like a pertinent question. "Considering all this."

"Well, watching these videos, Lloyd, my professional diagnosis is that you are immortal," he says, but then he turns and flashes a light in my eyes. "How's your pain tolerance so far?"

"It's fine, actually," I say, and I mean it. I've been a little surprised how little pain there has been of late. I had thought that would be a bigger problem. Maybe I'm sprinting too fast to notice.

"Well, that's good," he says. "But mentally? You're fading. You're obviously fading. I think you know you're fading. Have you had any rage moments yet?"

"Rage moments?"

"You're reaching the stage when you're going to have moments where you can't control your emotions. You'll start screaming at some guy for taking the last fresh strawberries at the supermarket, that sort of thing. It's very common. People go all Hulk Smash. Have you had any yet?"

"I don't think so," I say. "I hope not. I don't even like strawberries. No. No Hulk Smash."

"Know that they are coming," he says. "Honestly, you need to not take these moments where you're as lucid as you are right now for granted. If you're blanking on how you're getting from one place to another, you're skidding fast."

"Well, I wouldn't call it blanking, it's more like a jump cut, like a—"

"It's not good, Lloyd," he says. "You're approaching the end of this. Like, fast."

"Is that your official diagnosis?"

"You don't have to be a doctor to see it, Lloyd," he says. "You look like shit."

"Now, *that* sounds like an official diagnosis," I say.

He stands up, clears his throat, and straightens his jacket.

"Lloyd," he says, and he is not smiling, "you are running out of time."

"I'm doing my best," I say, and yeah, I think I am.

"I don't know if your current mental state is making it easier or harder for you to, uh, finish the job, such as it were, but soon it's not going to matter," he says. "Looking at you? I'd say in, oh, two or three weeks, you're not going to be able to get yourself out of the house, let alone get yourself killed."

"Uh-huh," I say. I wonder if I'm about to have another jump cut. Hopefully I wake up clothed this time.

He turns around, walks to the corner of the examining room, picks up a clipboard, pretends to look at it, then sets his right arm on a stool. He looks as serious as I have ever seen him, and this is a man who just told me not all that long ago that a tumor was eating my brain.

"And if you're running out of time, Lloyd, *I'm* running out of time," he says. "I can give you some medication to help a little bit with the blackouts, and if you end up having some pain, we can do something about that too. But you know what the best thing you can do for yourself is?"

"What's that?" I say, as if I don't know the answer, as if this isn't what this whole goddamn thing has been about since the beginning, maybe since the beginning of time itself.

"You need to hurry up and fucking die, Lloyd."

He takes my hand and tries to shake it, but all I can give him is a limp flop in return.

"Ten-four," I say.

55.

show up at the office to talk to Ellis. She left me a terse text when I got home . . . yesterday? I think it might have been yesterday? I am having trouble with the times, and the dates, and all of it.

> Need you to come in today.
>
> I know it's your off day.
>
> I can see you've been busy.
>
> Come in.
>
> Try not to drive your car off a bridge on the way here.

So I'm here, but she's not. Perkins is standing by my desk, and I expect him to bust my balls, but he takes a little step back when he sees me.

"Christ, man, you all right?" he says, looking a little scared. He pulls my chair out for me. "Take a seat, man."

I sit and lightly wave at him like there's a mosquito near my nose. "I'm good," I say. "Where's Ellis?"

Perkins turns toward Ellis's office and jabs his thumb over his left shoulder.

"She ran out real quick about half an hour ago," he says. "Couple of the guys said something about the mayor wanting to see her about the letter, but they're probably full of shit."

"The letter," I hear myself saying. I am finding it increasingly difficult to feign interest in boring conversations of late. "What letter?"

"Oh, shit, you don't know?" he says. "Ha, holy shit, it's the only thing people are talking about around here that isn't you! The AJC got a letter from that old killer guy, the one from the seventies. Or the eighties, or whenever." He pulls out his phone, taps on it for a couple seconds, and puts it in my face.

"See?"

I take it, but then I drop it. It skitters across the floor.

"Jesus, Lloyd," he barks, though it's more like a yip from one of those dogs they create when they breed a big dog with a poodle. "That's my phone, man." He picks it up and gives a little *wheewww* when it doesn't seem to be cracked.

"Anyway, the guy who killed those women all those years ago, I guess he sent a letter to the newspaper," he says. "We definitely know he's an old guy if he thinks people still read newspapers, eh?"

"Are you talking about the Dumpster Diver?" I say. CERTAIN HOMICIDE, the note said. I slump down in my chair.

"Yeah, that's it," he says. "She had to go deal with that. She ain't here."

I try to pull myself up in my chair, but I slip and nearly fall off it. Perkins takes my hand and pulls me up.

"Man, Lloyd, I think you need to go home," I say, and I am certain he is right.

stare at my keys.

I have lived in this house for many years. I remember my old bedroom with the window that faces the street, where I would stay up late and listen to the sounds of Atlanta, the car horns, the screeching of tires, the clatter of weekend activity, the parties that Dad would sometimes put on his uniform in the middle of the night to go break up. After he died, and after Mom got sick and we moved her to hospice, I transferred all my stuff into their bedroom. That was Jessica's and my bedroom for a few years. It never felt weird that it had been my parents' bedroom—it's not like they had ever let me sleep in there anyway. And then Jessica moved out, and it was just my room. It did feel strange, still does, to have a room that was clearly constructed with a married couple in mind end up only having one sad divorced guy in it. I never changed much. Mom's dressing table, where she would primp and try on tasteful jewelry for all the Police Benevolent Association banquets, still sits in the corner where she left it. Jessica used it during the few years she was here, but I didn't touch it after she left. Now it's just a place for old magazines, loose change, and a reading lamp I never turn on. What use do I have for a dressing table? My old room is now Bishop's room, though he likes to crawl in bed with me when he stays here. Or at least he used to. He's a little big for that now.

This is my house. My whole life is here. I brought my son straight here from the hospital. I put together his crib here, stayed up all night just staring at him as he slept in it, watching him, making sure he was still breathing, certain that the only thing I was put on this earth to do was to keep him safe. I buried his pet hamster Darryl here, right in the backyard, in a shoebox I painted black; Bishop made sure he had some grass in there to eat if he got hungry. I had my college graduation party here. I asked Jessica to marry me here. My dad died here; we had his visitation here. I wonder if we will have mine here. My whole life is here. It is our family home. It outlived my father. It will outlive me.

And I stare at my keys.

I do not know which one opens the door.

Is it the blue one? It might be the blue one? I had that one made at Home Depot a few years back, I remember that. One of those machines did it—you just stick your key in there and it plunks down three copies for ten bucks, you can even get an American flag design on one if you want to. There are no hardware stores where a guy goes in the back and grinds you a key anymore. You just put your credit card in a machine and press a button and then your new keys come out like Funyuns from a vending machine. They don't work half the time when you get home.

It's not the blue one. How about the rusty brown one? It looks old. That's probably the one. Nope: not the brown one. I drop the keys on the front mat, the novelty one Bishop got me for Christmas a few years ago that says DOORBELL BROKE. YELL "DING DONG!" REAL LOUD. I pick them up, then drop them again. There's another rusty brown one. Or is that the same one I just tried? I stand up. It doesn't work either. I try the other brown one. I think it's the other one. It might be the same one.

I take a deep breath and close my eyes. It must be one of them. You have opened this door thousands upon thousands of times in your life, Lloyd. You know how to do this. Which is the key? Just think. Or maybe don't think. It's not like you ever had to think before. Maybe the trick is not to think this time.

There's a red one—well, it's kind of red, maybe more of a lavender one. I fidget with it for a second—I have too many keys on this key ring—and then right before I try to put it in the keyhole, the door opens in front of me.

Standing in front of me is Gary. He has the same dumb affable grin on his face he always does. I am not sure why he is in my house. Why is Gary in my house? I'm pretty sure he doesn't live here. He never moved in. I would remember that.

"Lloyd, hey," he says, putting his hand out in front of him like we just ran into each other at a coffee shop or something. "Sorry, I didn't mean to startle you. We just all heard you out here, and we were going to be waiting for you when you came in. But then you seemed to be having some trouble, so they sent me out here to get you."

Oh? "Oh?" I ask.

"Yeah, uh, I think everyone wants to talk to you," he says.

"You're in my house?"

His grin falls, but just for a moment.

"Yeah," he says. "Here, just come in, Lloyd. We can all explain."

He opens the door wide and extends his arm to welcome me into my own home. It's the green key, of course it's the green one, duh, it has always been the green one. I grab it, I raise it in the air in victory, and I step inside.

57

Jessica is sitting on the couch. She is wearing a wrap dress, a nice one, pretty fancy for sitting on my couch. She looks sad, but there is warmth in her eyes. There always is. There's an open spot next to her: that must be where Gary just was. Bishop, bless him, is sitting on the arm of the couch rather than on the couch—he always does that, you can always count on a teenager to ignore the place specifically designed for them to sit and choose instead to lope awkwardly and uncomfortably on something they're going to break if they're not careful. He is chewing on a banana and flipping a fidget spinner around with his right hand. His teacher gave him one of those so he would stop tapping his foot in class. There's always a little bit too much current running through Bishop's brain. The feet are the only real logical place for it to escape.

Next to the couch, on my left, the couch's right, is my chair—it was my dad's chair too, an old hairy Barcalounger with a plastic cover on it, one Jessica put on years ago, presumably so I didn't get rabies from whatever had been living in there for several decades. Anderson has wedged himself into my chair, which may well buckle under his weight. He looks sweaty and uncomfortable.

"You're in my chair," I say, without really thinking.

"I told him that," Bishop says, finishing his banana. "You don't sit in a man's chair, dude."

Anderson grimaces as he uncorks himself from the depths of my poor chair. That thing may never be the same—I bet half the remaining springs just snapped.

"Hey," he says, giving me an awkward nod. I don't think he is enjoying being here. "Sorry about that, my pops hates when I sit in his chair too."

"How's your quad?" I ask.

"Not even limping," he says. "Three stitches, that's it."

"Badass," Bishop says, and then covers his mouth with his hand.

I take a breath, and I look around at these four people in my house. Why are these people in my house?

Gary sits down next to Jessica, puts his hands in his lap, and says, "OK." He then turns his head to her.

She clears her throat. Everyone is looking at me.

"Lloyd, would you like to sit down?" she asks.

"Uh, I think I'd like to stand, if that's all right. Unless this is an impromptu game of Family Feud. Is Steve Harvey back there?"

Bishop snorts, and Anderson gives him a funny little slap on the back of his head. I wink at Bishop. He looks at me.

Sorry, Dad.

What is this?

He shrugs. But I see something in him I rarely see. I see worry.

"Fine then, stand," Jessica says. "So, then, now that we're all here . . . Lloyd, what in the world is going on with you?"

I take a step backward. "Wait . . . is this an intervention?"

"No," she says. "I do not think you have a drinking problem, Lloyd."

"So what is this?" I ask, though it is dawning on me that of course I already know.

"Well, Lloyd," she says, waving her arm to include everyone else in the room, "we are trying to figure out why you seem to be trying to get yourself killed."

I cough, louder than I meant to. It is stunning to hear her just go out and say it like that. Was I that obvious? Wait, does she know about the tumor? She can't possibly know about the tumor.

"I'm sorry?" I say.

She takes out her phone and hands it to me. "What exactly is *this*?" I take the phone and press play on the video she has cued up. I see myself in the hallway of the GSU Urban Life Building, looking up at the wild-haired man with the gun. Was there a kid still in there I somehow didn't see, filming me? Where are all these phones *coming* from? I look at myself, frozen. I am surprised to see that I look . . . angry. The video unfreezes, and I begin to sprint at him, screaming. The screen freezes again. The words HAPPYCOP DESTROY flash across. Another headbanging bunny pops up in the corner.

I hand the phone back to her.

"That man could have killed you," she says, her voice rising. "Just like the man whose house you barged into out of nowhere. Or the man who you crashed your car *over a bridge* trying to catch. Look at this one!"

She tries to give me the phone again, but I push it back to her.

"C'mon, Jess. I'm a cop, you know what the job is."

"Bullshit," she says. Her eyes are widening and the pitch of her voice is getting higher, and I realize she is deeply upset. It gives me pause, but only for a moment.

"We were the first responding officers near the Bedford Pine Apartments. We were right by there, weren't we, Anderson?" I say, looking at him for some backup. Isn't your partner supposed to give you some goddamn backup?

"Uh," he says, looking nervously at me, then Jessica, then Bishop, then me again. Some nutter with a gun in a pharmacy probably seems a lot less harrowing to him now that he's dealt with the loony birds in this house. "Yeah, he's right, we were first, or maybe second, on the scene on that one."

"I'm trying to get the kid some action," I say to Jessica, trying to roll with it, just making up all this crap as I go. "Anderson, you said yourself the job was sleepy sometimes."

"That's bullshit!" Jessica says again, and now she is standing.

"You know it's bullshit, Lloyd." I am worried she is going to cry. Gary touches her hand lightly, but she slaps it away. She points to Bishop, who is now standing behind the couch, biting his fidget spinner.

"You have almost left this son of ours without a father three times in a week, Lloyd!" Now she's definitely yelling.

I look at him, and it's so hard not to break down that I have to turn away.

"Mom," says Bishop, who has moved closer to Jessica and is now putting a hand on her shoulder because Bishop loves his mother and he is a good person. "Mom, it's OK. It's OK. He's here. Dad's right here, look, he didn't leave us, he's fine. He's right there, aren't you, Dad?"

I try to smile. I have never felt sadder and smaller and more stupid in my entire life. I wish I could just tell him. I want nothing more to tell him, to give us both a chance to say goodbye. But then this all blows up. Then this will have all been for nothing.

I cough.

"Yeah, see, Jess, I'm right here," I say. That much, this second, is true. It's a relief to get to say something to all the people that I love that isn't a lie.

Jessica is not satisfied with my explanation. She is looking at me strangely. She cocks her head to the left, like a confused dog, like she is seeing me in a way she has never seen me before. And she is right. I was not a good husband to her. I was distant, and ineffectual, and too lost in my own life to be what she needed in hers. I was simply not enough for her.

But I never lied to her like I am lying to her right now. She seems to know this. And she is insistent about it in a way that is increasingly inconvenient.

"So let me get this straight," she says, calmer now, but sharper, clipped—focused. She has honed in. "You're claiming—you, *Lloyd McNeil*—that the fact that you have had three near-death experiences in a week, that you are hurling yourself into insane danger, that you"— and here she picks up her phone and shakes it at me like she's about to roll craps—"Are all of a sudden some sort of *folk hero*, you're telling me this is all happening because . . . you're trying to train your partner?"

Anderson clears his throat again, and if he could fit through the storm window, I think he'd jump through it. I should probably ease up, if just for his sake.

"Well, it's not just that, obviously," I say, and I pause.

I look at Jessica. I look at Gary. I look at Bishop. They are all safe and happy, and they're going to remain so. If I can pull this off, with the remaining time I have, which of course requires I get the hell out of this room at some point, something that I must allot might be impossible, they're even going to have some real money to make their lives easier. They're going to go on without me.

But what are they going to think of me when I'm gone? Are they going to think of me as this sad, tired, thinning person with cracked ribs who can't remember which one of his keys opens his front door?

Or are they going to think of me as *fucking Rambo*?

I feel a heat rise.

"You know what?" I take a step forward and straighten my shoulders. This is my house. This is my fucking house.

"Lemme tell you all something," I say, and I look at Jessica, then Gary, then Anderson, then back to Jessica. "I don't know what's so fucking surprising that I might not be the pussy you all apparently thought I was. You want to know why I'm out there risking my life? Because *I fucking can*. You see any of those people standing here? That asswipe who was going to kill his wife and son? That shithead who stole a baby away from its mother? That maniac who was going to shoot up a bunch of college kids? You see them here? You see them standing in front of you? You don't. You know why? Because I *kicked their fucking ass, that's why*."

Anderson takes a slight lean toward me, but I snap my head toward him. He stops. *You stay right there, kid.*

"I'm supposed to sit here and apologize to all of you for not being a pussy," I shout, and I'm aware I'm shouting, there's spittle going everywhere, "but I'm not going to. I went out there and saved a bunch of lives by stopping a bunch of bad guys, and you're all acting like *I'm* the asshole? You want to know how I'm feeling? I'll tell you how I'm feeling: *I feel fucking amazing.* Do you know how it feels to look at a man who is going to hurt someone if you don't stop them—and then you stop them? To put your nose right next to his? To look him dead in the eye and not budge? To see that moment when he realizes that you're not afraid of him? When you see that he's afraid of *you*? It's incredible. It's incredible! And you, *you*, all of you, you think so little of me that when I do something good, when I do something strong, you can't believe it, you think I must be having some sort of midlife crisis, or a stroke, or God knows what you think, because none of you can sit for a moment and, for fuck's sake, just give me a *second of goddamn respect for once in your goddamn lives.*"

I gasp and try to catch my breath.

Hulk Smash, I believe that's what Dr. Lipsey called it. *Hulk Smash.*

The room is silent. I stop. I realize I am standing over Jessica, who is cowering. Bishop is next to her, his arms around her. I realize that he is scared of me. I have scared my boy.

Gary stands up, in between them and me, and puts his arm on my shoulder.

"Hey, man," he says, soothing, calm—it's nice, he has a nice voice when he tries. "I think maybe we should go get a glass of water or something." He pats my elbow. "You all right with that, Lloyd? That might be a good idea."

I turn to him. The heat has subsided. Hulk just smashed.

"Yeah, Gary," I say, doing everything I can to remain standing. "Yeah, that might be a good idea."

He puts his hand on my back and guides me to the kitchen as my loved ones lie in ruins behind me.

sit next to the sink with Gary, drinking water out of a plastic cup I brought home from a Falcons game a few years ago. Do THE DIRTY BIRD, it says. The water is the coldest water I've ever tasted, it might just freeze into an ice cube in my mouth. I can feel it cut sharply against an old filling. Gary puts his hand on my back again.

"There, man, drink up," he says. "Take your time. Here." He takes a warm wet washcloth out and places it on the back of my neck.

I take a deep breath. What have I done? I think of Dr. Lipsey. *You are running out of time.*

"Thanks, Gary," I say. "Jesus, man, I'm sorry."

"It's fine," he says, taking the empty cup from my hand and refilling it from the Brita in the fridge. His voice is even and soft. Last year Bishop turned me on to this wellness app where actors read you soothing stories in a calm voice to help you fall asleep. Gary sounds like that. "Don't worry about it. We're all just worried about you. You've had a long week."

I drink more of the water. My heartbeat is returning to normal. I turn to the kitchen doorway, which is now blocked by my partner.

"Hey," I say.

"Yo," he says. "You good?"

"Yeah," I say. I turn to Gary. "I'm good. Thank you, Gary."

Gary nods. "You might want to talk to Bish, though," he says. "He's a little shook up."

Bish.

"I should probably apologize to your wife too," I say. "And you, for that matter. I'm sorry, Gary."

He shakes my hand. "It's no problem, Lloyd." He tries to hide the fact that he is looking at me up and down, and he fails. He can see I look like shit as well as anybody else can. "You've been through a lot. We're here, man."

I turn to Anderson.

"Yo," I say. "Now I know why you weren't at the office today."

"Oh, you were in?" he asks, and his face, hangdog this entire time, lifts a little. "That letter has everybody all worked up, right?"

"Was supposed to meet Ellis, but apparently she was out dealing with all that," I say.

"Lotta history there," he says, trying to be subtle. "Bet we catch that dude now. They always screw up when they resurface. Gotta be kind of exciting for you, yeah?"

I'm not sure *exciting* is the word I would use. "Something like that," I say, massaging my left temple. We're off track here.

"How long you all been planning this?" I ask. "And whose idea was this event?" I am a little curious.

"Um . . ." Anderson looks at Gary, who is still lurking in the door-way and listening intently, like there's a good episode of *Law & Order* on. He looks back at Anderson, then back at me.

"It was Bishop," Gary says. "He made Jess text everybody last night."

Bish.

"Pretty rough for a kid to watch his dad almost die in a different way every time he scrolls up on his phone," Anderson says. "He was just worried about you."

"We all are," Gary says.

I cough.

"Thank you guys," I say. "I mean it."

I give Anderson a little mock punch to the stomach. "But seriously," I say, "it's fine. OK?"

Anderson sighs. "OK," he says. "But if it's all the same to you, I'd rather not get shot again today."

He moves out of the way, and I cross through the doorway. Bishop and Jessica are sitting on the couch, opposite each other, both sitting cross-legged. They stop their whispering when I enter.

Bishop leaps up.

"Dad!" he says, and he runs to me and hugs me like he's afraid I might fly away. I pull him as close as I can.

"I'm sorry, Bish," I say, and I look over his shoulder at Jessica. "And Jess, I'm so sorry. I had no right to talk to you like that. To any of you."

Her face is red and splotched, and her hair has fallen out of her carefully manicured ponytail.

"No, I'm sorry," she says. "We shouldn't have sprung this on you. You've been through so much."

"Stop it," I say, and I let go of Bishop and turn him to face me. I can feel myself start to choke up. A lightning bolt starts to crackle in the back of my skull. "You all came here to help me, and I thanked you by losing my shit on you. I'm so lucky to have you guys. I . . . I don't know what to say."

"Just . . . just be careful, OK?" she says, and then she blows her nose. "We all need you here, you know."

But you don't. I turn to Bishop.

"I love you, Bish." What more is there to say?

"I love you too, Dad," he says, and he hugs me.

Gary comes in from the kitchen behind me. "I think this is maybe enough excitement for one afternoon," he says, and yeah, I guess it is the afternoon. "Maybe we should let Lloyd rest."

Bishop won't let go of me.

"Can I stay here, Mom?" he asks.

"Gary's right," she says. "Your father needs some rest. I think we all do."

He squeezes me. He is big enough now and I am broken enough now that it hurts a little, but it is good, it is very good.

"It's fine," I say to Jessica, feeling the bolts intensify but wanting him never to stop. "We'll watch a movie. I can bring him back over tomorrow. Though he needs to not leave his socks in the couch."

"Are you sure?" Jessica says.

You have no idea how sure. I nod.

I kiss Bishop on his forehead. His skin is still oily and slick.

"Gross, Dad," he says, wiping his eyebrows.

"Bish, I swear, you're forty-five percent zits," I say. "Do you ever wash your face?"

Everybody leaves. It is just us.

59.

I am glad I apologized to Jessica, to Gary, to Bishop, to all of them. I was harshest with Jessica—she did not deserve that, she has never deserved it. I did that in our marriage occasionally, not often, but enough, when I lost a little bit of control, when my frustration would bubble up from my subconscious, and it'd boil over and I'd yell at her over something that wasn't her fault. I wasn't violent, I wasn't cruel, and all told I probably wasn't even that scary. But it would happen from time to time, and she deserved better than that, she always has. She is one of the few people who has ever cared enough to push me to that point, to still be around when the parts of me that I try to pretend aren't there come out, when Major McNeil and all that he wrought comes out, and for that I have rewarded her with anger. I am sorry. I told her I was sorry, and I meant it. She did not deserve that. She was only there to help.

But.

It must be said.

In that moment: I did not lie to her. I did not lie to any of them.

Because it is true. It feels good. All of this feels good.

I have spent my whole life being afraid. Being afraid of my dad. Being afraid of not living up to his name. Being afraid of people seeing him when they see me. Being afraid of standing up for myself. Being afraid of getting hurt. Being afraid of not being there for my son. Being afraid of being a bad father. Being afraid of not making any sort of mark on the world. Being afraid of being a nobody. Being afraid of having people think less of me. Being afraid of being a joke. Being afraid of being a pussy. Let's face it: I've always been afraid of being a pussy.

But this—this mad experiment, this doomed last stage, this last big swing to do something important and powerful and lasting—this feels great.

My God: *It feels fucking amazing.*

I have had to lie to them so much. I have had to lie to the people I love more than anything in this world, the people who care so much about me that they will confront me and will break into my house and will not leave until they make sure that I know that they love me and they do not want me to die. Since I found out that I had mere months left to live on this planet, that everything I've ever valued or loved is about to vanish forever, I have had to look at these people closest to me and lie to their faces about everything. I haven't given them the opportunity to change my mind, or to help me, or even to be able to tell me goodbye. I have just lied straight to their faces about the only thing that really matters.

But right there? Back then?

I didn't have to lie. I wasn't lying. I was telling the truth.

But: only a little bit of truth. Not the real truth. Not all of it. Not enough. That's the little trap I've set for myself here: a discovery of some basic inner truths at the exact moment when the only thing I can do is lie. My last moments with them will end up being nothing but lies. These are lies for a good reason. These are lies for the people—the boy—I care about most. But they are nevertheless lies. They are my only way through this. It is too late now. With any luck they'll never find out how many lies there have been. The only truth that will matter is what I've done. I am sorry I could not do better. I am sorry the only thing I can do in the end is lie.

60.

We lie in the grass in Piedmont Park, no blanket, just two Mc-Neils down there in the dirt, staring up at a blue sky, surrounded by empty Grindhouse hamburger sacks. The clouds float lazily by. The air is crisp. I am breathing as easily as I have in weeks. Bishop, with a piece of cheese on his cheek somehow, fidgets a little but keeps his eyes to the sky.

"Do you think Gary's music sucks, Dad?" Bishop says, out of nowhere.

"Don't they just play Grateful Dead songs?" I ask, trying to tread carefully. "That band is not really my thing."

"Yeah, they go on forever," he says, chuckling. "Also I don't get all the dancing bears."

"I don't either, Bish," I say.

He clears his throat.

"He asked me if I wanted to play with his band sometime," he says. "He gave me a tambourine. It might be fun." He pauses. "Would that be OK?"

"You don't have to ask me if you want to play in Gary's band."

"Oh, I know," he says, sitting up. "I just wanted to know if you were, I don't know, cool with it."

"Of course," I say. "Why wouldn't I be cool with it?"

He squirms a little, and then I sit up.

"Bish, it's fine, obviously it's fine," I say. "Gary's, uh, kind of a dork, but he's a good guy. Though do you know how to play the tambourine?"

"I mean, all you have to do is hit it with your hand, right?" he says, and I can't help but laugh.

"That would be the body part I'd use, yes," I say. "You'll do great. My little rock star." I tousle his hair and then look back up at the sky. Two birds chase each other above us.

I hear a rustling to my right, then some whispers, then some more rustling. I roll to my right and see two girls, around college age. When they see me turn to them, they quickly look away. I adjust so I'm peering at them out of the corner of my eye, and I notice them looking back and forth between their phone and the two of us.

I nudge Bishop.

"See those girls?" I whisper. "I think they're checking you out."

"That's creepy, Dad," he says, but he's now looking at them too. One of them spots him and waves. She pokes her friend, who shrugs. They stand up and begin walking over to us.

I poke Bishop. "Oooh, oooh, here they come," I say, and he tenses up. I'm a little worried he's going to jump up and run away, but they're on us before he has a chance to lam it.

The first girl is wearing a sweatshirt that says MATTOON on it that's four sizes too big for her and shorts that are four sizes too small—clearly a college student.

She peers down over her sunglasses, which are in the shape of stars with sparkles affixed to them.

"I'm sorry to bother you, but . . ."

She pauses, gets out her phone, scrolls for a second, and puts it up next to my face.

"Are you Happycop? You look like Happycop!" She turns to her friend. "Mary-Margaret, Mary-Margaret, it is him! Happycop is here, look, look!"

Her friend hops down next to me and puts the phone on the other side of my face.

"Oh my God it is!" she says, giggling and jumping up and down. "Happycop smash!"

They instantly, almost simultaneously, point their phones at me. "Happycop is in Piedmont Park!"

Almost out of instinct, like I have been doing for years, I smile as wide as I can.

"Good to see you, fellow citizen!" I say, hoping my smile doesn't look too painful. "Just your friendly neighborhood public servant, here to keep the peace."

"Oh my GAWWWWWWD!" one of the girls screams. "That's so awesome. Happycop, you are the best! It's really you!" It is always remarkable to me how amazed people are to realize that the things they see on their phone also in fact exist in real life.

"Is this your son?" the other one says. I can *feel* Bishop blush.

"It is, yeah, this is Bishop." I stand, put my hand on his left shoulder, and guide him to his feet. He glances around us, probably looking for a tree to climb up and hide in.

"Hey," he says, chin down, to his chest.

"Hi!" the first girl says. "You're cute! Happycop's kid is cute!"

"Happyson!" the other one says, and they both giggle.

She jumps a little in the air. "Oh!" she says. "Can I get a selfie?"

"I want one too!" her friend says. "Happycop selfie!"

"Happycop and Happyson selfie!"

They put their cheeks up to mine and point their phones in front of us. They smell nice. They smell like everything in their lives is just getting started.

"Bishop, get over here," I say, motioning for him. He shuffles our way but still stands about two feet away.

"C'mon, Happyson!" one of the girls says, putting her hand around his waist and pulling him toward her. He lets out an involuntary yelp. The girls both laugh and smile for the camera.

Each of them gives each of us a hug. "Celeb sighting!" one says, and she gives a little peace sign. "You two have a great day! I can't believe we saw you here!" The other grins at Bishop, and he thinks I don't notice but I see him grin back.

"Good to see you fellow citizen," says the other one in a stilted, robotic voice. "Here to keep the peace." They both cackle and bound back to their blanket in the other direction, armed with a fantastic story to kick off their countless adventures.

I clap Bishop on the back, and he makes an awkward shrug, but he's also positively beaming. We lie back in the grass and look up at the sky.

His arm brushes against mine. One of the harder things to get used to when your kid is this age—when he's growing faster than you're used to people growing—is the adjustments you have to make for the physical space between you. For years, to Bishop, I was a giant who held his hand. He slowly, then suddenly, caught up to me, and the space that we had both grown accustomed to occupying began to be filled by his increasing mass. I always have the urge, when we are together, to engulf him in my arms like I once did, to fully envelop him, to make him feel as if there is nowhere safer on this earth. But there is more of him now, and neither one of us have quite adjusted. Sometimes when we walk alongside each other, our arms scrape each other in a way they never have before. He is outgrowing me. He needs more space than I know how to give him. I scoot over the best I can.

As I maneuver, there's an odd snapping sound in my knees, and a sharp crack that sends a bullhorn of pain up from the bottom of my spine. My rib injury, whatever's going on with that, briefly alights. I groan louder than I mean to.

Bishop's head snaps toward me.

"Whoa, Dad, that sounded terrible," he says, and he looks worried in a way that no thirteen-year-old should ever look worried. "Is that from the wreck? Did you ever go to the doctor? You should go to the doctor!"

Trust me, kid: way ahead of you on that one.

"It's fine," I say. "I'm just getting old. This'll happen to you someday too."

"Not if I don't drive my car off a bridge, you crazy man," he says, lightly popping me in the shoulder, which, amazingly, hurts. I can't believe my son's little light pop in the shoulder actually hurts.

"It was more an embankment," I say.

"Whatever," he says. "I saw it like everybody else did. That was intense, Dad."

"Your mom shouldn't let you have TikTok on your phone."

"I don't!" He turns his phone around and flips past a bunch of apps. "That's how they spy on you! I saw it on Martar. That's where all my friends saw it too."

"Martar?"

"Oh, it's the new app, just came out, all my friends were using it, though now they're more into Wrizzd," he says, and one of the nice things about dying is that I'll never have to hear either of those words again. "But it's on all of them. You're everywhere."

"I really wish you weren't watching that stuff," I say, and I feel like the world's worst parent that it never once occurred to me during any of this that Bishop might find what I was doing before I died, that he'd have to see me like that. My father once came home with a black eye, and he wouldn't tell me why, and I stayed awake all night staring out the window, afraid someone was going to come inside and kill him. "Those videos make it all look like a bigger deal than it was anyway." What's one more lie at this point?

"Yeah, Dad, but it's, like . . ." He stumbles and looks down at his feet, and I see real fear in his eyes, because of course I do, he's terrified his father is going to die, and the worst part about it is that he is right to be terrified, he has no idea how right he is. "I mean, you know, it's just . . . well, *why?*"

Why. The question kids need the answer to the most, the one we so desperately don't want to give them.

Why? Why, Bishop?

There's no why. You want to know *why?* That's the secret, Bishop. *Why* isn't real. It's just what happens. That's all there is. Why are there wars? Why will your heart get broken? Why will you and me and everyone you love die? Why did we have to bury that rabbit you found in the backyard? Why are people cruel to each other? Why do people lie the most to the people they love the most? Why does it hurt when you crash your bike and skin your knee? Why is everyone always in so much pain? Why are we so afraid all the time? Why are your eyes blue when mine are hazel and your mom's are brown? Why are you allergic to penicillin? Why did a man wave a gun at his family? Why did a man steal a car with a baby inside? Why did a man show up with a rifle at a college campus? Why is my brain being eaten by an evil tree? Why do bad things happen to good people? Why do bad things happen to bad people? Why are any of these bad things happening?

The answer is that there is no why. I'm dying. Forget that: I'm almost dead. You're going to grow up without your father, the man who loves you more than anyone has ever loved anything, and this loss will follow you the rest of your life, you will be eighty years old and someone will ask you about your dad and you will tell them "He died when I was young" and they will say they are sorry and in that moment they will know you have felt real loss and that you have suffered and that part of you forever changed in that moment and there was nothing you could do about it because it just happened and it was no one's fault your dad just got a brain tumor and died and there was no why and there never was a why and there never will be one. I don't know where I am going to go after this, but I know that you will not be there, and therefore I know it will be worse. There is no why. It's all just desert out there, Bish. It's all sand and wind and bones and dirt, on and on, until you can't see any farther.

That's your answer, Bish. I wish you hadn't asked.

"Just doing my job," I say, unable to look at him. "I'm doing what cops do, you know how it is."

He stares at me. A tear starts to form in his left eye. In my last moments with him, I've lied to him. And he knows it. He will think of me when I am gone, and he will remember this moment, and he will know that I was lying, that he gave me every chance to let him in and I shut him out. He knows all of this.

He is not looking at me with fear, or sadness. He is looking at me with disappointment.

"Dad, you know, it wasn't Mom that called everyone over to your place," he says, halting, a cough in the back of his throat he's trying not to let out. "It was me. It was my idea."

"I know," I say, grateful I don't have to lie, but only for a second, because right now the only thing I can do for him is lie. "I appreciated that. I'm honored you're worried about me. But really: it's fine. I'm fine."

Except I'm not. Except I'm crying. I didn't know I was until Bishop wiped my face with his sleeve. But I am.

The tear fully leaks out of his left eye. He puts his arms around me. He has gotten so big.

"It's OK, Dad," he says. "Whatever it is, it's going to be OK," and I hope he doesn't think he's lying, I hope he believes every word of it.

"Well," I say, blowing my nose into an old handkerchief I carry with me—Major McNeil said to always have a handkerchief and a pen on your person, and I will forever comply. "I'm sorry about that. That was sudden. It has been . . . Bish, it's been a long few weeks."

He shakes his head, trying to clear it. He even taps his right ear with his palm like he's trying to get water out of the left one, and puts his arms to his side.

"This month is crazy," he says, and I can see that he has decided to let me off the hook. "Do you believe we have midterms?"

I cough and grin. "I didn't realize they had midterms in the seventh grade," I say.

"Dad, they're already making us do college prep," he says. "It's not like when you and Mom were in school. It's so competitive!"

"You're going to do great," I say, and I've never been more certain of anything.

I look back to the sky. I put my arm on his knee. He stops.

"Hey," I say, hoping to give myself another second more to figure out what else I'm going to say. "I'm a very lucky father to have a son that cares about him enough to get everyone in his life to break into his house and tell him he looks like shit."

"You do look like shit," he says, and then covers his mouth in cartoonish mock shame.

"Yeah, well, you have cheese on your chin," I say, which he does, somehow, still. We finished eating an hour ago.

He wipes it and misses entirely.

"I just want you to know that I appreciate it, and I appreciate you, and everything about you, all the things you do, all the things you are, all the things you are going to be and all the things you can be," I say, and I'm laying it on too thick, babbling like an idiot, trying not to cry again, just trying to get through this and do it as right as I possibly can and I might as well just say it all I'm not going to get it all right but I gotta say it I gotta just go he's gotta know it's the only thing that matters it's the only thing anything in my life is ever going to be about. "You are the best thing I'll ever be a part of, Bish."

Babbling like an idiot. Just letting it all out. I don't mind. He doesn't seem to mind either.

We both sit up. I hug him. My arms go all the way around. He is not so big now. He is the little boy in his giant's arms.

"Just always know that, and no matter what happens, don't ever forget it," I say. "I love you, Bishop. I'm your father. And I love you."

"Jeez, I love you too, Dad," he says. "Like, duh." And he lets go and then he smiles at me and then we look up at the sky one last time and I shut my eyes and I don't remember when I opened them again.

61.

I'm sitting in Bertha at the station. She's purring, calm, in control as ever. She is not fazed by any of this.

How long have I been here? Let's retrace. Bishop and I went home. I lay down on the couch and fell asleep for long enough that it was darker when I opened my eyes than it was when I closed them, and then I closed them again and when I opened them it was bright again. Jessica must have come and gotten Bishop at some point. Did I notice?

My phone had a lot of messages on it, I remember that part. I must have been out for a while. Anderson texted "im sorry i sat in your chair" with a google-eyed emoji face. Bishop sent me a clip of Brad Guzan when he had hair—he looked weird. There were a bunch of spam texts; apparently the scammer tried to pretend he was my pickle-ball partner. That the spammers are trying pickleball cons now is a solid sign that stupid fad is just about over. Gary texted to let me know he left his sunglasses on my counter, if I could bring them by next time I come to pick up Bishop that'd be great.

Sergeant Ellis! That's why I'm here. I look down at my phone to refresh my memory.

Sorry I missed you earlier.

I'm in now whenever you're ready.

And now I am here. I do not know what she wants. But Sergeant Ellis is not a dramatic person. If she says something's urgent, it's urgent.

I set my phone down and face forward. The sun is bright. It hurts my eyes. I close them.

There is a tap on my passenger-side window. I look to my right.

"Jesus, are you going to come in?" Sergeant Ellis says. She's in full uniform, though I can see a little smudge on her left lapel where she clearly spilled some peanut butter.

"No, I just drove here to admire the parking lot."

"You've been sitting out here in your car for twenty-five minutes."

"I have?"

She lowers her sunglasses and cocks her head slightly. "Yes," she says. "I've been watching you from the window for the last fifteen."

"That's pretty creepy," I say, having no idea what she's talking about. "Stop staring at me."

"Just get out of the damn car and get inside, Lloyd," she says, and I do, and I do.

62.

walk by my desk on the way to Sergeant Ellis's office. I've always taken a lot of pride in keeping a clean, organized desk—some of the guys in here have half-full Chinese food containers that are older than Bishop—but it's a disaster area right now. There are papers everywhere—what are these papers? How long has it been since I've been in here?

I pick up a sheath and look at the top one. I see a photocopied image of an old front page of the *Atlanta Journal-Constitution*. There is a picture of my father on it.

Sergeant Ellis quickly snatches it out of my hand.

"Eh?" I say, stepping backward.

"Just get in my office, Lloyd," she says. "We'll talk about it in there."

"Where is everybody?" I say. There's only a couple cops in here.

"Busy day," she says and opens her office door. "Gotta keep those streets safe."

She shuts the door behind me, walks behind her desk and sits down.

She sighs.

"So, I've got some thoughts about your little tough-guy act of late, Mr. Happycop," she says. "But there's something we need to go over first. It's why I wanted you in here."

She opens up a cabinet in her desk, takes out a clear plastic letter-size envelope, and puts it in front of me. "You need to see this."

I look down at the envelope. There's a piece of unlined printer paper inside it. There is writing on the paper, in big block letters, precise, almost as if it has been stenciled. I start to read it, but the letters go off the page for a second. That's been happening a lot lately too, like everything I try to read briefly tries to run for the border.

I focus hard, and read.

63.

i have seen your happycop. he is quite a happy
cop, yes he is. i recognized him instantly.

it is the younger mcneil is it not? i bet happycop
cannot catch me any better than his father could.

did it bring it all back for you? such memories.

i felt an itch of the urge. just wanted to let you
know.

dd

64.

Huh," I say.

"Yeah," Sergeant Ellis says. "Huh is right."

I look at the letter. Its words hop and skip across the page. It has been nearly twenty years since anyone heard from this person—more than twenty years since he killed those women, destroyed so many lives, hollowed my father from the inside out—and here he is, resurfacing . . . because of me? He's right there, saying my name. I hadn't even considered he had any idea who I was. But he would, wouldn't he? Of course he would.

"What. . . . where the hell did this come from?" I ask, still gripping it, like if I let go it will fly away.

"Would you believe he just emailed it?" Sergeant Ellis says. "The son of a bitch just addressed it to 'crimestoppers@atlantaga.gov.' No shit. It came from a Hotmail address, dumsterdiver2024@hotmail.com. The guy set up a Hotmail account, scanned in a picture of the letter at the library, and emailed it to us."

"You have got to be kidding," I say. "This can't possibly be real."

"It is. Look at what else was in the email."

She brings out another piece of paper in a plastic bag and hands it to me. It's a 1990s-era Georgia driver's license, signed by Governor Zell Miller, with the picture of an attractive middle-aged woman on it: Helen D. Watsma, 3452 Woodward Way NW, Atlanta GA. She was an organ donor.

"That's the second victim," I say.

"Yep," she says. "He kept the ID all these years. The IDs for all the other women were also missing. He must have kept those too."

The back of my throat has suddenly gone dry. I scratch my neck and squint.

"When did you get this?" I ask.

"Overnight," she says.

I catch myself shaking the plastic bag, fidgeting with it, tossing it from my left hand to my right, and put it down on the table. It is, after all, evidence.

Wait, is it?

"Hey, why is this in a plastic bag?" I ask. "Didn't you just print it out on an office copier?"

"You're a better cop than you think you are sometimes, Lloyd," Sergeant Ellis says, chuckling. "Yeah, I did that so people wouldn't tamper with it. We're keeping this under our hats for now."

I stare at the letter again. I cannot believe that it is real.

"So do you have any leads?" I ask.

Sergeant Ellis laughs. "Uh, yeah," she says. "I'm pretty sure I already know who it is. I know everybody else forgot about the Dumpster Diver killer, but I didn't. We've been collecting string on this for a while. Which is where you come in, Happycop."

I blink hard.

65

Your dad had a lot of information on this, you know," she says, pulling a thick file out of her desk and placing it in front of me. I flip through it: sketches, surveillance photos, and pages of notes on my father's old steno paper, scribbled in his unmistakable handwriting. He was a crisp perfectionist in real life, but his handwriting was scattered, messy, and borderline unreadable, at least to the untrained eye. But I could always see what Dad was trying to say.

Ellis is right: he had been much further along on the Dumpster Diver than I, and certainly the *Atlanta Journal-Constitution*, thought he was. A psychological profile. A detailed DNA analysis. Surprisingly, an actual list of names. Lampton. Daulerio. Mascion. Templeton. Walker. Simpson. There are even transcripts of interviews with several suspects. Dad did them himself.

"Whoa," I say.

"Yeah, Major McNeil was a lot of things, but he was no dummy. He was making some real headway on this. He got closer than any of us have in the years since. He clearly spooked the guy, which I presume is why he vanished for so long."

She pauses. "We'd have had him years ago, had the major . . . well, I don't need to tell you," she says, trailing off.

"Yeah," I say, and scramble to gather the words that are racing off the page. I can't stop staring. These were the final moments of my father's life. This was the last thing he did.

"It was he who nailed down the geographic area of town the guy was from and brought in so many suspects to talk to," she says. "We've always assumed the killer was one of those suspects, but we never had enough on any of them to get warrants, let alone charge them. None of the DNA tests ever panned out either. We even tried that 23andMe shit. Nothing."

Dad always put a slash through his 7s and wrote all of his *s*'s, and only his *s*'s, in cursive. They always looked like little ocean waves.

"But then you came around," she says. "Or, more accurately, Happycop did."

I look up from the notes and stare at her more dumbly than I meant to.

"This guy has been quiet for nearly twenty years, but seeing you got the old itch back," she says. "This was something your dad predicted. It's right there in the notes." She pulls out one of the pages of Dad's scribblings and puts it in front of her face. "Yeah, right here. *Suspect desires recognition. If provoked correctly, he will tell **us** who he is.*"

"And I'm the provocation?" I ask.

"The combination of your sudden, uh, *fame*, and you being the son of the cop who scared him so much he went into hiding was too much for him to resist," she said. "So he sent this note. But he was pretty stupid about it. This supposed mastermind turned out to just be a Boomer who doesn't know how computers work. He's basically your grandma getting taken in by a Facebook scammer."

I chuckle. "Eventually we all get old and have to ask our kids how to use the remote," I say. Ellis tries to grin.

"When did he send this?" I ask.

"About two weeks ago," she says. "Not long after you arrested that guy at his apartment complex. In the early days of your TikTok fame. You weren't quite viral yet. That wasn't until Bertha and the bridge. But people were talking. And he apparently heard it."

She turns back to her computer.

"Once we nailed down the library he sent this from, we were able to narrow it down," she says. "Only so many people still alive from that time who would still be in town, would know anything, and, of course, would have the woman's ID."

"Did he really send this from the library?" I ask.

"East Point Branch," she says. "Forensics even knows which computer he used."

"Wow," I say. I am still looking at Dad's handwriting. It was even shakier than usual toward the end.

"So it turned out the library branch eliminated two of the three guys I'd been collecting all my string on, based off your dad's work," she says. "One has been in Florida all month. The other lives entirely on the other side of town and doesn't even have a library card."

Sergeant Ellis sits in her chair and leans back. She puts her arms behind her head and smiles.

"Well, this is why I wanted to see you," she says. "Because I think you should come get him with me."

I'm not sure I heard her right.

"What?" I say. "Me?"

"Yeah, of course you," she says. "We're going to arrest him. You and me."

I'm so confused I can only rest my head on my chin.

"You have to admit that it's perfect," she says. "The cop who couldn't catch the Dumpster Diver killer gets vindication from his son, who nabs him." She winks at me. "Alongside the zone commander who has the dad's old job and might make a great chief herself someday, of course."

"Hmm," I say, catching on as slowly as it takes me to catch on to anything anymore, which is pretty damn slow.

"And you're not just any son either," she says. "You're the world-famous Happycop. You really are everywhere, you know. PR wants me to make you give a big interview to the *Journal-Constitution*. But this is a much better idea. It'll be good for the force too. They've gotten into this whole Happycop business, you know. Cops have TikTok too.

They've seen you run into buildings and kick down doors and drive off embankments like everybody else has. You have to realize that most of your fellow cops, they think you're a hero now too. Jeez, even Perkins was raving about you the other day, the little shit."

"Wow," I say. This had not occurred to me.

"You're doing all the things they all tell themselves they would do, if they were in your spot, but deep down know they won't," she says. "Everybody loves a hero cop. Especially a cop."

Huh. "So we just hunt this guy down together?" I ask.

"I wouldn't say 'hunt,' Lloyd," she says. "He's at his house right now."

"Wait, you know his name?"

"Harold Templeton," she says. "His name is Harold Templeton. What a dumbass name for a serial killer, right?"

Harold Templeton. There is something surreal about the Dumpster Diver killer having an actual name, a stupid boring nothing name, a name that's on a credit card, a name with a social security number, a name he signs checks with. Hello, *Harold.* He's been walking around this earth all this time, being Harold, being a dumb guy named Harold.

"Worked as a meter reader for the electric company for years," she says, reading off a file she has brought up on her computer screen. "Low-level stuff. You're only supposed to do that job for a few years before getting promoted, but ole Harold did it for twenty years. He retired three years ago. Divorced, years ago, no kids. Lives alone up near Doraville now. In his mid-fifties. House is paid off. Mostly seems to sit around and post on Facebook all day. Loves Jimmy Buffet. Worried about immigrants. Wants the Braves to keep the Tomahawk Chop. Thinks today's kids just don't work as hard as his generation did."

"Typical old white man," I say.

"Hey, he's not *that* old," she says. "You and I will be there before you know it."

The circumstantial evidence that it's him is substantial. He's the only one who could have sent the note; its metadata matches not just that computer but a Gmail address he registered from his home IP address. He is a regular at that library. He lived just outside Little Five Points twenty years ago. Sergeant Ellis speculates that if he'd ever been fingerprinted—we don't have any prints in our files, he has no criminal record—we'd already have all the physical evidence we need.

I look at her screen, and then back at Dad's notes.

"This looks pretty locked down cold," I say.

"I couldn't have done it without the first McNeil," she says. "Or the second one."

She pauses and shifts her eyes left and right.

"So we are just gonna go," she says. "You and I. We go in first. We'll tip off the press, so when we bring him out, they'll get the picture and video of you and me next to him while he's cuffed and caught. People will eat that up. They will love it."

"Jesus," I say. "I don't think I realized you were so strategic about this stuff."

She smirks. "I think you did."

The idea makes sense. I don't know how I feel about it just yet. I keep looking at Dad's notes. As close as he came to a last will and testament.

Perhaps this will be mine. If you're the sort of guy trying to get himself killed, after all, surprising a serial killer might not be the worst way to go about it. Maybe he'll get us both.

"So whaddya say, Lloyd?" she says. "Is Happycop up for saving the day again?"

I look down at the desk, and then back up at her. She looks so strong. She's going be an incredible chief. Dad would be proud of her. Maybe he'd be proud of us both.

"I suppose that's how this story always had to end," I say. "Sign me up."

THE TEN GENTLE EDICTS OF LLOYD MCNEIL

Edict No. 9: Try to go quick.

My great-grandmother, your great-great-grandmother, was a woman named Sandy Lamm. She was a farm mother from South Georgia, a tough-as-nails old bird who had eight children, lost three others and, according to my grandpa, could lift a hog over her shoulder with her left arm while beating the shit out of two of her kids with her right. I was terrified of her. She'd lost her husband years before I was born, one of those World War I vets who smoked five packs of unfiltered Pall Malls a day and eventually died from his fifth heart attack at the age of forty-seven. She was a widow for nearly fifty years, which, according to my mom, meant that for nearly five decades she spent most of her time telling every other mom in the extended family all the things they were doing wrong.

Mom said that one time, a couple of weeks after I was born, she brought me to meet the extended family. Mom had a tough birthing experience with me; apparently I came so fast that they didn't have time to give her an epidural or any pain medicine. Mom hadn't practiced any of the breathing exercises, so she was so overwhelmed by the contractions that she just passed out in between each one. By the time Mom had a chance to tell this story to Great-Grandma Sandy, she had it practiced and honed. She knew when to pause for dramatic effect, when to hit the laugh lines, when to smile, point at me, and say "But it was all worth it," and everyone would awwwww. But at the end of the story this time, with the whole family rapt in the kitchen, hanging on every word, Great-Grandma Sandy grunted.

"Eh," she said, shrugging, as sharp and ornery at eighty-four as ever, "I did that eleven times." She paused. "Not in some fancy hospital either."

By the time Great-Grandma Sandy reached her nineties, she couldn't stay at home by herself anymore. She was starting to get dementia, and by the time she tried to drive her car to visit her friend Mary, who had been dead for twenty-four years, and ended up in a ditch outside a Pep Boys, it was universally agreed that she needed to be put in an old folks' home. I guess that's not what they call it anymore. It's now a "retirement community," or an "assisted living facility." But it'll always be an old folks' home to me. I'm sure that's how Great-Grandma Sandy saw it. Mom said she was snarling and hissing and growling like a rabid old cat when they checked her in there. She actually made Mom's mom cry. "She called her a cunt," Mom told me. "I don't think my mom even knew she knew that word."

As the years went along, Great-Grandma Sandy's dementia fully took over, and she wasn't calling anybody any awful names anymore, least of all her own daughter. We'd all go see her every once in a while, and she was always a little bit quieter and frailer than the last time we'd seen her. After a year or two, she stopped recognizing any of us, and after another year we all stopped visiting her entirely.

When I was about eight years old, a new pizza place opened up just down the road from the old folks' home. Mom started feeling guilty that she hadn't checked in on Great-Grandma Sandy in so long, so she dragged me with her to visit. We needn't have bothered. Her room was cold and dark and silent but for Great-Grandma Sandy's low, sad wisps of breath, just an old woman who'd died years ago, but no one had the decency to tell her body about it. She was propped up in a chair, but her head lay on her chest, barely moving. I wondered if someone got her out of bed in the morning, just took her to the chair, and let her sit there until it was time to move her back to bed at night. That's probably what happened.

Mom took my hand and walked me over to her.

"Grandma," she whispered. "It's Alice, your granddaughter. I'm here with my son Lloyd. We just wanted to come see you."

Great-Grandma Sandy didn't look up. She didn't move a muscle. She just lay there in the exact position she was in when we entered the room, and surely would be in the rest of the day. We stood there for a few seconds, not sure what to do, and then Mom turned to me. "OK!" she said, cheerily. "Are you ready for lunch?" "Pizza!" I shouted, putting my hands in the air. When we left the room, we heard Great-Grandma Sandy, or what was left of her body, make a sad, empty fart, with the power and force of someone opening a Ziploc bag. We didn't even look behind us.

About six months later, she finally died. What a horrible word to say, right? She *finally* died. But that was how it felt to everybody. My mom told me the news when I got home from school, and while she was respectful enough not to actually say "finally," she certainly didn't tell me in a way that implied what she was telling me was some horrible, stunning news. In fact, I remember the exact phrase she used: "Honestly, it's a relief."

That's not the last time I heard that phrase when somebody died. You would be amazed, Bish, how often people say it. You live your whole life, you have all your hopes and dreams and fears, you make friends, you visit places, you eat a lot of sandwiches, you take a lot of naps, you do all the things that make this world so incredible and ridiculous, you, you know, *live*. You do it for years. You try to leave a mark. You try to leave the world a little bit better than when you found it. You try to help. You try to be helped. You try to make a difference. And what happens when you die? Well, after all the people you love leave you in a dark room by yourself so they don't have to deal with you anymore, they call your death a *relief*.

And—and this is the thing—they're right to. This is the worst part of death: what makes it harder on the person dying is actually easier on the people they leave behind. What's the thing Kurt Cobain wrote in his suicide note? *It's better to burn out than to fade away.* Well, Bish, I'm sad to say that the dead rock star was right. He wasn't right to kill himself: we lost a lot of great music. (I've always thought he'd have been a great middle-aged musician—I can see him making, like, a Tom Petty turn. But nevermind.) People shouldn't kill themselves. But when he died, people *cared*. If he died in an old folks' home, thirty years after he'd made his last album, we all would have shrugged. *I didn't even know he was still alive.* Instead people mourned him in the streets. When you go suddenly, it hurts people. They only appreciate you when they are shocked that you are no longer here.

One of the things that I have realized about myself, as I've been going through this process, as I've made my peace with this, as I've made the decisions I've had to make once I knew what was happening to me, is this: *I want to be mourned.* Bish, you should know that I feel bad about this. I don't want you to be sad, or anyone else to be sad. But I hope you will indulge me in feeling that, now I'm at the end, I'd like my life to be acknowledged a little? I'd like people to kinda miss me? I'd like to know I made some sort of mark on the world, that maybe it's a little different, maybe even a little worse, without me in it. Or, at the very least: I'd like my death to maybe not be a *relief?* I'd maybe like no one to say, "Finally!" That's not asking too much, is it?

I know this makes it harder on you. It would have been easier on you if I'd died like Great-Grandma Sandy, if you had years to anticipate my death, to process it, to come to terms with it. That's yet another horrible irony of death: What's easier on the living is harder on the dying. I'm going to go out fast, quick. My death will surprise people. *He was just here yesterday, I was supposed to see him next week,* they'll say, as if those things could serve as some sort of proof that a person couldn't be dead, as if the plans we make with each other in life are some sort of obligation that the dead don't realize they're supposed to be honoring. They might, if just for a moment, reflect on the world without me. That will be harder to process than if my light had gone out years ago, if my last contribution to the world was an oblivious Ziploc fart. I'm sorry about that. But yeah: going out like a door slamming has more dignity. It gives me more heft. I've always wanted to have some heft.

So I have to admit: I'm glad you will mourn me. I'm glad my death won't be a relief. I am indeed sorry about this. I am sorry about the pain. I am sorry you will hurt. But it's true. This is better than dying alone in a room and you thinking *finally* and then feeling guilty about it. I know you don't think that's what would happen. But it would. It's true. This isn't the worst way to go out. It really isn't.

I hope you will forgive me.

66

Not long before the end, Dad told me he loved me. It was the only time he ever said it. I'd never thought I needed him to, and I'd always assumed he wouldn't. But he did. It was an accident. But still, he did.

He was drinking, down there in the den, watching a Braves game. He would work all hours of the night at the end, trying to find the Dumpster Diver, and he must have felt like he was under siege from all angles. He didn't really talk much to me or Mom. On the rare occasions that he'd come home when either of us were still awake, he'd pass us, grunt, and head straight to the den, where he'd sit and drink and watch the Braves. I'd sometimes go down and sit with him, sit next to him really, and he'd nod to acknowledge that I was there but otherwise just growl at the television. The Braves were good back then, real good, they had Maddux and Smoltz and Glavine and Chipper and the whole gang, but you wouldn't have known it from Dad when he was watching the games. He was always angry at somebody, *why'd you throw that pitch, what the hell are you swinging at that for, would somebody around here hit the goddamn cutoff man?*

He was yelling at Bobby Cox for something when I came in and sat down next to him. I might as well have not been there.

"Stupid sumbitch," he said, stirring his glass with his finger. "What the hell is he thinking?"

"Who's winning?" I asked, a stupid question I knew was stupid before it had even escaped my mouth.

He turned his head to me, pointed at the scorebox in the corner of the television, gave a sarcastic scowl, and turned his head back to the screen.

We had not talked about everything swirling with the Dumpster Diver, the press, or any of it. What could I possibly say? He was Major McNeil. There was nothing I could tell him he did not already know—he always made sure of that. I wasn't on the case anyway. I was still going into the precinct for my shifts, but Ellis was working more closely with him than I was. It's no wonder I was so stunned when Ellis told me how close he'd gotten to finding the guy. It's not like he was going to tell me anything.

We sat and silently watched the game. I didn't know anything about baseball. The game droned on. After about a wordless half hour, he stood up, walked over to a bar cart, took out a bourbon bottle, and for the first time in a couple of innings, looked at me.

He shook the glass in his hand. "You?" he said.

I'd never had a drink with my dad before. It was one of those things that didn't even seem possible, like dividing by zero, or leaping into a black hole.

"Sure," I said, my voice cracking as I tried to sound gruff and grown-up, an eight-year-old boy in a twenty-four-year-old's costume. He pulled a glass from under the counter, held it up to his face, and peered at it, as if he were trying to read its fine print. He poured a small amount of bourbon in it, about a quarter of what was in his glass, walked it over to me, and handed it over. He sat down. Without taking his eyes off the television, he lifted his glass in my direction. It took me a second, but I clinked it, and he took a sharp gulp of his, clicking his teeth and inhaling tightly.

After a minute or so, I couldn't take the quiet anymore. I brought up the only person the two of us shared an acquaintance with outside of this house. "How's Ellis holding up?" I asked. She was seven months pregnant at the time and working just as many hours as Dad was. "She's as big as a house already."

"Good," he said, and the right side of his face loosened a bit, only for a second. "She's having a boy."

"Oh, that's great," I said.

"I told her to make sure he doesn't become a cop," he said, so casually it was obvious he didn't think he was saying anything that noteworthy at all.

All these years later, I still can feel the wet hot shame splash the back of my neck. It came on so fast I flinched.

All I could think to say was, "What's that?"

"Oh, you know what I mean," he said, at least acknowledging, for a second, that I was his son and I was also a cop and that perhaps those two facts might be somewhat connected. "I just mean that it's a tough job. She should hope her kid does something else. I didn't mean . . ." He trailed off and looked at me briefly. It almost looked like he was feeling regret. It was very strange to see him look that way.

"It's fine," I said, trying to move on as quickly as humanly possible. "I think I know what you meant."

He coughed a couple of times, hard, almost like he was barking, and then he hit the arm of his chair with his open palm.

"That kid," he said, and I remember that he was slurring—I'd never heard my father slur before—"Is gonna think he has to be a cop just because his mom was a cop, and he doesn't have to be. No one has to be."

He turned to Braves manager Bobby Cox, who was sitting in the dugout and chewing mindlessly, a big dumb cow in a hat. "They'll screw you in the end, no matter what you do. That kid should just do what he wants. You could have, you know."

I sat silent, staring at the television. And then he said it.

"Parents are gonna love their kids no matter what they do, so they should just do what they want," he said, waving the hand not holding the drink in the air, swatting imaginary flies. "People would be a lot happier if they just did what they wanted." He paused and coughed again. He looked at me, only for a second, before turning away. His eyes were hollower than I'd ever seen them. When I think of him now, I do not think of the picture outside Ellis's office. I think of this man. Those eyes. "No matter what they do," he said, back talking to Bobby Cox. "No matter what."

I looked at the back of his head. He'd said the word *love*. In that moment, I vowed to say it to my own son as often as I could. Just hearing it once, in passing, could fill you up right there. What could saying it a million times do?

I knew at the time that "parents are gonna love their kids no matter what they do" wasn't the same thing as "I love you"—it was only barely in the same zip code—but it was as close as I'd ever gotten.

"That's good to know, Dad," I said.

I was about to say something else, Lord knows what, when a player for the Cardinals hit the ball real hard off a pitcher for the Braves, and Dad yelled "Oh for crissakes Millwood!" at the television, and then he spilled his drink and cursed a whole bunch more. I got up to grab a towel to help him clean it up, but he waved me off and said "I got it, goddammit," and after that he decided it was time for bed, they were playing terrible anyway, and I said good night, and then he grumbled, almost embarrassed, "I'm sorry, Lloyd," and then he said good night and about two weeks later he was dead and now I live in his house and often fall asleep in that same chair and a few weeks from now I'll be dead too and maybe in twenty years it'll be Bishop falling asleep in that chair himself.

This was not the last conversation I had with my father. But it was close. And it might as well have been.

I do know, deep down, somewhere, that he loved me. He didn't know how to say it. But I did hear it. It was as close to hearing him whistle as I ever got. He never found any peace in the end. Maybe I can.

67.

Sergeant Ellis is in my kitchen. She is in full uniform. Is it a work-day? I try to remember. I'm not wearing my uniform. Did I know she was coming? I don't like wearing my uniform much lately if I don't have to. It's hanging off me too much these days. I tuck my shirt in, and it nearly goes down to my knees.

Sergeant Ellis snaps her fingers at me.

"You with me, Lloyd?"

"Yep, sorry," I say. "We're clicking a little slower around here lately."

"So, big day," she says, taking a small step back to look at me. I'm wearing rumpled jeans with a tear in one knee and an old Atlanta Thrashers T-shirt, and I just looked down and realized I'm only wearing one sock. "We need, uh, to get you ready. Are you ready for this?"

Today is the day. I'm more ready than she knows. And certainly more ready than I look.

"I am, I yam what I yam," I say, another of those things that just comes out. *Cognitive issues*, Lipsey said. "I probably need to get changed, yes?"

"Yes," she says, and I can tell it's taking considerable effort for her not to roll her eyes. "It's a big day, Lloyd. This is what we've been waiting for. Is your uniform pressed like I suggested?"

"Did you tell me to do that?"

"Christ, Lloyd," she says, and goes into my bedroom. To both of our surprise, my uniform is in fact pressed, ironed, hanging up, crisp as it was the first day I put it on. I have no idea when I did that.

I start to take off the T-shirt, and Sergeant Ellis takes a step backward and begins to walk out of the room. But then I groan—my ribs are really killing me, they're a little worse every time I wake up—and the shirt gets caught around my left arm, and I stumble and almost fall over.

She steps forward, looks at the red and blue bruises splotching my midsection, and sighs. "Here," she says, and she gently puts her right arm on my back and lifts the shirt over my head. "I got you."

"Thank you," I say, and then she helps me get dressed and, God help her, without a word, guides me through putting on my uniform like I haven't done it ten thousand times, like I'm not falling apart, like it's the most normal thing in the world.

We stand in front of the full-length mirror, another thing Jess put in here years ago that hasn't moved once since. I'm a good seven inches taller than Sergeant Ellis is, but she has forever seemed larger, more formidable, more *composed*. She's just more than I am. She always has been. I am grateful.

She straightens my tie and wipes some lint off my right breast pocket. She looks at the mirror.

"We look sharp, Lloyd," she says. "We're gonna look great for our big day."

"Atlanta's Finest," I say.

She turns to face me and lightly puts her hand on my chest. She unclips my name plate and places it on my dresser, then takes something out of her pocket. It's another name plate, older, slightly rusted, with chips on the edges, like it had been dropped, or maybe even thrown.

It says the same thing my name plate did: McNeil.

"I thought this would be something you might want to have with you today," she says, and she pins it on me. "He'd certainly want to be here today."

I look down at it. She's certainly right about that. He'd much rather be the one doing this today than trust me to do it. But he's dead. And I'm not. So she's stuck with me.

"Thanks," I say. "Nice touch."

"I thought so." She rubs her hands together. "So," she says, grinning. "Let's get moving."

I see my new cane lying next to the couch. I find myself needing it of late. You can just buy them at CVS, you don't need a prescription or anything. I lean over and grab it.

"Hey, careful there, old-timer," she says, taking my arm. "Maybe you'll be more careful the next time you drive your car off a bridge."

With her help, and the cane's, I push myself up.

"Now's as good a time as any," I say. Now's the only real time I have.

68.

Ellis drives. I sit next to her, staring at the window. I roll it down. The air is brisk. The breeze feels nice.

"We certainly didn't have any trouble getting a warrant," she says. "If we wanted to, we could storm in there right now."

"But we're not going to do that?" I say, looking back to her.

"No," she says. "You and I are going to see if he's up for confessing first."

"Ah," I say, and I'm waking up, I'm feeling stronger, this is starting to sound fun. "Well, that would certainly be convenient and helpful if he would do that for us."

"Hey," she says, "why not us?"

And so she lays out the plan.

His house is on a street called Spanish Oak Drive in Doraville, just a few blocks away from Honeysuckle Park. It's on a little hill, with old cracked concrete steps leading up to it, with no back exit, just a fifteen-foot-tall fence that separates his property from his neighbor's off Oakcliff Road. The only way out is the front. The SWAT teams will establish a perimeter just a block away, with eyes on that front door at all times. They've been staking the place out for a week, tracking all his movements, confirming his habits. He's not difficult to nail down. He goes to the grocery store, he goes to the library, he goes to a Mexican restaurant for happy hour on Tuesdays and Thursdays, and otherwise he's just home. He's just a guy who lives alone. There aren't many places for him to go, and there isn't much for him to do. That's probably why he got so eager to reach out to us in the first place.

"The idea has always been to wait for him to be home in the morning, ideally outside," she says. "He likes to water his plants and fidget with his pathetic excuse for a garden in the morning before he comes inside for lunch. He should be out there now, and you and I are going to pay him a visit."

"This is the big PR part you had in mind?"

"Of course," she says. "Who better? Lloyd McNeil, the son of the chief whose career was ruined by the Dumpster Diver killer, there to bust the man that his father never could. Except he's not Lloyd McNeil anymore, he's not Major McNeil's son, no, sir. He's Happycop! He's the hero. And here he is, saving the day again, solving the city's most notorious cold case."

"Uh-huh," I say, taking it in and unable to deny the logic.

"And look there, right alongside him," she says, "why, it's Sergeant Desiree Ellis, one of the highest-ranking and most respected Black female officers in the history of the department. Say, didn't someone say she'd make a great chief someday? Isn't the mayor set to select a new one just next year? My, I believe he is! Didn't we just see her, alongside the hero Happycop, carrying the Dumpster Diver killer out of his home in handcuffs? Who would be better for the job than her?"

I have long understood Ellis's ambitions. But this Machiavellian side of her is legitimately impressive. She always wanted this. It makes sense that I'd be useful in helping her get it. Perhaps even more than she currently knows.

Thus: we wait until he's outside, and Sergeant Ellis and I casually walk up to him. We tell him we're investigating some activity in the neighborhood and were wondering if we could ask him a few questions. Maybe we could come inside? Then we sit down and have a little chat. The SWAT guys will be everywhere outside, available to barge in as soon as Sergeant Ellis tells them to—it'll be as easy as a text. We have a warrant if we need it. But ideally: he'll want to tell us. Maybe it will be a relief. Maybe it's what he wants.

Either way, we've got him cold. Maybe he confesses. Maybe we see evidence right out in front of us. Maybe he lawyers up immediately and the SWAT team comes in. It doesn't really matter. All that matters, Ellis says, is that he's coming out, with us, with the whole world watching. "I've even got 11Alive News alerted that something big is coming so they have their people ready," she says. "Though some kid with TikTok will surely have it first, right, Happycop?"

She smiles. "And then," she says, "it's over."

"Wow," I say.

"Yeah, I'm a pretty smart lady, Lloyd."

I look back out the window, in front of us, and I see Spaghetti Junction, the spiraling, labyrinthine octopus of highways and on-ramps and off-ramps that connect I-85 and I-285, thirteen miles northeast of Atlanta.

"Want me to pull over?" she says, chuckling.

69.

Anderson looks funny to me in his SWAT uniform. He probably wouldn't look funny to you. He'd look terrifying to you. He's a mountain, so hulking and ripped at this point that I'm surprised they could find anything that would fit him. I wonder who makes SWAT team gear. I like to imagine it's someone's grandma, she's been knitting and quilting for years, someone calls her and gives her measurements, she heads into a closet filled with Kevlar, and she gets down to work. "Wow, this new guy's a big one," she says, peering over her bifocals at the order sheet. It's a funny thought. I'm sure it's an eleven-year-old in China, though.

The reason Anderson looks funny to me is that he is a lot of things—a good cop, a bodybuilder, a man with a profoundly hideous protein diet, a true-blue movie buff—but one thing he is not is a *soldier*. Anderson, I've learned during my time with him, is more than anything else kind. I don't mean that to say that soldiers cannot be kind, of course they can be, most are. Not all SWAT team members are soldiers. But they are dressed up to look like them. Every police department is always asking for SWAT team funding, and most guys just want it because it makes them feel like marines without having to go through the hell you have to go through to become a marine. They're all pretenders. They're just dressing up like tough guys.

The reason Anderson looks ridiculous in his SWAT uniform isn't that he's a pretender. He's bigger and tougher than all of them, when he needs to be. The reason is that he's *not* a pretender. The reason is that he's the real deal. I'd walk into any situation with him without all that crap on before I'd walk into one with any of them who do have it.

Today, he is not walking in with me. He nevertheless wouldn't be anywhere else. He is, after all, my partner.

"I see you've got a new appendage," he says, taking off his ridiculous goggles and skull cap and pointing to my cane. "Is that like your billy club?"

"'Ya gotta box their ears, son,'" I say, shaking the cane while trying to do a Cockney accent and very much failing. "'Gonna teach these young gits a lesson.'"

We are two blocks from the home of Harold Templeton, retired meter reader, oddly indiscriminate library computer user, apparent serial murderer of women. Anderson is towering over ten other SWAT team guys, most of whom are wearing their full tactical gear, goggles and all, while flipping through their phones. It's hot, it's the fall—it's always hot in Georgia anymore, why would the fall be any different? My uniform hangs off me, which keeps me cooler, or at least makes it so the sweat isn't showing through my shirt.

"How you holding up?" Anderson asks. "You're not still pissed at me for back at your house, are you?"

"Oh, come on, you're fine," I say, tapping some sort of black shin-guard he's wearing that's probably made out of Vibranium, or whatever that indestructible material that's only found on Wakanda is called. "Bish is a hard kid to say no to."

"No shit," he says, sipping from his Jittery Joe's mug. "We're all going to be working for him someday."

"Lord, I hope not," I say, looking around at the gaggle of middle-aged men dressed like Batman and holding HK416s. "Or at least not here anyway."

"I think we've had just about enough McNeils in this department," says Sergeant Ellis, turning from around the corner of the SWAT van. Upon seeing her, the whole SWAT team puts down their phones and straightens up. She pats me on the shoulder and shakes Lieutenant Anderson's hand. "Glad you made it out, Wynn."

"Yes ma'am," he says, and he looks at me for a split second before turning back to her. "Thanks for calling me."

Sergeant Ellis straightens her uniform, jumps into the bed of the van, and clears her throat. Everyone stands in rapt attention. This is a big day for all of us.

"All right, gentlemen, and I think you're all gentlemen, yes—"

A goggled figure waves its hand in the air sheepishly.

"Oh, yes, sorry, Officer Lapida," she says. "I forgot this was your unit. Anyway, we've got a limited window here, so let's get to it."

She looks down to me and waves me forward. She motions for me to take her hand, and I do, and she pulls me up into the truck. She's stronger than she looks. I dropped my cane, but Anderson grabs it and tosses it up to me. I catch it with my left hand. He gives me a little fist pump.

"You all know Detective McNeil, of course," she says. "He has become quite the little celebrity of late, it seems. He and I are running point on this operation. We have eyes on the suspect, who is currently inside the domicile. Regular surveillance over the last week has given us reason to believe that he will soon exit his home for basic yard work. When that happens, the operation will kick into gear."

She turns to me. Does she expect me to say something?

"Uh, yep." I nod, trying to look grave and serious. "Basic yard work."

Sergeant Ellis turns back to the team.

"When he is outside, Detective McNeil and I will approach him and tell him we are investigating a series of incidents in the neighborhood and that we'd like to come inside and ask him a few routine questions." Her voice is firm and clear and strong. She's good at this, always has been. They'll all walk through a wall for her. "Hopefully he will invite us in. He has no reason to believe we suspect him of anything, he has no criminal record, he will want to keep up appearances. Now, if he doesn't invite us in, well, that's why I have this." She pulls out a warrant signed by Judge Jones, a great guy who went to high school with Jessica in Athens—every time I see him, he asks how she's doing. He's really into the Georgia basketball team, he is always asking if I or Bishop want to use his extra tickets, just an absolute gem of a person, one time he—

"You still with us, Detective McNeil?" Everyone is staring at me.

"Yes, yes," I say, coming to. "Warrants? Warrants."

"As I was *saying*," she says, looking at me for a beat too long before pivoting back to the team, "hopefully we just go inside and talk to him before we make any arrest. It would be helpful to get whatever information we can before he realizes we're there for him. If he doesn't welcome us into his humble abode, I will cuff him right then and there, and that'll be the sign for you all to come in. But if he does, and we do get to talk to him, we will get everything we can out of him. When that, uh, stops becoming productive, when that particular stone begins to run dry, I will alert you all to enter the residence. And then . . . that'll be the end of it."

She turns again to me. I appreciate that she is making sure to include me, but she has this all pretty well handled.

"Lloyd, you have anything else you want to add?" she says.

I glance down to Anderson, the only guy with his goggles and skull-cap off, and I see him looking at me in a way I have never seen anyone look at me before: He is looking at me with *reverence*. I remember Sergeant Ellis's words. *They all think you're a hero.* Underneath those goggles, I realize, they're all looking at me the exact same way. That's why she has me up here, that's why she keeps prodding me to say something.

She believes I can inspire them.

My ribs are screaming. I keep losing my train of thought. If I didn't have this cane, I'd fall out of this van. I'm a little worried I'm going to pass out when we get in that house.

But I can do this. When called, I will serve.

I push myself up with the cane and look among the team. They're about to get the Dumpster Diver killer. This is the biggest moment of their careers. They will never forget this.

"Well, Sergeant Ellis," I say, taking a deep breath, knowing I'll need it. "We've been trying to get this guy my whole twenty-three years on the force. Many great cops have tried to track him down, to make him pay for what he's done, and none of them ever did it." I look at Sergeant Ellis, who nods approvingly.

"My dad," I say, feeling strong. "My dad gave his whole career to get this guy, died trying to get this guy. And now, right now, you, and me, and Sergeant Ellis, and all of us: we're going to finish this. We're gonna take this son of a bitch down. For all the cops who couldn't. For all the families who deserve justice. For this city."

I put my hand on Sergeant Ellis's shoulder so I can lift my cane in the air.

"For the city of Atlanta," I say, feeling like Braveheart. "And for my dad. Let's fuck this guy up."

The sea of goggles cheers. Happycop has spoken. My eyes meet Anderson's. He pounds his chest with his fist and extends his arm to me. I point to him with my cane.

Let's fuckin' go, he mouths.

I don't know if my dad would be proud of me. But here, at the end of it, I can say: I do hope so.

"Thanks, Lloyd," Sergeant Ellis says. "So everybody got that?"

The goggles nod as one.

Sergeant Ellis's radio crackles.

A muffled, pixelated voice.

"We have eyes on the suspect," it says. "He just came out the front door. He is carrying a watering can. Repeat, a watering can."

Sergeant Ellis pushes the button on her radio.

"Copy," she says. "We're on our way."

She turns back to the goggles. "You heard the man. Everybody get to their positions." She hops off the van and extends her hand to me to guide me down.

"What do you say, Lloyd? You ready to wrap this story up?"

I am. No matter what, I am. She takes my wrist, and we are off, together.

THE TEN GENTLE EDICTS OF LLOYD MCNEIL

Edict No. 10: Don't worry about what comes next.

You were not raised in a religious home. That's me and your mom's fault, though I guess it's more our parents' fault, or their parents' fault. It just was never a part of our lives, or our parents' lives, so it wasn't a part of yours. I know it was sort of unusual to grow up in the South and not have church be even slightly a part of your life. I'm sure all your friends thought it was weird. But we wouldn't have known what to tell you, even if we had thought we should tell you something. We just left it out. There are better legacies we have given you, and surely worse ones as well.

To me, all the church stuff is, in the end, just about what happens when you die. That's the point of all of it, isn't it? They can talk a big game about being good to your neighbor, about loving the invisible man who lives in the sky, about doing right by the Bible, but most of the things they tell you to do, it's all stuff a good person should try to do regardless. Be nice to people, forgive, be kind . . . all the Jesus business, that's just what you're supposed to be doing, whether you're Lutheran, Baptist, Presbyterian, Catholic, Jewish, atheist, whatever. Even people who live their entire lives on that island in the Indian Ocean, you know the one, the one that civilization never reached and they all walk around naked and live in huts and just eat whatever fish they can find, even they know that's how you should treat people. You don't need any God to tell you that. Maybe you choose not to do it. Maybe you're a dick to everyone. But you know you're being a dick. You know you're doing something you shouldn't. No one requires a book, even the Good one, to learn that. You just know it.

No, the church business, the Bible, all the *rules*, it's about death. It's about what comes next. Basically, people need the church like they need cops: they need something to make sure they do the right things, because if they don't, they'll go to jail—or, in this case, hell. The whole thing is about punishment. It's an implicit understanding that if you don't set up some sort of consequences for bad behavior, people will just get up to whatever they want to and not give any of it a second thought. Sure, you can get away with whatever you can in this world, and we might not be able to punish you, particularly if no one ever finds out, but the church is there to say, sure, maybe we won't get you in this life, but the big guy upstairs, he sees everything, he *knows*, so if you don't act right, he'll make sure to get you in the next one. All of it comes down to that. *What happens when you die?* The church says if you're good, you get everything anyone could ever want, and if you're bad, you'll suffer the worst torture, they'll literally set your ass on fire, and it will happen for the rest of eternity. You don't come up with those sorts of polar opposites if you're not trying to keep people in line. It's white or black, yes or no. You get everything, or you get the worst thing imaginable.

And it's all about that question, the one that obsesses everybody, even the people on that island: What comes next when you close your eyes and never open them again? We got all the smarts anyone could imagine, we can cure disease, we can create a baby in a test tube, we can invent a bomb that will kill everyone on the planet, we can fly someone to outer space and then send them an email, but we aren't any closer to the answer to that question than we were when we were drawing on cave walls with rocks. It's the one thing we can never know. Is it any wonder we've created entire belief systems to try to come up with something? That we've patterned our entire lives around our lack of understanding of what happens when they're over?

As you'd probably expect, I've spent a lot of time pondering this lately. The big question, the one unknowable—well, I'm not the brightest bulb who ever walked this earth, but sometime soon, sometime *very* soon, I'm going to know something that the biggest genius in history never knew and never could. The thing that has obsessed every human since the beginning of time, the thing that drives us and terrifies us, the thing that separates us from the beasts—the knowledge that someday our eyes aren't going to open again, I'm about to find out the answer. I'm right on the cusp. I'm so close.

What I've learned—and what you need to know—is that . . . it doesn't matter. I don't even care. Isn't that wild? Life is so short, and the arc of time is so long, that in many ways every person on earth is just sleepwalking through that very brief period in which they are not dead. What's going to happen when this is over? Does it make a difference? It's not like there's anything I can do about it now. If I started getting really into Jesus now that I know I'm about to die, well, that's kind of cheating, isn't it? I'd have a hard case to make once I got up there. *Hey, I never thought much of you, or your dad for that matter, until I was about to die, but when I found out, I thought, well, I better cover my ass.* The die is cast at this point. Either I did what I was supposed to do, or I didn't. There is something after this, or there isn't. I'm about to find out. But right now, I'm as dumb as the rest of us. There's nothing I can do to change that, or any of it.

Death—avoiding it, worrying about it, doing what you can to deal with it—is the center of everything in this life, and what I'm saying, what you need to listen to, what you need to understand, is that it shouldn't be. I'm right on the doorstep of it, at the point when I should be the *most* concerned about it . . . and I don't care at all. It doesn't make a bit of difference. Maybe when I wake up, I'm in heaven, or I'm in hell. Maybe when I wake up, I'm haunting my old house. Maybe when I wake up, I'm a bumblebee flitting around. Maybe when I wake up, there's one hundred virgins waiting for me. (Which: Gross. That better not be what it is.) Maybe I don't wake up at all. I don't have any control over any of it. What I realize now, at the end, is that so much of my life, and I think everybody's life, has been about trying to avoid that fact, to pretend that the illusion that we could ever control it could possibly be real. We constructed our whole world, our value systems, our entire way of thinking, around something that we couldn't do anything about—about something we don't even slightly understand. Why was I thinking about any of this? Why were any of us? What a stupid waste of time. What a dumb way to spend a life.

So hear this: Stop. You're going to die. Hopefully it will be a hundred years from now, and thankfully it'll be long after I'm gone, but it's going to happen, because it is going to happen to everyone. It has nothing to do with how you live your life. That's what you think about when you're about to die: how much more living you should have done. That's my lesson from this. That's what I understand now. When you're at the end, when it's about to go down, you don't think about what happens next. You think about what already did. You think about what you would have done differently. You think about how much you should have appreciated what all of it was—how lucky you were just to get to experience any of it at all.

This is my lesson, Bish, and it's a big one: Just live. You are experiencing the very short period in which you are alive. It'll be gone before you know it. When it's over, it's over, that's it, that's the end, that's all it is, it's just the shutting off of some lights before bed—it's just boring. I'm right here, about to be there, and I cannot emphasize enough how much it doesn't matter. I'm gonna die, and I don't care, not anymore. Whatever goes down, goes down.

Don't worry about death. Just live. You won't regret it.

70

He's right there. I'm looking at him, with my own eyes, from across the street from his home, as he handles weeding shears with big bulky brown garden gloves. That's the guy who killed those women. That's the guy who destroyed my father. That's the guy who vanished for almost twenty years. That's the guy who, apparently, returned for me. That's the guy we've all been trying to get.

There is nothing remotely scary about him. He's younger than I realized, or at least younger-looking: I imagined him being more feeble, shuffling around his front yard, clipping at a bush, occasionally swatting at a bug. But he's a strong fiftysomething, wearing a maroon sleeveless tank top and khaki cargo shorts with all sorts of buckles and pockets. He has white hair that's too long for his haircut, which he combs over and down to try to cover the third of his head that has no hair at all, a pool of baldness that's like a still pond surrounding a lonely only-slightly-shaggy stone in the middle. He's got a gut, but not a flabby one; it's thick, like he's got a kickball in there. He moves around his garden with purpose, precision, and focus. He clips his hedges, then pauses for a moment to scratch the back of his neck, and then his ass.

That's him. He's right there.

"I'm going to approach first," Sergeant Ellis whispers to me as we peer around the corner of a mailbox, about a hundred feet away. "You follow behind so I'm the one he sees, in case he recognizes you and freaks out. And let me talk."

His back is turned to us. As we get closer, I see the shirt isn't maroon, it's red. He has just sweated entirely through it, so it looks maroon. My cane clanks with each step, and I try to lighten it so he doesn't hear it as we approach. He doesn't notice. He doesn't notice much of anything. We are a hundred feet away, and then we are seventy-five feet away, and then we are fifty feet away, and then twenty-five, then twenty, then ten, and then we are right behind him and he still has not turned around or gotten any sense that anyone else is in the front yard at all. I can see the droplets on the back of his neck, next to a gnarly black wart just under his right ear. He has a long scar that runs from his right elbow to his wrist. He is wearing loafers with no socks. He is the murderer of several women, he's the man we've all been looking for, and he's just right there, wet and warty.

"Ahem," Sergeant Ellis says. "Sir?"

He does not respond. His left hand shakes slightly. He just keeps staring at his bush.

"Sir," she says, louder this time. "Sir, hello?"

His ears rise, slightly, and I see the side of his face twitch.

"Sir?"

He moves his right foot toward us, lopes his left one around toward it, and begins to slowly turn in our direction. His body pivots before his face does, the gut nearly poking Sergeant Ellis in the side, and his eyebrows both rise as he faces and finally sees us, two police officers, dressed up neatly in pressed uniforms, standing in front of him.

His mouth curves in surprise, but then it settles into a look of apology.

"Oh," he says, in a deep voice that's ostensibly friendly but has a hint of annoyance to it, like we interrupted him in the middle of something important. "I'm sorry. I didn't hear you. Hello."

Sergeant Ellis gives me a quick glance out of the corner of her eye but then is right back on him.

"Hello, sir," she says, calm and firm. "We are from the Atlanta Police Department. I'm Sergeant Ellis, this is Detective McNeil. We'd like to ask you a few questions."

I see him look at me. There is a flicker of recognition. I saw it. He knows I saw it. He turns back to Sergeant Ellis, and his eyes go blank. He catches himself and smiles. "Oh, yes, of course, it's nice to meet you," he says. "I'm happy to help however I can. Would you like to come inside?"

He then turns and begins walking toward his front door—faster than I would have thought him capable. I instinctively push forward after him—faster than I would have thought myself capable.

"Sir!" Sergeant Ellis says, and she begins to rush forward as well, but I am faster than she would have thought me capable too.

The man speeds toward his front door. The guy is motoring, he's like an Olympic speedwalker, I can see the sagging but still formidable muscles in his back contort and contract. He hops up the first step on the stairwell to his small porch and takes the next two in one little hop. I am shoving hard enough to be matching him step for step.

He then arrives at the front door, pauses, opens the door with his left hand, and extends his right arm theatrically toward us.

"Uh, come on in," he says. "After you."

Ellis goes in first. I'm right behind her.

71

It's not that big of a house. It is striking how oddly un-lived-in this house is. Ellis told me earlier that he has lived in this house for fifteen years, but it looks like a place for a traveling salesman who spends his entire life on the road and only drops in here every month or so to do laundry and check his mail.

I look to my left, down a hallway with ugly shag carpeting and a side table littered with loose change, rubber bands, and about six different sets of keys. The house is clean and well put together, but there is an odd dark stain on the wall above the table, particularly strange because the rest of that wall seems to have been recently painted. The lamp on the table is homemade, with an old electrical meter as the base and a light bulb outlet welded into it, with no lampshade. There's a small sofa next to it, and I see it and instinctively take a step back.

Four Cabbage Patch Kid dolls are sitting there, in formation. They are all outfitted with little waitress uniforms with the Waffle House logo on them. They each have a name tag, but the names are scratched out.

I catch Ellis's eye. She scrunches up her nose and turns toward the kitchen on our right. There, Harold Templeton is sitting at his kitchen table, calmly, his hands in his lap, looking up at us.

"Hello," he says. "Is there any way I can be of service to you?"

I look back to my left, down the hall, past a wall with no pictures, and see a small spare bathroom. There are no lights on, and no one in there. I turn back to Sergeant Ellis. She steps forward and pulls out a chair at the table. She motions me to take out the one next to it. She sits down, and I put my hand on the back of my chair and prepare to do the same.

"Yeah, so we don't want to take up any more of your time than we have to," she says, leaning backward, casual, unthreatening.

"Oh, please, it's no problem at all." His eyes wander toward me, then back to Ellis, then back to me. He stands up abruptly, but then catches himself and smiles. "Can I get the two of you a coffee? I should get you a coffee, you'd probably like a coffee." He turns toward his refrigerator.

There's a little twitch in his right hand. I don't know why I saw it, what drew my eyes to it—it's minor, little, not much of anything. But it's a little twitch, like he's opening a lock, and he spreads his fingers out and stretches them, clenching his knuckles quickly. They make quick light pops, and his hand does the key-opening twitch again.

A lightning bolt flickers up the back of my neck. I stare at his hand.

Ellis says over his shoulder, "We're all right, actually, thank—"

He snaps suddenly toward her and yanks open a drawer under the kitchen table. Ellis yells "Hey!" and pulls back in her chair, but her legs catch on the top of the table. A revolver appears in his hand, and he lunges toward her.

But I'm already there. I don't know how I got here. I don't remember moving. I did not choose this. I did not make a heroic gesture. I am just here. I just jump-cut from that place to this place. I am here. I am in front of her. How long have I been standing here?

Maybe I have always been here.

The gun is now pointed at me.

They say it happens in slow motion, but it doesn't, it happens fast, it happens so fast that you can't really follow what's going on, one thing happens and then another happens and then there is a flash and then there is another flash and then I am on the floor.

72

When we took Bishop home from the hospital, I stayed awake with him every night for a week. Jess couldn't get him to latch on to her breast, so we went to formula immediately, and I volunteered to be the one to feed him every three hours so Jess could sleep. I wanted to help her out, to do my part, but the real reason I volunteered to do this was because I was unable to take my eyes off him. I couldn't look away. It floored me, *floored, floored me*, how instantly everything that had happened to me in my life up to that point became unimportant, even frivolous. All that mattered was that this person, this thing that had not existed seventy-two hours beforehand and now was the person that I loved more than anyone had ever loved anything since the beginning of time, was safe. I had to keep him alive. I had to protect him.

So I sat across from his crib, every night for a week, and just stared at him. I would watch his little chest, concave, exposed, ribs thin as tissue paper, rise and fall, and rise and fall, and rise and fall, and if it took a second longer for it to rise than it had the last time, I would rush to the crib and put my ear to his mouth to make sure he was still breathing. I began to believe that if I left the room at any point, if I took my eyes off him for so much as a second, that would be the moment I lost him, the moment when the whole world fell apart, *fell, fell apart*. As long as I was there, as long as I was watching, he would keep breathing. As long as I didn't look away, nothing could happen to him.

After the first week I slowly stepped away and eased back into my life. At first I just left the room for a few minutes at a time. Then I could watch a movie on my iPad in the hallway outside his door. Then I'd be all right with napping for an hour or so, I'd just be out, *out, out, I'd be out*. Eventually I was able to get back into bed with Jess. After a month, I'd swaddle him and we'd both be out for eight hours; we were always lucky, he was such a sound sleeper. But that was my first lesson of parenthood, one that I both accepted and tried to resist for the next thirteen years of Bishop's life: he didn't need me as much as I needed him to need me. If you left him alone, were just there when he reached out for you but trusted him to stay alive, *alive, alive, stay alive*, on his own without you, he would not only be fine—he'd be better. He knew that I would always be there, and that allowed him not to require me to be there. I needed to fall back for him to be who he was. It has allowed him to thrive.

This is all anyone could ever want for their children. It's important. It's wonderful. But it just kills you, *kills you kills you*. Your child discovers him or herself in a new place and takes all you have tried to teach them, all the preparation you tried to lay down for them, *lie down, lie down, just keep those eyes closed*, and they use it to build themselves a life in that new place. That's the goal. But the new place they are building is a place that doesn't involve you. They can breathe on their own. They always could.

What is the beginning of their story is, in many ways, an end of our own. The journey he's about to go on, the journey that is already well on its way, that journey has to involve me—the person who loves him more than anyone has ever loved anything—less and less with every passing day. I have always to fade, *fading, fading* from the story so he can write his own. His world belongs to him now. To be who he wants to be, to discover what that is, he has to slowly separate himself from me. Every day, he gets a little bit further away. The more he becomes himself, the more I have been able to feel him slipping, *slipping slipping*, through my fingers.

But I am strong, because he is strong, and free because he is free. I have given him all I can. He can do the rest by himself. I wonder if he always could.

It is his world now. My God, it's going to be incredible.

strong strong i am strong

73.

I am moving. I am moving fast!

I open my eyes, but it is extremely bright, so I try to cover my face with my hands but something is stopping them, someone is pulling them back, and there is noise and there are loud beeps and a man with a deep voice and a cool African accent, he sounds like Dikembe Mutombo, tells me to settle, he is soothing, I find him comforting, I will settle if he asks me to again.

I turn my head to my left. My eyes adjust. Ellis is sitting next to me. She is holding my left hand in hers.

"Shhhh," she says. "Shhhh. You're fine. You're OK. You're alive, Lloyd. We're all right here."

I have always been scared of her—she has always been strong, stronger than me, more than I was. But she is now alit. There is a small blue flame behind her, and she is settling me.

I'm in a car. No: I'm in the back of a car.

I'm in an ambulance. That makes sense.

"Easy, Lloyd," she says. "Easy. It's going to be all right."

I turn to the man with the deep voice. He has put a wet rag on my forehead and is gently holding his hand over it. "You are safe here, you are safe," he says. "I am Derek. You are safe."

We hit a bump, and my cot rises a little in the air, and Derek slips for a second. He gets back to his feet and puts his hand back on the rag.

"Sorry about that," Derek says. "This is a bumpy ride."

"Thank you, Derek," I say, and I close my eyes.

have gotten my bearings. I can tell from the annoyed grunts of the ambulance driver that we are stuck on I-85 on the way to Emory. Not even an emergency vehicle in full alarm stands a chance against Atlanta traffic.

I look up at Ellis. "So, uh, did we get him?"

She smiles, but there is an emptiness in it. She is still in shock herself.

"We did," she says. "After you jumped in front of me," and she pauses here and takes a little breath for herself, "I was able to take him down."

"Take him down?"

"I shot him," she says.

"Dead?" I say.

She glances away from me, toward Derek, then down at the floor of the ambulance. "Seems that way," she says.

The three of us sit silently for a moment.

Ellis coughs, and turns to look up toward the driver. "How are we not moving?" she says.

The paramedic turns around and shrugs. "People can't get out of our way if they can't move their cars," he says. "I'm doing the best I can."

A lightning bolt hits, and it reminds me that I'm still alive and can feel pain, which is when it occurs to me that my left arm really hurts.

"Ow," I say, leaning my head toward my left shoulder.

Derek leans down to me. "Is your pain all right?" he says. "I've given you two milligrams of morphine, but I can give you more."

"If we're stuck in this traffic any longer, you're going to have to give me some," Ellis says.

I shake my head at Derek. "I'm fine, thank you." My head's screwed up enough right now, I'd rather not fog it any more than it already is.

"That's where he got you," Ellis says. "He missed your head by"— she takes her left hand and puts it on my nose, and puts her right hand above my shoulder, then puts both hands in front of my face—"That much."

"You're a hero," Derek says. "You jumped in front of a bullet for your partner."

"She's not my—"

"I'm his boss, actually," Ellis says, turning to me. "But Lloyd, I do nevertheless appreciate you, well, you saving my life."

My eyes moisten a bit, but then I narrow them at her. "Hey, you're the one that just saddled up all chill at the kitchen table of a serial killer," I say. "'We don't want to take up any more of your time than we have to.' Pretty casual there, Ellis. Who would have thought the serial killer might have a gun?" I lift my hand and flick her on the elbow. "Brilliant plan."

Ellis looks down and shakes her head. "Shut up," she says, not looking up. "It worked, didn't it?"

"Says the lady that didn't get shot," I say, flicking her elbow again.

"He is a hero," Derek says, putting a straw in my mouth. "You were willing to sacrifice everything."

Ellis lifts her head up, suddenly at full attention, and snorts.

"Well, I'm not sure *sacrifice* is the word I'd use here," she says.

"I'm sorry?" Derek says.

I look up at her. *I'm sorry?*

"I'm pretty sure Lloyd was doing exactly what he planned all along," she says. She leans over to me and whispers in my ear.

"You're a total dipshit, you know," she says, adjusting the rag on my head. "You are a stupid, stubborn man."

75

We start to move, hit another pothole, and stop again.

"You've known me for a long time, Lloyd," Ellis says as Derek leans toward us but tries to make it look like he isn't. "We've been through it all. Remember Home Depot?"

I nod to her. I start to feel like my body is slowly lifting up from this cot, floating.

"And you know that I am a good cop, yes?" she says. "Or at the very least not an idiot."

"Of course," I say, my mouth so dry, more bolts creeping in, but hanging on every word.

She puts the straw back in my mouth. I take a light sip, and then she puts it to her lips and takes one herself.

"At first I couldn't figure any of it out, Lloyd," she says. "When you filed your report from Bedford Pines, and it was so different than Anderson's, and the other cops, I didn't understand. Why would you put yourself in such a reckless situation? Since when do you kick down people's doors? Since when do you barge in when a guy has a gun? Since when does anybody? And even stranger: you tried to pretend it didn't happen. You downplayed it. You said it was nothing unusual . . . until you went out and just started hightailing it after a car thief. A car thief, Lloyd. In Bertha no less!"

There is a tinge of anger to her voice, but just for a split second. She's enjoying being Columbo.

She cocks an eyebrow at me.

"So that was weird," she continues. "I thought for a while that maybe the deal with the apartment complex, maybe Lloyd really is trying to give his kid partner something to do, maybe he's covering for him, I didn't sweat that. But then you drove Bertha off a damn bridge. The stadium embankment no less. I can't believe that didn't kill you. And that's what I thought: Is Lloyd *trying* to get his ass killed?"

I lean my head over to Derek. We have his total attention.

"So I started sniffing around," she says.

"Alex from the union told me you'd asked to see our contract," she says, and she sees my eyebrows rise. "Yeah, not much around there I don't hear about, Lloyd. And then I saw you checked out some documents about our insurance plans, and family bereavement."

I cough, and she grins. "Yeah, that's all on the record too. Didn't realize that, did you, pal?"

I try to meet her gaze. "I didn't, no," I say.

"So I put two and two together, like any normal cop would," she says, and she chokes a little on "together." "And I see you checking out the policy papers, insurance papers, payouts, at the exact time you are suddenly doing crazy-ass things on the job that you haven't done in the twenty years I've known you. And then I see them, I see what you're doing, and then if I needed any more proof, people are *taking videos of what you're doing*, and it's obvious: that fool's trying to get himself killed. For money."

There is a clanging on the floor. We both snap our heads to the noise. Derek has dropped a clipboard. It rattles against the metal frame of the ambulance.

"Sorry," he says, grimacing. He looks up to Ellis. "Please, uh, don't let me interrupt."

Ellis picks up the clipboard and lays it on the foot of my cot.

"I couldn't figure out why you'd do something so stupid," she says. "But it didn't take very long to figure out what would make you act like a crazy person. It would have to be for Bishop."

"Bish," I say out loud, I think.

"So the question is why," she says. "You're not suicidal, as far as I can tell, and even if you were, you'd never leave Bish alone like that. That's what I couldn't figure out. Why would you want to get yourself killed, even if it were for some insurance money?"

She leans down and lifts my chin up toward hers.

"But for that, I didn't need to be much of a cop," she says. She rubs a hand through my hair, then over my knee. "All I had to do was look at you."

She brushes a strand of hair out of my face, and it gets stuck on her hand.

"What is it?" she says. "Is it cancer?"

It will feel good to say this.

"Brain tumor," I say. "Glioblastoma, they call it." An evil tree. "I found out about a couple of months ago. The day Morgan found me on the hood of my car."

"Oh," she says, flinching. "Oh."

"Sarge, my teeth are falling out," I say, all at once, and it makes me burst into sobs. It feels like it's happening outside me, like I'm watching myself do it, like it's somebody else.

She puts her arm around my neck, puts her forehead on mine, and rubs a spot behind my left ear. My sinuses clear, and bloody snot falls out of my nose. She gives me a tissue out of her pocket.

I blow my nose. I'm having trouble figuring out where my face ends and the towel begins.

"So you tried to die in your uniform," she says. "For Bishop."

My eyes meet hers.

"Yes," I say. It does feel good to say it.

"Well," she says, with a twinkle in her eye. "You did a real shit job of it."

"It's surprisingly hard," I say.

76

We break through the traffic and are finally moving. The sirens wail and the lights flash. Look at this, all for me.

The twinkle is gone from Ellis's eye.

"After it all, you're just like him, you know," she says. "You McNeil men think you have to do everything by yourselves. We didn't know your dad was even this close to nailing that prick until after he was already gone. All he would have to have done was ask for help."

Major McNeil asking for help. That'll be the day.

"And you tried so hard not to be him, and here you are," she says, her nostrils flaring. "Trying to do it all yourself while missing everything right in front of your goddamn face. You realize what a fundamentally moronic thing you're doing, don't you?"

"I couldn't leave him with nothing," I say, but my words sound weak, pathetic—turning to ash the second they leave my lips.

"So instead you just lie to him, and don't give him a chance to say goodbye," she says, and there's a growl in there. She's pissed. "What kind of dad hides that he's dying from his son? For some harebrained scheme. For some *illegal* harebrained scheme, I remind you."

My throat begins to constrict. I reach for the water, and Derek holds it for me.

"I didn't know what to do," I said.

"Christ, Lloyd, let us help you!" she bellows, and then catches herself and lowers her voice. "Ever heard of GoFundMe, motherfucker?"

"Whoa," Derek says suddenly. "Wait, I just realized: you're Happycop!" He claps his hands together. "Hot damn! Happycop's in my ambulance!"

He stops himself.

"Oh," he says. "Oh, OK. OK. I understand what you are all talking about now."

I smile. "Great to meet a fan," I say.

"Well, I'm glad you two find this funny," Ellis says, and I lock back in on her. "But you know what people might do for Happycop? They might make sure his son is taken care of." She snarls a little, starts to choke up, then gets back in control. "We all would have."

I look at her. How long has she had my back? How long have they all have?

"I'm sorry," I say.

"I'm not the one to apologize to," she says.

77

A couple of years ago, I fell asleep on my couch next to Bishop while watching a movie. He stayed awake and turned on the Xbox, playing a video game in which you shoot zombies deep into the evening.

Late at night, probably into the morning, I woke up with a shot, so violently that Bishop jumped and sent his controller flying across the room.

"Jesus, Dad," he said. "Are you OK?"

I was having a dream, I told him. In it, Major McNeil, my dad, was riding a horse. I was driving Bertha, and he was ahead of me. I hit the gas, but no matter how fast I got Bertha going, the horse would just speed up even faster. I saw the back of my father's head, but he did not turn around. I began to catch up, and was just about to pull up next to him when the horse zagged off course and into a ditch, sending my father flying. He did not flail, he did not struggle, he simply soared through the air. He landed silently ahead of me.

I sprinted out of the car toward him. But he was not there. He was gone.

"That's scary," Bishop said, and he must have meant it, because he paused his game. "Why were you trying to catch him? Were you trying to tell him something?"

I hadn't thought about it that way. I didn't know why I was chasing him. I was just chasing him. I didn't know what I'd do when I got there. I just wanted to get there.

"I don't know," I said. "I guess maybe? But then when I got there, I couldn't find him."

He unpaused the game and started playing again.

"I have a dream like that about you and Mom sometimes, where I'm trying to chase you guys," he said, tossing a couple of Skittles into his mouth.

"But I always find you."

I do not know what I would have said to my father. But I know I would have said something. Because I could have. Because he would have been there.

But he wasn't.

There will be a time when Bishop longs for his father, when he has a million things he wants to tell him, when he is chasing him. He will not be able to find me. I will be gone.

But I am here now. He can find me right here. Right now.

Another lightning bolt. They are cascading, but it feels true, it feels like the heavens landing, letting me know how foolish I have become.

But also letting me know that I do still have time.

"Hey, Ellis," I say.

"Yeah?" she says, as we pull off I-85 at Spaghetti Junction, the roads in the sky. Are you looking? Do you really see?

"Anybody grab my phone out of that mess?"

She reaches into her pocket. "Got it right here," she says, and she places it gently in my palm.

I put it close to my face. It is hard to see.

I press a button. I press another. I bring it to my ear.

"Bish," I say when he answers. "Hey, Bish."

"'Sup, Dad."

"'Sup."

AFTER

It's a balance. You release with your left while you press with your right.

I'm trying.

You're pulling with your left too quickly and not giving it enough gas. That's why we're jumping forward.

It's hard.

You'll get the hang of it. It takes a while. There's a reason we're doing this on a country road. Fewer people you can kill.

Shut up, Dad.

Sorry.

OK, here goes.

Whoa. Don't go so hard on the gas.

It's fun!

It is fun. But take it easy.

So that's second gear?

Yes. So after you make this turn and come back around, you can speed up and get up to third.

Do I need to go down up here when I tur—augh.

It's OK. You didn't give it enough gas that time. That's why you killed it.

Do I just restart it?

Yes, but—

Oh, crap, that sound was terrible, what did I do?

You have to push in the clutch before you turn the key.

Got it! Here goes.

That's it. Now speed up a bit, you're going so slow that bugs are coming in through the window.

I got it. I got it.

Now keep going. Up to third now.

Ooooh, all right, I get it, I get it. Let's goooo.

You feel that pressure? That's Bertha wanting to go into high gear. Get ready to hit it.

Is it ready now?

Not yet. A little bit more.

Now?

Wait . . . wait . . . OK, now!

We're going fast! We're going fast! Are we going too fast?

You're going great. Keep going.

Let's keep going. I want to keep going.

You can keep going.

Let's keep going.

Yeah. Let's keep going.

Acknowledgments

In February 2020, right before *everything*, I sat on a sofa in my childhood home with our close family friend Marlese Cook, who had lived there since my parents moved out twenty years earlier. She was dying of glioblastoma, which had killed my Uncle Dave just a few years earlier, and we both knew this would be the last time I'd see her. I held her hand, and she was scared, but she was also strong. Anyone who has ever had a loved one die from glioblastoma, including the people I spoke with for this book, has forever had their perceptions altered from the experience. I'm grateful to those who were kind enough to share their stories with me. I hope I did you and your loved ones justice. I also would like to thank those police officers, and their family members, who provided their experiences as well. I can never get a story as right as those who have lived it. I'm reliant on, and deeply grateful for, those who have.

I say this every book, and I mean it: I want to keep writing books for Noah Eaker, my editor and friend, until one of us dies. I can't imagine anyone being better at what he does than him. David Gernert has been my agent and guiding light for fifteen years, and he has now handed the baton to Mark Tavani, whose energy, empathy, and encouragement I'm elated to have alongside me for hopefully fifteen more. Thank you as well to the whole Harper crew: Edie Astley, Kate D'Esmond, Samantha Lubash, Joanne O'Neill, and Miranda Ottewell.

One of the most difficult parts of this book to write were the Lloyd Edicts, because they required me to think about what I would want my two sons to know most after I'm gone. I thus corralled a Council of Dads for their input. We should all have a Council of Dads at our disposal when we need one. Thus, thanks to my Council of Dads: Matt Adair, Mike Cetera, Scott Duvall, Tim Kelly, Bryan Leitch, and Tony Waller.

Special thanks must go to David Barbe, Amy Blair, Greg Bluestein, Joan Cetera, Tommy Craggs, A. J. Daulerio, the David family, Joe DeLessio, Denny Dooley, Bertis Downs, Roger Ebert, Dave Eggers, Aileen Gallagher, LZ Granderson, Tim Grierson, Will Haraway, Benjamin Hart, John Heilemann, John Hendrickson, David Hirshey, Jenny Jackson, Carrie Kelly, Kim Keniley, Stephen King, Andy Kuhns, Jill Leitch, Mark Lisanti, Russell Little, Matt Meyers, Bernie Miklasz, Christi Moore, Chris Morgan, Adam Moss, Leandra Nessel, Ragan Odle, John Parker, Matt Pitzer, Michael Ripps, Lindsay Robertson, Andrew Simon, Sallie Starrett, Trevor Stevenson, Wynne Stevenson, Susan Stoebner, Kingsley Strong, Chris Suellentrop, Michael Tyler, David Wallace-Wells, Kevin Wiegert, Ben Williams, and Kevin Wilson.

The best way to be a good parent, I've found, is to have good parents, and I've been lucky to have truly great ones in Bryan and Sally Leitch. Getting to spend this last near decade living near you for the first time since high school is a gift I'll always cherish. (And Go Illini, of course.) I will be turning fifty about seven months after this book is published, which means I'm roughly a third of the way through my life. I can't wait, then, to spend those next one hundred years with my wife, Alexa, and my sons, William and Wynn, at my side. Though if I continue to publish a book every other year, one of them is probably going to kill me before I get there. Everything I do is for you, because of you, and with you. Thank you.

About the Author

Will Leitch is a contributing editor at *New York* magazine, a columnist for the *Washington Post* and the founder of the late sports website Deadspin. The award-winning author of the novels *How Lucky* and *The Time Has Come* and two works of nonfiction, *God Save the Fan* and *Are We Winning?*, he writes regularly for the *New York Times*, NBC News, the *Atlantic*, and MLB.com. He lives in Athens, Georgia, with his wife and two sons.